OF TREASONS
BORN

OF TREASONS
BORN

A NOVEL OF
THE TREASONS CYCLE

J. L. DOTY

OPEN ROAD

INTEGRATED MEDIA

NEW YORK

Cover design by Michel Vrana

ISBN 978-1-5040-1208-9

Published in 2016 by Open Road Integrated Media, Inc.
180 Maiden Lane
New York, NY 10038
www.openroadmedia.com

OF TREASONS
BORN

CHAPTER 1:
GUILTY

"All rise."

The hand and leg manacles hampered eleven-year-old York Ballin, and his attorney had to help him stand. Next to him, Cracky, Ten-Ten, and their attorneys stood as well. It bothered York that the older boys looked frightened.

As the judge entered the courtroom, York tried to look sorrowful and repentant. He was counting on the judge being too soft-hearted to throw the book at a poor little boy raised by foster parents, and he'd practiced looking pitiable.

The judge sat down behind the bench, then shuffled a small sheaf of papers for a second before looking at Cracky, Ten-Ten, and York. When he spoke, his voice sounded hard and unyielding. "Charles Towk, Robert Tennerin, and York Ballin. The three of you made a conscious decision to steal a woman's purse, and when she resisted, you, Charles Towk, struck her over the head with a still unidentified blunt object. She died of that wound, and a jury of your peers has found you guilty of felony murder, a capital offense. Mr. Tennerin and Mr. Ballin, that you did not personally strike the blow does not lessen your culpability in the matter."

From the moment Cracky whacked that woman over the head, York knew what a mistake it had been to listen to the two older boys. "Easy money," they'd said. "Nobody gets hurt. You just gotta be lookout."

"I've considered your sentences carefully. Mr. Ballin, while you have not been before this court as repeatedly as Mr. Towk and Mr. Tennerin, you have appeared here twice for shoplifting and petty theft, so I'm not going to waste time with long explanations. It is my responsibility to ensure that predators like you three are not free to victimize the law-abiding public. Mr. Towk, I sentence you to death in a low-gravity gallows. May whatever god you honor have mercy on your soul."

Cracky leaned forward on the table in front of him and started crying—big gulping sobs, tears streaming down his cheeks, snot flowing freely from his nose.

"Mr. Tennerin, I sentence you to death in a low-gravity gallows. May whatever god you honor have mercy on your soul."

Ten-Ten shouted, "You can't do that! I didn't hit her!"

"Silence," the judge snapped. "Be silent or I'll have the bailiffs restrain you."

He looked at York. "Mr. Ballin, like your two friends I consider you nothing more than a set of genes that need to be removed from our gene pool. Because of your age, the law won't allow me to give you a death sentence, but I can still put you away where you can never harm anyone again."

York's stomach muscles tightened. This wasn't going to be good.

The judge shuffled the papers again, then carefully read from them. "I sentence you to life without parole at hard labor on a prison mining asteroid, the location of which will be determined by the penal system."

"But I didn't kill her," York said. "I just wanted—"

"Shut up," the judge barked. "There'll be no more discussion of the matter."

He stood, turned, and marched out of the courtroom.

Two bailiffs descended on York and almost picked him up

by his arms as they hustled him through a side door and out of the room. His feet barely touched the floor as they half-carried him to an elevator, then down to the basement level. At the end of a long corridor, they stopped at a metal door and nodded to another bailiff seated behind a glass partition. He did something, and the metal door slid aside to reveal a hallway with more metal doors on either side, each with a large number stenciled on it. One of the bailiffs holding him said, "He's a minor, so we got to put him alone."

A metallic-sounding voice came from the speaker above them. "Put him in three."

As they marched him down the hallway, the second door on the right slid aside with the clatter of steel gears. The cell had two bunks folded up against one wall. One of the bailiffs pulled the lower one down and they sat York on it, then removed the manacles. Then both guards backed out of the cell without saying a word and the door clanked shut.

York had been counting on the fact that the judge couldn't give an eleven-year-old boy the death penalty, but for all intents and purposes he'd done just that. York knew he wouldn't last a year on a mining asteroid.

He lay back on the small bed and tried unsuccessfully to sleep.

York had only been in the cell for a couple of hours when the door clattered open and two bailiffs walked in. Holding manacles, one said, "You got visitors."

They manacled his hands and feet and marched him out of the cellblock, then down a series of long corridors and into a small room where Maja and Tollem waited, both seated at a plain, rectangular table. York's foster parents weren't much to look at; tired, one might say—tired eyes, skin, hair, clothing. As the bailiffs hustled him into the room, Maja scowled at him while Toll stood and started to step around the table.

One of the bailiffs stepped between York and Toll, held out

an arm, and said to Toll, "No. You stay seated on that side of the table; we sit him down on this side. You talk, but you don't touch, you don't exchange anything. If he wasn't a minor, you'd be talking to him through a blast-proof partition, but we can't let him among the general inmate population."

Toll sat back down beside Maja, and the bailiffs pushed York down into a chair opposite them. Toll leaned forward and said, "We're trying to get hold of your attorney, see what we can do."

Maja's scowl deepened. "That lawyer ain't going to give us shit for time. We don't have no money to pay him."

York knew that story all too well. Maja and Toll had tried to make it as croppers, but even with a government subsidy, they'd barely put food on the table from one day to the next.

"But we gotta do something," Toll said, his voice rising into that pleading tone York knew so well.

Maja leaned back and looked at York, making no attempt to hide her contempt. "We don't gotta do shit. He fucked up and got himself into this. Maybe if the money hadn't stopped when he was six, we might have some now to help him with."

That was all York had ever meant to Maja: the money, the mysterious bank transfer that had arrived every month, then stopped, for some reason, shortly before his seventh birthday. She hadn't been mean or abusive, just sour and hateful, with never a kind word for anyone. On the other hand, Toll had always been friendly, but they'd both lived under Maja's thumb.

Maja and Toll argued back and forth for about a half hour, then the bailiffs escorted York back to his cell.

York sat on the bunk in his cell and tried to remember when he'd first come to Maja and Toll. He'd been four at the time, clutching desperately to a man's hand. He recalled that hand now; not a father's hand, not someone he loved or longed for, but a face and a voice that was at least familiar when he'd needed familiarity most.

Somewhere deep in his memories there was someone he'd thought of as *Mother*, but he could no longer picture her, couldn't even recall the color of her hair or eyes, nothing. Maja and the man that brought him talked money, though York hadn't understood any of it at the time. They came to some agreement and the fellow left. York never saw him again.

During the two days he spent in the holding cell, he repeatedly tried to contact his attorney, but the man wouldn't take his calls. Then they transferred him to solitary confinement in the maximum-security block of the county magistrate's court. Sitting there with nothing to do, staring at the walls of his small cell, he lost count of the days.

They came for him in the middle of a dark and rainy day: two bailiffs who locked him into manacles again. He assumed they'd drive him out to the spaceport, then put him on a shuttle up to Dumark Prime, the big satellite station that served all the shipping in the Dumark system. There, he'd be transferred to some sort of ship for passage to one of the mining asteroids. He was too numb to pay any attention to his surroundings until they marched him into a room and sat him down in a chair at a table. Seated opposite him was his attorney, who looked quite frightened and ill-at-ease, and an older man with salt-and-pepper gray hair wearing an expensive business suit. Standing to one side were a woman and a man, both dressed in some sort of military uniform.

The woman said, "I don't like this."

The fellow in the expensive suit looked her way and said, "I'm sorry, Captain, but you have no choice."

She said, "The Admiralty has no—"

He raised a hand, silencing her with a gesture. York got the impression that she was not one to take orders easily. His attorney sat silently through the whole exchange, and was careful not to make eye contact with anyone.

The fellow in the suit turned to York's attorney and said, "Please proceed."

The attorney had a comp terminal in front of him. He spun it around and slid it across the table to York. "Sign that," he said.

There was some sort of document on the screen of the terminal. York looked at the page count, saw that it was quite long, and in any case, even if he could read, he probably wouldn't understand it. "What is it?" he asked.

"It's the only chance you've got to stay alive, so just sign it, dammit."

The guy in the expensive suit said, "You're joining the navy—for the rest of your life. You know full well you won't last a month on a mining asteroid, so we're giving you a second chance. The navy has its own rather harsh code of justice, and you may not survive that, either, but you have a better chance there than on a prison asteroid."

When York hesitated, the fellow added, "If you don't sign it, we'll just fake your signature, and you'll be in the navy anyway."

York looked at his attorney, then at the woman and man in uniform, then back at the suit.

The bailiffs had to remove his wrist manacles so he could lift his hand and press his palm against the screen of the terminal. Then they took a DNA sample to file with whatever it was he'd signed. After that, the suit said to the woman, "He's all yours, Captain."

The woman turned to the man in uniform standing beside her and said, "Master Chief, get him aboard ship."

"Aye, aye, ma'am," the fellow said, and practically lifted York out of his chair.

The fellow called *Chief* then fulfilled York's earlier expectations. They took him to the spaceport where they boarded a military boat of some sort, but they didn't stop at Dumark Prime. When the boat came to rest and Mr. Chief marched York off it, he had a brief glimpse of an open deck that someone called Hangar Deck, with a lot of navy uniforms bustling about. The captain went her way, and Mr. Chief quickstepped York down through the bowels of the ship. He turned him over to another fellow, also named Chief—York assumed they were brothers or something. The second Mr. Chief walked York into another cell, removed his manacles, and locked him in.

A cell was a cell, small and cramped with a sink, a toilet, and some sort of bed flat against the wall, like a big picture hanging there. He could tell it was a bed because it had blankets on it, held in place and prevented from falling to the floor by a shallow gravity field. But since it was flat against the wall, he figured it was folded up, and he had to figure out how to unfold it if he was going to sleep in it.

He examined the periphery of the bed carefully for some sort of latch or release mechanism, spent a good half hour doing so and never did find a way to unfold it so he could lie in it. He did discover some controls that contracted or extended the gravity field that held the blankets in place. He finally pulled the pillow, sheets, and blanket off the bed, laid the pillow on the floor, wrapped the blanket around his shoulders, and lay down to sleep.

He was a man who had kept himself alive all these years by never being curious, or at least never acting on that curiosity. It was the busiest hour of the day in the bar in the spaceport on Dumark Prime, which he liked. Most of the bar's customers glanced frequently at the wall clock, some planning to board an outbound ship, some to meet inbound acquaintances. It was also a place that didn't have a group of regulars, just nameless, transient people all waiting for something, and he liked that, too. He could wait and remain anonymous.

He took a seat at the bar and ordered a drink and lunch. He was hungry and thirsty, but he would have ordered something either way; all part of fitting into the surrounding terrain and remaining anonymous. He had finished half the food when a younger man in an expensive suit took the seat next to him. "Carson," the fellow said, "how'd it go?"

Carson wasn't his real name, but it worked for the purposes of this job. He'd change his identity before going through customs and boarding an outbound ship. He said, "Everything went as planned, Mr. Tolliver." Carson had no doubt that Tolliver was not the young fellow's real name, either. "The identity codes you gave me elicited the . . . appropriate responses from the authorities and the navy."

The bartender came over and Tolliver ordered a drink. Had Carson been a curious man, he would guess that the younger man was all navy, probably an attaché of some sort working for someone very high in the Admiralty. Definitely not Admiralty Intelligence; AI tended to have a more thuggish, heavy-handed approach. Had Carson been a curious man, he would wonder why Tolliver would go to the trouble to travel to a backwater agroplanet to oversee a relatively simple clandestine operation, and why they'd pay Carson to travel such distances when they could have easily used local talent. Had Carson been a curious man, he might have wondered about these things, but acting on that curiosity in any way would probably get him killed.

Tolliver asked, "So the boy's on his way?"

"That he is," Carson said. "Though he has only a slightly better chance of surviving the navy than a prison asteroid."

Tolliver tossed back his drink and stood. "It wasn't your responsibility to worry about his survival, just see to it he signed those papers and got on that ship alive."

He turned and walked away, leaving a small comp card on his seat. Carson picked it up and put it in his pocket. It would contain access codes to a bank account supplying untraceable electronic funds.

Had Carson been a curious man, he would wonder why they were going to all this trouble for an orphaned boy from a backwater agro-planet. But Carson took great pains to never be curious.

CHAPTER 2:
A PRISONER

"Wake up, kid."

York opened his eyes and found Mr. Chief standing over him, a small package under one arm, the cell door behind him open.

"Couldn't figure out the grav bunk, eh?"

York unwrapped himself from the blanket and stood. "Grav bunk?"

"Here, let me show you."

Mr. Chief stepped up to the bed, reached down, touched the controls, and extended the gravity field a bit. He turned around, leaned his back against the bed, and did a funny sort of pivot. When he was done, he lay against the surface of the bed, flat against the wall and held in place by the gravity field, like a painting on the wall of a man lying in bed.

York glanced over his shoulder, noticing that no one stood between him and the open cell door.

"Don't even think about it, kid. You're on a ship and there's no place to go."

York turned back to Mr. Chief.

"And the captain would be pissed if you tried. You don't want the captain pissed."

The man reversed the funny pivot and once again stood upright on the floor. He opened the package and handed York bright, fluorescent-yellow coveralls with the word PRISONER sten-ciled on the back. "Put that on."

York stripped down in front of Mr. Chief and pulled on the coveralls. The man then locked him in hand and leg manacles, marched him out of the cell, and put him at the back of a line of three men and a woman wearing similar coveralls.

"Sturpik," Mr. Chief said as he turned his back on them. "Tell the kid the rules."

The man in front of York turned around. He was tall, with greasy black hair; a two-day-old stubble of beard; sharp, pinched eyes; and sunken cheeks. "We're going to the mess hall to eat. You're one of us—a prisoner. You don't do shit, you don't say shit. You stay in line, you take what they hand you, you sit down, you eat it. When we're done, we get up and march back here. Got it?"

"Yes, sir," York said, not sure he was going to like this navy thing. But it still had to be better than a mining asteroid.

"You don't call me *sir*, neither."

Sturpik turned around and now all York saw was his back.

"Okay, you pieces of shit," Mr. Chief said. "Let's go." He shouted, "Prisoners on deck," then marched forward. The five prisoners followed him.

York quickly learned that the leg manacles forced him to shuf-fle forward in a series of short, quick steps, though he was no worse off than the men in front of him, even if his legs were a bit shorter than theirs. They climbed up a plast ladder to another floor, then shuffled down a hallway with floor, ceiling, and walls all made completely of plast. When they approached other men and women in uniform, Mr. Chief called out, "Prisoners on deck," and the others stood aside to allow the prisoners to pass.

They entered a large cafeteria with a lot of uniformed people seated at plast tables. Everyone but the prisoners wore khaki, dark gray, or black uniforms, making the bright yellow of the prison-ers' coveralls stand out even more. A line of uniformed men and women snaked past a long, plast counter where they were given trays of food. When Mr. Chief shouted "Prisoners on deck," the line parted and the five of them were allowed to step in. A fellow behind the counter handed each of them a tray, Mr. Chief escorted them to an empty table, and they sat down with Mr. Chief standing over them.

One of the men whispered, "Rotten crap for food."

Mr. Chief said, "Button it, Thurgood."

The "rotten crap" they ate was far better than the rotten crap Maja had served, though York thought it wise to keep that opinion to himself.

York had left his civilian clothes in a heap next to the bunk, but when he returned to his cell they were gone.

"You won't need those anymore," Mr. Chief told him.

York's days turned into a monotonous grind of sleeping and staring at the walls of his cell. The daily trip to the showers broke up the monotony a bit. Each morning, Mr. Chief marched them up there just before the second-watch rush—York wasn't sure what *second watch* meant—and he learned quickly that he had a half-minute under chem wash to scrub down, then one minute of warm water to rinse off. But since he was low man on the shit list, they made him shower first, and *"warm"* didn't apply to anything that came out of the spigot. The other four prisoners showered after him, which got them lukewarm water. York learned that part of their responsibility as prisoners was to warm up the showers for second watch.

His third day in the cell, Sturpik marched up to the showers with them but wasn't present when they went up to the mess hall. When they assembled for lunch, York learned he'd been released and returned to duty.

At regular intervals, a speaker somewhere in the cellblock came to life, and a voice announced something to do with the ship, usually with a string of words that meant absolutely nothing to York. In the middle of York's fourth day in the cell, he was waiting for the march to the mess hall for lunch—anything to break up the monotony—when the speaker came to life.

Up-transition in ten minutes and counting. All hands stand by.

It was the first time York understood anything that came out of the speaker. He'd heard of *transition*; it had something to do with traveling as fast as light—or faster, or something like that—and he wondered if it would make him sick or something. He noted the time on a small digital clock above the door to his cell, but he needn't have bothered. The speaker gave a five-minute warning, then a one-minute warning, then a countdown from ten seconds. When the speaker said *zero*, York felt an odd little flutter crawl up the back of his spine, but that was all. He shrugged it off and continued his wait for lunch.

The next day, after the morning shower, Mr. Chief pulled York aside while he locked up the other three prisoners. He gave York khaki coveralls with his last name stenciled above the left breast pocket. The word PRISONER was not stenciled on the back of the coveralls. "Put that on," he said. "You ain't a prisoner no more."

York said, "Yes, sir, Mr. Chief," and started stripping down.

"You don't call me *Mr.* Chief. You call me just plain Chief, or Chief Zhako."

When York had finished putting on the new coveralls, Zhako clipped an ID card to his chest. York glanced at it and saw his own picture prominent on its surface. His reading skills were limited, but he knew enough to make out the details of his own identity. Beneath his picture were bright-red letters that said UNCONFIRMED.

"It's got a DNA trigger in it," Zhako said. "Touch it with a finger."

York reached up and tapped it lightly, and the word UNCON-FIRMED disappeared.

Zhako said, "It needs to make contact with your skin to get a sample and confirm your identity. If anyone else touches it, it goes inactive and unconfirmed until you touch it again."

Zhako spun about. "Follow me."

Chief Zhako led him down steep ladders to two floors below the cellblock, which surprised York. The cellblock was located so far down in the ship he'd assumed they were as low as they could get. Zhako stopped outside a funny-shaped, open plast door and turned to York. He lowered his voice and said, "Listen to me, kid. Nobody but me, the master chief, the captain, and the XO know what you did as a civilian. And if you keep your mouth shut and work hard, no one ever needs to know. On the other side of this hatch, you get to start over, a second chance, so be sure you do something with that."

"Yes, sir."

"And don't call me sir."

York kept his mouth shut and didn't say anything.

Zhako nodded once and turned back to the *"hatch"*—York was beginning to realize he'd have to learn a whole new language. He followed Zhako through the hatch into a long, narrow corridor that curved slowly to the right. The curve was quite shallow, but the room was long enough that he couldn't see where it ended. Several groups of men and women were busy at one thing or another. They walked past one group that had some sort of apparatus disassembled, with tools and mechanical parts spread out on the floor. York spotted Sturpik in another group, though he didn't acknowledge York as they passed him. York noticed several small, round hatches spaced about five meters apart in the wall on his left, and they appeared to extend the entire, unknown length of the curved room. One group of five people paused and looked their way as York and Zhako approached. A woman stepped forward, wiping her hands on a greasy rag.

She said to Zhako, "So this is Ballin?"

Her eyes settled on York and he saw no kindness there.

Zhako said, "Spacer Apprentice York Ballin, this is Petty Officer Straight, your new boss. From now on, you do what she says."

She leaned close to York and said, "And you do it when I say, and how I say."

York wasn't sure if he should call her ma'am, or sir, or what, so he kept his mouth shut as Zhako marched away and the woman and her four companions gathered around him. Straight introduced her crew. A girl named Zamekis appeared to be in her late teens, and a fellow named Marko seemed to be the oldest among them, with a man named Stark and a woman named Durlling both of ages somewhere between the two. All of them had some sort of insignia on their sleeves, where York's sleeves were bare khaki.

"Marko," Straight said. "Tell Spacer Apprentice Ballin what he just became."

The older fellow stepped forward. He gave York a kindly smile and said, "Come here, Ballin."

He turned and walked over to one of the round hatches in the curved wall, so York followed him. He slapped the wall next to the hatch and said, "This here is *Dauntless*'s inner hull."

York asked, "Dauntless?"

Marko frowned. "You don't know the name of your ship?"

Straight said, "He was pressed into service. Probably picked up in a sweep of undesirables."

Marko nodded; that seemed to satisfy him and the others. He held out his hands in a broad gesture. "You're now part of the crew of *Dauntless,* an imperial medium cruiser, and as I said"— he slapped the wall again—"this is her inner hull, and this hatch leads to one of the pods on the outer hull. You know what a pod gunner is?"

York shook his head. "No—" He'd almost finished by saying *sir*.

"Well, kid," Marko continued, "a pod gunner is almost the lowest form of life on ship. But you know what's lower than a pod gunner?"

York shook his head again.

Marko grinned. "Us. We're lower-deck pod gunners, and that makes us even lower. But there is one thing that's lower than a lower-deck pod gunner, and that would be an apprentice lower-deck pod gunner. We only got one of them. Care to guess who that might be?"

York said, "Me?" It came out in a squeak.

Marko nodded. "You got that right, kid. You're so low, you're lower than the lowest. But when we're done with you, you're gonna be a lower-deck pod gunner."

Straight said, "Give the kid his first weapon."

Marko picked up a bucket of water and a sponge and handed them to York.

Straight said, "Dirt's your biggest enemy, Ballin. So take no prisoners."

He asked, "What should I clean?"

Straight grinned. "Everything."

York got down on his hands and knees and started scrubbing the floor.

Straight and her crew broke for lunch, and while someone always complained about the food, York thought it quite good. After lunch, he went back to scrubbing the floor. They broke for dinner, then York followed them to the bunk room, and while the rest of them played cards or lounged about through the evening, Straight put him to work scrubbing the floor there. At the end of his first day as the lowest of the low, he was ready to drop into bed. He could barely keep his eyes open as they pointed him to a square, boxy recess in the bunk room.

"There's your coffin," Straight said.

At the look on his face, she grinned. "Pod gunners don't get a real bunk on a ship this size. You get a stacked coffin and stim-sleep. Hope you aren't claustrophobic."

York laid down in the coffin, it cycled closed, and he felt it moving as the ship's systems stored him somewhere. And then he dreamed: about Cracky and Ten-Ten, about Maja and Toll, and the man who brought him to them. And in all of his dreams, a shadowy image of his mother hovered in the background. He tried to see through the haze of the dream, hoping to recall her face, but she remained wrapped in dark shadows.

When he awoke, he sat up and slammed his nose into the top of the coffin. He tasted blood streaming out of his nose as the lid opened to a room full of bright lights and Straight's crew.

"Ah, kid," Marko said, helping him stand, holding a somewhat clean rag to his nose. "We all made that mistake at one time or another. You'll catch on."

York scrubbed a lot of floors, though he learned they weren't called floors on a ship, they were decks. And the walls weren't walls, they were bulkheads, just like doors were hatches and rooms weren't rooms: big rooms were decks, like Hangar Deck, and Pod Deck, and Lower Pod Deck. Then he learned that some rooms were rooms, like the Engine Room. And some doors were doors, not hatches, like those on the officers' staterooms. It left him quite confused.

"Hey, kid."

On his hands and knees scrubbing the deck, York craned his neck to look up. Sturpik stood over him. York rose to his knees and said, "What can I do for you?"

Sturpik leaned close to him. "Watch out for Straight. She's a mean bitch, and snotty, and she ain't doing her job."

York hadn't formed an opinion of Straight one way or another. "What do you mean she ain't doing her job?"

Sturpik gave York's bucket a nudge with his toe. "She's supposed to be training you. You call this training? What are you learning you didn't already know?"

York couldn't deny the truth of that. "I don't have any choice, do I?"

Sturpik shrugged and rolled his head from side to side. "You got more options than you think, kid. When you get some time off, look me up."

Sturpik was right. York had done nothing but scrub decks for days now. "Thanks," he said.

"Don't worry about it, kid. Us gunners, we gotta stick together."

Sturpik wandered away, and York went back to scrubbing the deck.

For ten days, York scrubbed decks from the moment he climbed out of his coffin until the moment he climbed back into it. Then one day after evening mess, as he picked up his bucket, Straight said, "Belay that, Ballin. XO wants you to start learning the regs."

"XO?" York asked.

"Executive officer."

York returned the bucket to the maintenance closet and reported back to Straight. She and seven other petty officers shared a small bunk room where they slept in real bunks, not coffins. She had York sit next to her on her bunk, handed him a small reader, and said, "Read the first paragraph out loud and tell me what you think it means."

York looked at the jumble of symbols on the screen, and his gut tightened with fear. The first word he recognized. "The . . ." And the next few words. "naval . . . code of . . ." The next word was *long*, with a few characters he didn't recognize. "Uh . . ."

He noticed several of Straight's roommates had paused and were looking his way.

Straight's eyes narrowed and she said, "You can read, can't you?"

York said, "Uh . . . a little."

"Ah, shit!" Straight said as she raised both hands and rubbed the sides of her temples.

After that, York's evenings were spent learning to read and write, with *The Naval Code of Regulations* as his primary lesson book.

CHAPTER 3:
GOTTA DO FAVORS

York came up out of stim-sleep to the sound of a loud horn blaring an irritating burp. The lights in his coffin flashed to full brightness, and a disembodied male voice said, "*Watch Condition Red. All hands, this is not a drill. Repeat: This is not a drill. Battle stations.*"

No one had told York about *battle stations*, but any idiot could figure out it wasn't good. As the rookie in Straight's crew, he was assigned the top bunk, which meant he had to wait longest for his coffin to cycle out of storage. He waited while the horn continued to blare and the male voice repeated the call to battle stations. Then his coffin suddenly cycled into the bunk room and his reflexes took over. He'd practiced this move a dozen times now and was getting reasonably good at it. He sat up and at the same time killed the grav field in his bunk, let the deck gravity start him into a fall toward the deck. By hooking one hand on the edge of his bunk, he spun himself so he landed on his feet like a veteran, almost. He followed the others as they ran out of the bunk room. And now what?

He stood there in his underwear, watching people rush about. Everyone had some purpose or destination to get to, everyone but him. Marko and Straight dropped into seats at a large console nearby. Marko glanced over his shoulder at York and said, "Get to your battle station, goddammit!"

York said, "What's a battle station?"

At that, Straight looked over her shoulder and said, "Ah, shit!"

That seemed to be the only thing she ever said regarding York. Her face screwed up into an angry scowl as she said, "Get over here."

York hotfooted it across the deck. She slapped him in the back of the head, pointed to the deck, and said, "Sit down against the console and stay there."

York dropped to the deck and pulled his knees up to his chest.

When the loud horn stopped blaring, York closed his eyes and tried not to listen to the sounds around him. He heard the slap of booted feet crossing the deck at a run, heard a shout here, a grunt there, the clatter and whine of some mechanism being activated. But one by one, the sounds died and an oppressive silence settled over the ship.

A woman's voice echoed around them coming from a speaker somewhere—York had learned it was called allship. She identified herself as the captain, said something that York didn't understand, then the silence returned and nothing happened for what felt like the longest time.

York started as a vibration rippled through the deck where he sat, and the air echoed with a sound like a deep bass drum. It was repeated five more times.

"Stay calm, kid," Marko said. "That's our main transition batteries echoing through the hull. That means we're throwing shit at them, which is better than them throwing shit at us."

"Who is 'them'?" York asked. "Who are we fighting?"

"Feddies," Marko said, and glanced his way. The look on York's face must have prompted him to say more. "Warships of the Federal Directorate of the Republic of Syndon—feddies."

"What for?"

Straight gave him an odd look, and Marko said, "Don't know. War's been going on since before I was born, probably be killing each other long after I'm dead."

York wasn't sure what to think of that, and in the silence that followed he found he was holding his breath, had to force himself to breathe, but not overdo it. He heard the bass drum sound again several times, more silence, more drums, then a long, drawn-out silence. Then a voice over allship, "*Stand down to Watch Condition Yellow. All clear.*"

Marko leaned back from the console in front of him and let out a long sigh. He looked at Straight and said, "Did you forget to assign the kid a station?"

Straight glanced down at York, a sour look on her face. She said it again, "Ah, shit."

"Don't get mad at the kid," Marko said. "It wasn't his fault."

"We aren't that far out," Straight said. "I didn't think we'd get into it yet."

She stood and said to York, "Come with me."

He jumped to his feet and followed her. She led him to a console with an empty seat. "This is your duty station. Any watch condition other than green—I don't care if it's yellow, red, or as brown as the shit in your pants—you run like hell to this seat, you sit down, you strap in, and you don't touch nothing."

She turned around and marched away, leaving him standing there. He wasn't sure what he'd done wrong, but there was no question Straight was not happy with him.

Seated at the empty console during his free time, York struggled with the regs, which is what the veteran spacers called *The Naval Code of Regulations*. Too many of the words were big and long, and he had to sound them out carefully, never sure if he did it right. But after a month of sweating over the words during every moment of free time, he was getting better.

"Hi, kid."

He'd been so focused on the small reader screen he hadn't seen Sturpik approach. Next to the older man stood a younger fellow York guessed was probably in his late teens. He had blond hair cut in a buzz cut and a pimply face.

"This here's Tomlin," Sturpik said, introducing Pimply Face. "Tomlin, meet Spacer Apprentice York Ballin."

Tomlin stuck his hand out and York shook it.

Sturpik said, "We seen her hit you. I told you Straight's a mean bitch."

"She didn't really hit me," York said. "She just slapped me up the back of the head. My foster mother used to do that all the time."

Sturpik ignored him and glanced around in a way York had seen too many times on the streets, the way one of the older boys looked to see if there were any police near. Tomlin did the same, then held out his hand, palm up. On it rested a clear, cylindrical, plast container about the size of the tip of his thumb. Again, he glanced from side to side and said, "Need a favor, kid. Hold on to this, will you?"

Inside the clear plast, York saw some sort of greenish-black tarry substance. He shook his head and said, "I don't think I should."

Sturpik confirmed York's suspicions when he said, "Get that out of sight or you'll get us all in trouble."

Tomlin closed his hand around the container and shoved it in a pocket in his coveralls.

Sturpik glanced around again and said, "We need you to hang on to that for us. Just hold on to it for a bit for safekeeping."

York didn't know exactly what the tarry stuff might be, but he knew he didn't want anything to do with it. "I don't think I should—"

"Hold on, kid." Sturpik leaned close to him and spoke softly. "You got to do favors for people. Otherwise, they don't do favors for you."

That was one of the rules of the streets York knew well.

Sturpik looked at Tomlin. "Give me a moment alone with the kid."

Tomlin nodded, turned, and walked away.

Sturpik lowered his voice to a whisper. "You gotta do favors, kid. You don't do favors, it makes people unhappy. They start thinking you're maybe not willing to help out a friend. You see, I'm gonna do you a favor right now. I'm gonna give you some real valuable advice."

"Okay," York said, realizing he didn't have much choice in the matter.

"Straight's making you look weak, kid. You look weak, and everybody's gonna take a piece of you. You gotta stand up to her—just once will do, show her you ain't one of the weak ones."

That's the way it had been on the streets: There were predator and prey, and no in-betweens. If you didn't establish that you were one, then you were automatically classified as the other. York thought the navy would be different from the streets, but he was learning otherwise.

Without waiting to hear agreement from York, Sturpik turned around and walked away. York knew he hadn't heard the last of this.

"Tri . . ." York said, struggling with the word on the reader.

Seated at the console next to him, Zamekis said, "Tribunal."

Before York had come along, Spacer Third Class Meleen Zamekis had been the low rating on Straight's crew. Zamekis was a fair-haired girl in her late teens, and it would have come as no surprise if she decided to make York's life difficult. He'd seen that on the streets a few times, where the shit always flowed down-hill. But Straight didn't tolerate any excessive hazing on her crew, so Zamekis didn't have a backlog of petty mistreatment that she needed to pass along. Straight had ordered Zamekis to help York with his reading, and she was quite nice about it, had confessed that it was easier duty than many of the alternatives.

York got through several sentences without struggling too much, and just as he came to a word he didn't know, Marko approached the two of them saying, "Zamekis, Ballin, come with me."

Zamekis looked up from the reader and said, "What's up?"

Marko smiled at York. "Ballin here is gonna get his first gunnery lesson."

Marko led them to Straight, who waited with the rest of her crew at one of the round hatches set in the inner hull. Straight scowled at York and asked Zamekis, "How's his reading coming?"

The girl nodded. "Not bad."

As York stopped in front of Straight, her crew gathered around behind him. She asked, "Marko tell you what's up?"

"He said I get my first gunnery lesson."

She grinned and looked at the hatch next to her. It was round with a large valve wheel in the middle of it. "This is a pod hatch. It's powered and can be controlled from here, the bridge, or engineering."

She slapped a switch just above the hatch. The valve wheel in the center of it spun and the hatch popped open, swinging out on heavy plast hinges. "It defaults to manual, so if you hit the switch and it doesn't work—like if this section has lost power or something—you turn that wheel, then you can pull it open."

She stepped aside and said, "Take a look."

York peered through the hatch and saw a round plast tube large enough to crawl through, about three meters long with plast hand grips running its entire length.

"We call it a zero-G tube. Why do you think we call it that?"

York shrugged and guessed, "There's no gravity in the tube?"

"Sort of," she said. "The whole ship's under several thousand G's[*] right now, so if we didn't have compensation everywhere, we'd just be red stains on the deck. Deck gravity is compensated so we feel one G. Out in the tube, it's compensated so you feel zero-G; it's easier and faster to crawl through the tube that way. There's a gravity shear at the hatch, so don't let it scare you. And whatever you do, when you pass through it, don't blow lunch, cause you'll be the one has to clean it up."

---

[*] See Appendix: Some Notes on Time, Gravity, and the Imperial Naval Academy

She leaned down and looked into the tube with him. At the far end, he saw what looked like another hatch. "That's the outer hatch that lets you into the pod itself. Normally, once you're past the inner hatch, you seal it before crawling to the pod. But this time, I'm gonna be right behind you, so we'll leave it open."

Following Straight's orders, York crawled up into the hatch and through the gravity shear. It felt strange but didn't bother him. As he floated toward the pod, using the handgrips to propel himself along, he heard Straight crawl into the tube behind him. When he reached the pod's hatch, she said, "Just hit the switch to the side."

The switch was a large red button on the inner edge of the hatch. He pressed it and the hatch popped open toward him.

Straight said, "There are fail-safes built in so it won't open if there's a serious pressure differential on either side. Go on and strap yourself in."

The inside of the pod was a cramped maze of instrument clusters and screens surrounding an acceleration couch. York had to twist around, then get his butt aimed at the couch and pull himself into it. By that time, Straight had crawled halfway into the pod, and in the tight confines, the very short distance separating them was almost intimate. For the first time, it hit York that Straight was a girl—woman—with all sorts of curves and bumps, and quite attractive at that. She wore her brown hair shoulder-length, and always tied back in a ponytail.

After she showed him how to buckle into the couch's harness, she helped him pull on a headset and adjust a wire-thin pickup just to one side of his mouth. "We don't fit you with implants until you make spacer first class—if you survive that long."

She showed him how to boot the pod's system and bring it online, gave him a rundown on the controls he'd need to operate, then closed the hatch and left him there alone. A few minutes later, he heard her voice in his headset. "Okay, Ballin, we're going to start with basic operational procedures. We can see the inside of the pod, so if you have any questions, just point and ask."

York spent the next three hours going through the pod's boot sequence, learning to read debug dumps and diagnostic data. Then Straight had him shut the pod down, open the hatch, and crawl back down the zero-G tube. So far, it had been a lesson in computer science, and he had yet to see what pod gunning had to do with gunning.

"Now we're going to see how fast you can be on-station from a dead sleep," Straight said. "Get in your coffin, and when I wake you, you run like hell to get into that pod and have it booted and online."

York climbed into his coffin and cycled it into storage. He never felt anything when they turned on the stim-sleep, he just simply began dreaming. Then he awoke to the sound of the alert klaxon and Straight's voice.

When his coffin cycled out of storage, he hit the deck running. As he sprinted toward the pod hatch on the inner hull, he noticed that most of the occupants of the Lower Pod Deck had paused to watch him. He dove through the first hatch, sealed it, climbed up the zero-G tube, through the pod hatch, and when his pod had finished its boot sequence, he was online.

"Just over two minutes," Straight said in his headset. "Not real good. We're going to have to improve on that. Come on back out."

Back on the Pod Deck, Marko said, "Here's the drill. You get in your coffin, and when we wake you, you get to your pod and get it online as fast as you can. And as soon as it's online, you shut it down and get back into your coffin as fast as you can. Then we're going to repeat the whole thing, and see how many times you can do that in one hour."

York got into his coffin and the stim-sleep took over. Then he awoke to the sound of the alert klaxon, jumped out of his coffin when it opened, scrambled across the deck to his pod, and brought it online. "A minute and a half," Straight said as he shut the pod down. He climbed down the zero-G tube, across the deck, and back into his coffin.

He got his time down to a little more than a minute on the fourth scramble, but on the fifth he was feeling winded and his time went back to a minute and a half. By the tenth, he staggered like a drunk across the deck, gulping for air, and then, at some point, he lost count. By that time, he was stumbling over his own feet, his coveralls soaked in sweat, and he had trouble with the straps on the acceleration couch in the pod. When he climbed out of the zero-G tube, he fell out of the hatch on the inner hull into a heap on the deck. He struggled to his feet and heard Marko shout, "Time."

He stumbled across the deck toward the bunk room.

"Hold on there, Ballin," Straight said. "That's enough."

York stopped in the middle of the deck, bent over, and put his hands on his knees. He gulped for air, couldn't get enough into his lungs.

Marko pushed him into a seat at the command console, and as he took deep, heaving breaths, he realized the deck was crowded with gunners, all watching him. Marko handed him a glass of water and slapped him on the back. "Twenty-six scrambles, kid. Twenty-six in one hour. You broke the ship record by two. We'll make a gunner out of you yet."

Zamekis let out a cheer. Several others joined her. Some gunners shook York's hand, while others patted him on the back, and a strange feeling washed over him. He'd never felt this way before, and realized that for the first time in his life he'd done something he could take pride in.

CHAPTER 4:
ILLICIT FAVORS

York was in the mess hall with Zamekis and Marko when the alert klaxon blared and allship called them to battle stations. The three of them sprinted out of the mess together, but when they hit one of the steep ladders between decks, the two more experienced spacers just grabbed the rails, threw their feet out, and slid down to the next deck. York had seen others do that, had tried it a couple of times himself, but he was still a bit awkward and fell behind as they raced deeper into the bowels of the ship. When he got to the Lower Pod Deck, Marko and Straight were already seated at their command console, and as he shot past them, Straight gave him a nasty look. He dropped into the empty console seat—his battle station—and strapped in.

In York's only previous experience at battle stations, as he'd waited for something to happen, he'd thought the ship had been silent. But he realized now it was only the silence of anxiety and fear, beneath which he heard a faint, low-pitched rumble, possibly the ship's engines. If he listened closely, he could just make out Marko and Straight subvocalizing commands into their implants. He closed his eyes and heard the whine of some sort of mechanism. The bass drums—the main batteries—started up, and the rumble of the ship's engines changed pitch. Then Straight said something about *incoming*, said it loudly and excitedly, and the hull echoed with a cacophony of sharp pops.

He'd been warned about that, knew that he was hearing the sound of the pod gunners firing at incoming ordnance. When he'd asked Zamekis what it would sound like if the ship took damage, she'd said, "Can't really describe it, Ballin, but you'll know it when you hear it." She'd also warned him that acoustic baffling in the ship's hull meant he'd only hear damage if it was close by, or catastrophically major. "In that case," she'd said, "just bend over and kiss your ass good-bye."

The main batteries went quiet for a while, then started up again; the whine of the ship's engines changed pitch; and the pops of the pod guns ebbed and flowed. The main batteries never fired more than three or four rounds before going silent for a bit. About an hour after York had strapped down at the console, while waiting for them to start up again, he realized they'd been silent for some time. And the number of rounds fired by the pod gunners had dwindled to just a pop here and there. Then they stopped completely, and the pitch of the ship's engines dropped an octave or two. As he'd noticed earlier, the ship didn't go completely silent, but the noise level had dropped to that low-level background that required him to concentrate if he wanted to hear it.

"All hands, Watch Condition Yellow. Stand down, but remain on-station until further notice."

York fired up one of the screens on his console and pulled up a copy of the regs to practice his reading. He was struggling over a difficult word when something smacked him in the back of the head. He looked up to find Straight standing over him.

She snapped, "Next time, get here faster."

Standing behind her, Marko frowned. "The kid tried like hell."

She turned on Marko angrily, gave him an unhappy look, then walked away.

*   *   *

York was about to cycle into his coffin for the night when Zamekis interrupted him. "Hold on, York. We're not done yet. We still got important duty."

"What's that?" he asked.

She gave him a furtive grin and said, "You'll see. Follow me."

They met up with Marko, Durlling, and Stark, all of whom were wearing khaki coveralls with no rank insignia. The sleeves of their coveralls ended just above the elbows in ragged, frayed cloth, as if they'd been torn away, rather than cut cleanly. York figured he'd learn what was up by keeping his mouth shut and following orders.

Marko slapped Zamekis on the back and said, "Tonight's your night, girl."

Durlling and Stark shook her hand and congratulated her for something. At the look on York's face, Marko said, "She got her first confirmed kill today."

York followed them as they went aft. They climbed up three decks, went farther aft, then back down two. York was thoroughly lost by the time they stopped at a closed hatch. It was a large hatch, door-size, and York had learned enough to know it should be open when not under an elevated watch condition.

Marko knocked on it, which was odd. A few seconds later, the valve wheel spun and the hatch popped open just a sliver. York saw the glint of someone's eyes as they looked out at them, then the hatch swung fully open. York followed his companions through the hatch. The lights were dim, and there were quite a number of spacers present.

Just inside the hatch, Marko, Durlling, and Stark paused and rolled up the chopped-off sleeves of their coveralls. Marko had a dozen scars on his upper arm just below the shoulder, odd chevrons of scar tissue that ran in a line down his arm. Durlling and Stark had similar scars, though Durlling had fewer than Marko, but more than Stark.

The chief who'd admitted them announced loudly, "Gunner Thaddeus Marko. Thirteen and a half chevrons."

That number matched the number of scars on Marko's arms. The chief made similar announcements for Durlling and Stark, but when he announced Zamekis, he finished with "No chevrons, but she's drawing blood tonight."

That brought a raucous round of cheers. He introduced York simply as "Gunner Apprentice York Ballin." He finished by shouting, "Someone get 'em some beer."

Someone handed York a cup of dark-brown liquid with tan foam on top of it. He took a sip, tasted strong beer. He hadn't had any alcohol since his arrest on Dumark, and thought he might enjoy himself.

Marko, Durlling, and Stark were greeted warmly as they moved among the spacers, while Zamekis was jostled about in a friendly way, with lots of crude jokes and swearing. Everyone about him spoke with excessive profanity, and he realized it was some sort of tradition. York was halfway through his beer when the ranking chief shouted, "Listen up. I want the following front 'n' center." He read off a list of names, no rank, and each young spacer called shot forward accompanied by loud jeers and crude epithets, along with a steady stream of accusations concerning their ancestry and their sexual preferences—usually something to do with certain exotic animals. Each had full-length sleeves on their coveralls.

Zamekis was one of the names. Marko sat down on the deck next to York as she jumped up and ran forward.

Marko said, "This is called gunner's blood, York. Every gunner gets a half-chevron for each confirmed kill. It's the only rank that counts among us gunners. Straight's got no chevrons, and since she's not riding a pod no more, she'll probably never get one."

One by one, each candidate was escorted to the center of the room, their station chief recounted the particular kill that had earned the scar, usually with some flair and a certain amount of embellishment, and of course accompanied by a lot of crude cheers and shouts. Then they cut away the candidate's sleeves with an old, steel knife—York now understood why the sleeves ended in ragged cloth. The chief then used the knife to make a half-chevron cut in the skin high up on the arm. They let the wound bleed nicely, let blood stream down the arm all the way to the fingertips and drip onto the deck. Then they washed the blood into the deck with a splash of the black beer, and the next candidate stepped forward.

"We always do the new bloods first," Marko said. "It's a tradition. We add chevrons to the old bloods after them."

The chief ordered additional ratings, spacers already wearing cutaway sleeves, front 'n' center. York got a second beer while they added chevrons to the old bloods. He watched the ceremony closely, and at some point, though he couldn't say when, he found himself hoping that someday he'd get to stand up there and get a chevron or two.

As the pod cycled through its boot sequence, York listened to Straight's voice in his headset. "Okay, Ballin, you've done pretty good on the comp stuff. Seems you've got some talent there. So let's see if you can hit what you aim at."

York would never admit it to his new friends, but he found the inside of a pod rather cozy, like being wrapped in a cocoon of instruments. The acceleration couch conformed comfortably to his backside, and he had control of local gravity, temperature, humidity, and lighting. It felt strange to have such control over his environment.

Marko said, "In a real firefight, you stay away from any target you're not allocated. If Fire Control doesn't give it to you, you ignore it. And if they do give you one, more often than not you'll just let your onboard computer handle it without intervention. But making that kind of decision is still way over your head."

York kept the lighting low and liked the temperature a little cool. He kept his right hand near, but not on, the targeting yoke, wouldn't touch it until they told him to. He rested his left hand on the console near the controls for rate of fire and primary muzzle energy. His computer tracked the motion of his eyes and super-imposed a targeting reticle wherever he looked on his primary screen. If he'd been fitted with implants, the computer would have had a direct feed from his cerebral cortex, allowing faster response that included algorithms to anticipate his moves.

Straight took up the dialogue. "Today, we're going to give you one target at a time. They're all yours, and you're to use the pod's manual fire controls on each. No decision making. Just aim and shoot. We've walked you through this enough that you should be able to handle that much."

A stationary yellow blip appeared on one of York's screens.

"That's an enemy warship at four hundred megaklicks. And here comes your first target."

A yellow blip split off the enemy warship coming their way.

"Don't fire on it until it's been allocated."

The target came in at over three hundred lights and the distance dwindled quickly. York knew it was all simulation, but it felt so real his heart began to pound. At ninety megaklicks, the blip flashed an angry red, and following his eyes, the targeting reticle locked onto it. He gripped the targeting yoke, touched it delicately, and the pod spun wildly, the target slicing completely off his screen. He tried to bring it back, but he only caught a glimpse of the red blip as it zipped across the screen and off the other side.

Straight said, "That was sloppy, Ballin. Let's try again."

York didn't do any better on the second target. Every time he touched the targeting yoke, he overshot, completely missing it.

After he'd missed the third target with the same wild, out-of-control aiming, Marko said, "Hold on a minute. What's the gain on your gravity servos?"

York looked up at the panel over his head, still wasn't used to all the readings available there. He found the reading he needed and said, "The gain is set at a hundred percent."

Straight didn't laugh openly, but he heard her chuckle. She said, "Your crewmates are having a little fun with you. They've got your gain maxed out, which destabilizes all your controls."

Marko said, "Don't worry, kid. We all took our turn."

Straight and Marko helped him set the gain properly, and he did much better after that.

York sat at one of the tables in the lower-deck bunk room studying the operations manual for a defensive Perimeter Ordnance Delivery system, or pod. Three spacers sat at a nearby table playing cards.

There were no real bunks in the lower-deck bunk room, just the access feeds to coffin storage. Beyond that, the bunk room appeared to be a place where gunners relaxed when not in their coffins or on duty. It had a couple of plast tables with bench seats bolted to the deck; an access feed for the gunners' lockers, which were auto-stored much like the coffins; a caff dispenser; and a number of readers shared among the gunners. York was officially on duty, but Straight had ordered him to study the pod manual, and the bunk room was a good place to stay out of her way.

Under Zamekis's tutelage, his reading had improved and he only had a little difficulty understanding the pod's functions, found it far more interesting than the regs. He now understood there was a certain status among pod gunners, a rank that he could control by learning this stuff and getting confirmed kills. It didn't require approval or authorization by some officer he'd never met, and it couldn't be taken away. He was so immersed in the manual that he barely noticed the three spacers fold up their card game and leave. Now alone in the bunk room, he could concentrate even more on the manual.

A hand slapped something down on the table in front of him with a sharp smack, startling him. He looked up as Sturpik and

Tomlin sat down opposite him, the small plast vial of the tarry stuff resting on the table in front of him. Sturpik glanced over his shoulder at the open entrance to the bunk room and slid to one side a bit, placing himself between the vial and anyone who might come through the open hatch.

Sturpik smiled, though York saw nothing friendly in the man's face. "Well, kid, you ready to be a team player?"

Predator or prey, there was no question where Sturpik and Tomlin fit into the feeding chain. York said, "I really don't think—"

Tomlin interrupted him by closing his eyes and quietly shaking his head from side to side.

"Favors," Sturpik said. "You're at the bottom of the shit list on this ship, and you need friends. You won't make friends if you don't do favors."

Tomlin opened his eyes and said, "And holding that for us for a while will be a nice start."

Cracky and Ten-Ten hadn't given him much choice, either—predator or prey; be lookout for them, or victim to them.

"If you ain't gonna help us," Cracky had said, "then we gotta figure you're going to rat us out."

York had pleaded with them, told them, "I ain't no snitch."

Cracky had ignored him. "And if yer gonna snitch, then we gotta protect ourselves, gotta make sure the snitch ain't around to do any snitching. Yer either with us, or against us, Ballin."

York had reluctantly agreed to help them. It hadn't done them much good, hadn't done York any good, either.

Straight's voice startled all of them. "Ballin, you in there?"

Sturpik's and Tomlin's eyes widened; Sturpik looked at the vial of tarry stuff and hissed, "Get rid of that or you're going to get us all in a lot of trouble."

Without thinking, York reacted, reached out, and palmed the small vial just as Straight walked into the room. "Ballin," she said. "Time for more pod training."

Sturpik and Tomlin's eyes narrowed, looking at him angrily.

York lifted the reader and said, "Can I take a second to put this away?"

"Sure," she said. "But make it quick." She turned and walked out of the room.

Sturpik and Tomlin both smiled and nodded their approval, then stood and walked away.

York put the reader away, cycled his locker out of storage, and wrapped the vial in spare coveralls. He'd give it back to Sturpik as soon as he could.

CHAPTER 5: TROUBLE AGAIN

The alert klaxon woke York from stim-sleep, the lights in his coffin flashed to full brightness, and Straight's voice said, "Battle stations, this *is* a drill. Hop to it, Ballin."

York had to wait several seconds for his coffin to cycle out of storage. They'd taught him to sleep with a clean set of coveralls tucked under his arm so he didn't waste time searching for them. When his coffin cycled out, he hit the deck, got his legs into the garment, and sprinted out of the bunk room while getting his arms into the sleeves. He hit the switch on his pod hatch on the inner hull, dove through the gravity sheer as it cycled open, yanked it shut, and sealed it behind him. He grabbed a handgrip, straightened his body, and shoved off, using the zero-G to float the length of the tube to the outer pod hatch—another trick the veterans had taught him.

He hit the switch on the hatch and pushed through it as it opened. He'd learned to rotate his body so he was at the proper angle. All he had to do was tuck slightly and coast in zero-G until he dropped into the acceleration couch. Then with one foot, he kicked the hatch closed, hit the switch to seal and lock it, and strapped in.

Comp was already running his pod through pre-combat check. He scanned the readout, watched closely as the status check ran its course, and the instant it was complete he slapped the active switch. He was on station.

Straight's disembodied voice sounded in his headset. "Not bad, Ballin. A little over a minute, which is pretty good given that your coffin is always the last to cycle out."

Marko said, "Here's the drill, Ballin. You got an enemy warship at a hundred million kilometers, spitting transition shells at us at a hundred lights. How much time you got to make a decision?"

"A little under eight seconds," York said.

"Good. You've been doing your homework.

"Today we're going to walk you through a simulated engagement. And this time, when you think it's appropriate, go ahead and override."

For the last month, York had spent five to ten hours a day strapped into a pod learning and practicing. His training had started with the scramble to battle stations. He learned it was a tradition to put a new pod gunner trainee through that test. He then graduated to basic pod systems, had studied emergency procedures and backup systems. He'd moved up to pod control, had practiced targeting, aiming, and firing. It didn't seem that hard to him, and he was anxious to have a try at a real combat situation. He wasn't yet participating in full ship-wide drills, but that would come if he did well today.

He scanned his screens: guidance and ballistic control, ordnance, fire control, three tracking screens . . . a large yellow blip on his tracking screens at a hundred million kilometers. The yellow blip spit out a smaller yellow blip, a transition launch aimed at *Dauntless*; it spit out several in rapid succession. The simulation included all of the sounds of a battle, the hull thrumming with the sound of her main batteries, the pops of the pods around him firing at incoming ordnance, the sound of the ship's engines changing pitch as they maneuvered. One of the yellow blips turned red, indicating it had been allocated to him as a target. He tracked it, let it go, allowed the computer to control his pod and deflect it.

Over a period of an hour, they gave him forty targets, though he only found it necessary to override the computer on five. When they ended the simulation, he crawled down the tube to the Pod Deck thoroughly exhausted.

Marko helped him out of the hatch on the inner hull. "Not bad, kid. I would have overridden the third target we gave you, not let the computer handle it, but Straight disagrees, so it's a toss. Let's go review the whole thing."

As they turned to walk back to the command console, Marko hesitated, frowned, and said, "Hmmm!"

Straight stood near her console talking to Chief Zhako and an officer about Zhako's age.

"What's wrong?" York asked.

Marko's eyes narrowed in thought. "Zhako is master-at-arms. I wonder what he's doing down here? And with Pallaver?"

"Who's Pallaver?"

"Lieutenant Pallaver is our section head."

As York and Marko walked toward them, the three turned to look their way. None of them looked happy, and Straight looked just plain angry. As they approached, she snarled at York, "You idiot."

Marko asked, "What's going on?"

Pallaver ignored him and said, "Bring him."

Straight and Zhako each took one of York's arms and marched him in Pallaver's wake. The lieutenant led them to the bunk room where a couple of spacers waited near the locker access. They'd cycled one of the lockers out of storage and had it open, and as the five of them entered the room, one of the spacers turned and held out a pair of coveralls. He peeled back a few layers of cloth, revealing the small vial of tarry stuff. York's stomach knotted up.

Pallaver said, "We found this in his locker. Looks like a stim-hype. We'll have to analyze it to be sure."

He turned and towered over York. "Cuff him."

*   *   *

A cell was a cell. At least York now knew how to get into and out of a grav bunk. He lay there wondering how he could fix this. They hadn't questioned him yet, though he knew that would come. He considered telling them the truth, how he'd refused to accept the stuff once before, and then the second time Sturpik and Tomlin had practically forced him, had certainly tricked him . . . at least a bit. But as he thought about what he might say, it sounded whiney, like a phony excuse, which would only get him in more trouble.

In any case, those who ratted out their friends on the streets paid a painful price, ranging from a thorough beating up to and including a knife in the gut. And little by little, he was learning that these navy people had a bunch of unwritten rules not unlike those of the streets. No, he'd be a fool to squeal on his friends, though he reminded himself that Sturpik and Tomlin weren't his friends, but that really didn't matter, either. Friends or not, a snitch's life was short and unpleasant. He'd have to keep his mouth shut and pay the price.

About an hour after they locked him in the cell, some sort of mechanism in the cell hatch clanked loudly and the hatch swung open. York killed the gravity field on his bunk, caught the edge with a hand as he fell out of it, and pivoted so he landed on his feet on the deck. Zhako and Straight walked into the cell carrying manacles. "You idiot," Straight said as they cuffed his hands and ankles.

They marched him to a small room furnished with a plast desk and a couple of chairs. Pallaver and an older officer with gray in the hair at his temples were waiting there. They watched silently as Zhako sat York down in one of the chairs and locked his manacles to the chair so he couldn't move. The chair was bolted to the deck.

The older officer approached York with some sort of palm-size instrument in one hand. He gripped York's wrist and pressed the instrument against the back of York's hand. Then he raised the instrument and looked at it. "Passive scan says he's clean, but I'd still like to confirm that with a live blood sample."

Pallaver said, "Go ahead."

The older man said to York, "I'm going to take some blood."

He pressed the instrument to York's neck. It emitted a little puff of sound and he felt a momentary sting. The man raised the instrument and looked at it again.

"Well, Doc?" Pallaver asked.

The older officer shook his head. "He's clean. Nothing."

"How long?"

Still looking at the face of the instrument, the man shrugged. "This thing is sensitive enough to spot even trace elements. If he'd taken anything within the last two months, we'd know. And I'm including everything in that, not just the crap we confiscated. The only thing I see is some liver enzymes that indicate he had a small amount of alcohol a few days ago."

He looked down at York and asked, "Gunner's blood?"

York nodded and said, "Yes, sir."

The man looked again at his instrument. "And he didn't overdo that, either."

He turned to Pallaver and said, "I'm done here," then walked out of the room.

Pallaver, Zhako, and Straight surrounded York and stood looking down at him. Pallaver said, "So tell me, Spacer Ballin, where did you get that stuff?"

York had seen nothing to change his mind about the ramifications of squealing on Sturpik and Tomlin. "I found it, sir," he said. "What is it?"

Straight leaned down and put her nose a centimeter from York's. "What is it? You know fucking well what it is."

"Easy, Petty Officer," Zhako said, and she straightened up.

Zhako asked, "You don't know what it is?"

York shook his head. "Some sort of drug, I guess."

Straight threw her hands up in the air and said, "This is bullshit."

Pallaver said, "Back off, Petty Officer Straight."

She took one step back, folded her arms, and stood there staring at York.

"Okay, Spacer Ballin," Pallaver said. "You claim you found it and you don't know what it is, other than that it's probably some sort of drug."

York nodded, and Pallaver's brow furrowed. "Let's pretend I believe you about not knowing what it is. I certainly don't believe you just found it."

York stuck to his story. They attached some sort of instrument to him, looked at the instrument as they asked him questions, and agreed he was lying about finding it, but conceded that he didn't know what it was. After an hour, they finally gave up and locked him in his cell.

York spent his twelfth birthday in the brig, but after two days there, they released him into Straight's custody. As she marched him back to the Lower Pod Deck, she repeatedly slapped him in the back of the head and said, "You fuck up like this again, I'll have your balls."

As punishment, he'd been sentenced to unflavored protein cake and water for a tenday, and Straight had him back on his hands and knees scrubbing decks. Every fourth day, his watch rotation put him on first watch—graveyard. When not on an elevated watch condition, most of the ship's personnel slept through first watch, with just a skeleton crew on duty. York didn't really mind the quiet and solitude—he scrubbed the deck and stayed out of trouble.

A whirring and popping maintenance robot rolled by, cleaning the deck better than York. He'd seen several that watch and had come to realize there was no reason for him to be on his hands and knees other than sheer spite, or perhaps something to do with training, or some strange naval custom. When the robot got to York, it detoured around him.

He'd almost been part of something. *Lower-deck pod gunner* wasn't much, but it would have been a lot more than he'd had as a stray kid hanging out on the streets. And now he'd fucked that up, and probably wouldn't have even that.

"Hey, kid."

York looked up from the soapy deck, saw Sturpik and Tomlin approaching him. York rose up to his knees as the two men stopped about a pace away. Sturpik looked around furtively, then, satisfied they were alone, he reached into his coveralls and retrieved something wrapped in shimmering plastic. He unwrapped a sandwich and held it out to York. "Brought you something to eat, kid. I know that stuff they're feeding you tastes like crap."

York's mouth began to water. It had been tough choking down the unflavored protein cake. His appetite had disappeared, and he'd forced himself to eat something at each meal. But just before he reached out and took the sandwich, he realized he'd owe Sturpik a debt. He shook his head and said, "No, thanks."

"Aw come on, kid."

Sturpik held the sandwich out closer to York, and he got a whiff of real food. York's mouth watered even more, and he chose his words carefully. "No. I don't want no favors."

Both men's brows furrowed angrily. Sturpik lifted the sandwich to his mouth and took a bite. As he chewed, he spoke around a mouth full of food. "You think he's gonna be a problem, Tomlin?"

Tomlin nodded his head slowly. "Ya, bet he's not gonna pay us what he owes us."

York said, "I don't owe you nothing."

Tomlin leaned down close to him and said, "You lost our stash."

York became conscious of the fact that it was first watch, and that the three of them were alone in that section of deck, and that the two men each outweighed him by twenty or thirty kilos. "I didn't lose it. They confiscated it."

Tomlin leaned even closer. "That was prime stuff, and I don't care how you lost it. You lost it, so you gotta pay for it."

"I don't gotta pay for nothing. I didn't—"

Sturpik's boot hit York in the gut, sending a shock of pain up into his chest. He fell backward, gasping for air, landed on his back with his legs twisted beneath him. York couldn't get any air into his lungs as Tomlin lifted him by the front of his coveralls and raised a closed fist to hit him.

"No," Sturpik said, blocking his hand. "You don't want bruised knuckles when people start looking around."

Tomlin dropped York to the deck and they kicked him, no hands involved. York lost count of the kicks and at some point lost consciousness.

He awoke by himself, lying on the deck in a puddle of water. It took him a moment to realize they'd thrown the bucket of water on him before leaving. The water had a pinkish tint to it—blood. He struggled to his hands and knees.

He had a bloody nose, but mostly his ribs and chest and gut hurt. The two men didn't want him walking around displaying the obvious signs of a beating. That's the way it would have been handled on the streets.

He cleaned up the mess—Straight would give him hell if he didn't—rinsed out the bucket, and put it away. Then he cleaned the blood off his face, though he couldn't get the stains out of his coveralls. He climbed into his coffin, and stim-sleep sent him to some very unpleasant dreams.

York got to sleep in because he was working first watch, but when he climbed out of his coffin and hit the deck in his shorts, Zamekis happened to be in the bunk room, took one look at him, and said, "Holy shit, Ballin. What the hell happened to you?"

York looked down, saw that his chest, ribs, gut, and arms were covered with blueish-yellow bruises. "I fell down," he said. "Accident."

The look on her face said she wasn't buying his story. "What'd you do, fall down ten or fifteen times?"

"Fell down a stairwell." He wasn't sure there were any real stairwells on ship, probably just steep ladders and lifts, but it got him out of the bunk room and clear of her scrutiny and questions.

Working graveyard meant he was out of sync with Straight's crew, so the rest of them didn't see the bruises when he hit the showers. He noticed members of other gunner crews taking furtive glances his way, and he had to admit the discoloration stood out rather prominently.

Once clean and fully dressed, he sat at a table in the bunk room to study the regs. He learned the captain of a ship had quite a bit of latitude when dealing with drug abuse, especially if the ship was patrolling the front lines. York didn't understand why he wasn't still locked in the brig.

Marko sat down opposite him, leaned forward, and looked at the page he had open in the regs. He leaned back and looked at York for a long, silent moment.

It had become obvious that Marko, with all the chevrons cut into his arms, held considerable sway among the pod gunners. He wasn't an NCO, but York had seen him offer a "polite suggestion" to someone who outranked him, had seen him do it more than once, and they always listened very carefully.

"You know Pallaver was tipped off," Marko said.

"What do you mean?"

"He got an anonymous tip that one of Straight's crew was dealing stim-hypes. So they searched all our lockers. Now who do you think would know to tip off Pallaver like that?"

York knew it could only be Sturpik and Tomlin, but also knew he'd pay a brutal price if he told Marko that. "I don't know."

"I think you do."

York tried to pay attention to the regs, but couldn't escape the older man's stare.

Marko asked, "You know why they let you out?"

"No."

"Well, let's see." He lifted a hand, raised one finger, and said, "You're dealing, but you didn't have anything close to a salable quantity."

He raised another finger. "You weren't using, but dealers always use."

He raised another finger. "You haven't been on the ship long enough to make any connections, not that kind. And you were searched before coming aboard, so you didn't bring it with you."

He raised another finger. "And the stuff wasn't very good quality. Almost like someone knew they were going to lose it and decided to lose something they could afford to."

Marko stood and leaned on the table. "You were set up, kid."

He turned and walked out of the bunk room.

CHAPTER 6:
THE LASH

Predators didn't like witnesses—that was true on the streets and in the navy—so York did everything possible to never be alone. He studied the regs in the bunk room only if others were present, and if they got up and left, he followed them out. Once the bruises healed, he showered only at the busiest time of day, and he tried to spend as much time as possible in the more public sections of the Lower Pod Deck. If a crew member was busy repairing some piece of apparatus, he'd sit down at an empty command console nearby to study the gunner's manual.

Even when his watch rotation put him on first watch, if he wasn't scrubbing decks, he could usually find a place to sit down and do his homework within sight of someone. He knew he was "the kid," so no one really took much notice of him, and that was okay with him. But when scrubbing decks, he was stuck with the section of deck he'd been assigned, and if there was no one about, he couldn't just choose a different section of deck to scrub. For a while, he'd been lucky, but one night his luck finally ran out.

He was on his hands and knees scrubbing away, thankful that two spacers were running some sort of maintenance check on a command console nearby. But with about an hour left on first watch, they finished, packed up their gear, and left. York stood, picked up his bucket and the small duffel with cleaning solvents, moved to a section of deck near a large bulkhead, got down, and continued scrubbing there. If anything happened, he could put the bulkhead at his back so no one could come at him from behind. As he worked, he constantly scanned the deck and listened for the sound of boot steps, and only a few minutes after the two spacers had left, he heard someone coming.

When Sturpik and Tomlin came into view, he thought it suspicious that they showed up so soon after the others had left. He stood long before they got to him, reached into the duffel, and pulled out a heavy wrench he'd hidden there. He put his back to the bulkhead and held the wrench casually at his side.

"Hey, kid," Sturpik said as they approached. "What's with the wrench?" They stopped a couple of paces away.

York said, "I need it to do my job."

Tomlin's eyes narrowed angrily while Sturpik made an elaborate show of looking up and down the deck. "I don't see any reason for a wrench when all you're doing is scrubbing decks."

York shrugged. "I like to be prepared."

Tomlin lifted a foot to step forward. York stepped back half a pace and drew the wrench back, determined he'd go down fighting this time. He didn't say anything, just shook his head slowly from side to side. Sturpik put out a hand, halting Tomlin. He looked at the wrench, then into York's eyes. "Seems to me you got the wrong idea about us, kid."

York didn't relax, remained ready and poised to swing the wrench. He'd picked the largest one he could handle. "Seems to me I got the crap beat out of me last time we met, or did I just imagine that?"

"Kid, we were just helping you, just teaching you a lesson."

York shook the wrench a little, and Tomlin twitched. "I learned my lesson, and I don't intend to learn it again."

"You can't take both of us," Tomlin said.

"No," York said, "I can't. But I can hurt one of you really bad, and maybe do some damage to the other as well. And this time, you're gonna have to kill me."

Sturpik squinted at York, his head nodding up and down just a bit as he eyed him. "I don't think you learned the right lesson, kid."

"Maybe not the lesson you wanted me to learn," York said. "But I learned the lesson I needed to. And I don't intend to unlearn it."

Sturpik shook his head sadly. "You know, kid, it ain't us you gotta stand up to, it's Straight."

York knew that at some point he'd have to stand up to Straight—the law of the streets—but he also knew he needed to stand up to Sturpik too, even if it meant he got the crap kicked out of him. He didn't say anything.

Sturpik stared at him for a long moment, still squinting as if York were standing at a long distance. Then he took a step back and said, "Come on, Tomlin. Let's go get some breakfast."

Tomlin looked like he was itching for a fight, but he obeyed. He turned and the two of them walked away.

York decided it might be wise to carry the wrench at all times.

Even after York finished his tenday of unflavored protein cake and water, Straight still had him on his hands and knees scrubbing decks. And apparently, she'd decided his name was now Fuck-Up.

Come here, Fuck-Up. Do this, Fuck-Up. Do that, Fuck-Up.

Such orders were usually accompanied by a slap to the back of the head for emphasis.

Straight put him to work scrubbing the inside of the zero-G tubes. Water didn't stay in the bucket under zero-G, but they showed him how to override the gravity field in each tube before he climbed into it. He learned that adjusting the gravity to half a G made it easier to work in the tube and keep the water where it was supposed to be. He was in one of the tubes when the alert klaxon started screaming.

Much later, he learned that he should have put the tube on

maintenance status in the ship's system, though no one had thought to tell him that beforehand. Without that flag, when the ship went to an elevated watch condition, its combat systems automatically reset the tube's gravity to default combat status: zero-G.

York floated up off the handgrips, the water floated up out of the bucket, a giant, transparent globule, rippling along its edges. It broke up into smaller blobs that stuck to everything, his clothes, his face. He got a lung full of it, broke into a fit of coughing, struggled the length of the tube, tumbled out of the hatch on the inner hull, and landed in a heap on the deck spitting and choking.

"What the fuck are you doing, Fuck-Up?"

Straight stood over him, shouting. He climbed to his feet, still coughing solvent-laced water out of his lungs, as Straight bent to look through the hatch into the tube. "Holy shit, Fuck-Up, this tube's completely inoperable."

She looked at the hatch designation and spoke into her implants, "Marko, flag G-Sixteen as inoperable and take it off-line."

York had just gotten the coughing under control when she said, "You idiot," and slapped him in the back of the head.

He staggered, and all his frustration welled up. He turned to her, shouted "Leave me alone," and shoved her hard.

She stumbled backward, her leg caught the edge of a console seat, and she tumbled to the deck. She laid there, eyes wide, mouth open, saying nothing. In fact, everyone within eyesight had paused and was staring at them, and York realized then that he'd violated some rule, some regulation.

"Atteeuun'shuuuuun."

The shout startled York and he tried to assume the correct posture, but the manacles on his wrists and ankles prevented him from standing properly rigid with his hands at his sides. There was some sort of commotion near the front of the crowd, but the forest of tall uniformed strangers surrounding him blocked his view. He glanced at the female marine standing guard over him and, as if she sensed his gaze, she looked down at him, her face devoid of expression, her eyes cold and unsympathetic. "As you were," he heard someone say, and everyone relaxed.

"Spacer Apprentice York Ballin," someone barked. "Front 'n' center."

The female marine nudged York unkindly.

Edging forward among the elbows, he stepped out into the only clear space on Hangar Deck.

Behind a table sat three officers. York recognized only the woman in the middle. She'd been standing to one side in that small room when his lawyer had made him sign his enlistment papers. He now knew she commanded *Dauntless*. He threw his shoulders back, did his best to stand very proper and rigid.

The captain took no interest in him. Her hair was neatly trimmed, and she wore a freshly pressed uniform open at the collar. She glanced at a comp tablet on the table before her, leaned to her right for a moment to consult privately with the sharp-eyed male officer seated next to her, then turned her attention to York. She had soft, pleasant eyes, and York hoped he might have better luck with her than with the marine. "At ease, Spacer Ballin."

York pretended to relax.

"I am Captain Jarwith, and this is captain's mast. Do you know what that means?"

York shook his head. "I'm sorry, ma'am, no."

She nodded. "Then I'll explain. Captain's mast is an informal proceeding convened for the purpose of disciplining enlisted personnel. It allows me to correct certain deficiencies in my crew without resorting to a trial or court-martial. Do you understand?"

"Yes, ma'am," York said. No trial; it appeared the old broad would be an easy touch after all.

"Good," she said tersely. Again she looked down at the comp tablet. "Now, it's customary that a crew member's civilian past is not held against him, but I'm free to consider it if I choose. Four months ago, while stealing an old woman's purse, you struck her on the head with a blunt object, causing her death. I don't mind telling you, if you were to commit such a crime while under my command, I'd keelhaul you out to an appropriate set of coordinates then vent you."

York didn't like the way her voice hardened as she spoke. "I'm not the one who hit her. And what's keelhauling?" he asked. "And what's venting?"

Her voice cracked angrily. "Pray you never learn." She sighed and continued, "Because of your age, the civilian courts chose not to execute you, even though you had previously been arrested God knows how many times. And for reasons I still don't understand, they pressed you into the navy instead of sentencing you properly, most unusual since the press gangs don't ordinarily take capital offenders. But be that as it may, you joined this ship on the planet Dumark and since that time have been a continuing disciplinary problem for my subordinate officers. You're conniving, deceitful, and disobedient."

"But I—"

"Don't say anything," she barked angrily. "Your civilian rearing has taught you if you can get beyond the moment, then you can repeat any offense you wish as often as you wish, and probably get away with it. But here, that will not be the case. You committed an act of gross insubordination while this ship was on alert status. You disobeyed a direct order and struck the NCO in charge of your station."

"But she hit me first."

Captain Jarwith's eyes turned the color of steel. "I meant it when I told you not to speak."

She paused, looked at him carefully for a moment, then barked out orders in a sequence of staccato commands. "I sentence you to thirty days unflavored protein cake and water, and thirty days suspension of pay. During that time, you will be given the dirtiest, filthiest, most dangerous jobs on this ship, and when not on duty, you will be confined in the brig. Do you have anything to say for yourself?"

York stifled a sigh of relief. The punishment was a harsh one, but it evidently could have been worse. "No, ma'am," he said.

She frowned. "No doubt you think you can get around this punishment in some way. But you need to learn I have absolute power over your life, your very existence, and I will tolerate nothing less than absolute and instant obedience from the likes of you. And to teach you that lesson, I sentence you to fifty strokes of the lash."

York frowned. "What's the lash?"

Jarwith's eyes turned almost sympathetic, and there was no joy in her voice. "The lash is a strip of hardened plast two millimeters thick, one centimeter wide, and two meters long. Its method of use is . . . well . . . it's really quite impossible to describe." She looked at the female marine guarding York and nodded. "Sergeant."

"Aye, aye, ma'am," the marine snapped crisply, then literally picked York up by the manacles on his wrists. He struggled, but she cuffed him once across the jaw, then dropped him on his feet between the girders supporting two bulkheads. Two marines helped her manacle his wrists separately to the girders. York heard the unmistakable hum of a power knife as she cut away the back of his fatigues, then left him standing with his back exposed and his arms spread wide.

An ominous figure stepped into York's now-limited field of view. It was human in shape, but encased head to foot in mottled gray-black plast, with a face hidden behind the silvery glare of a helmet visor. It was the first time York had ever seen a marine in full-combat plast armor. Someone had made judicious use of black tape to obscure all identifying insignia, as well as the name stenciled on the marine's chest plate.

The marine saluted Jarwith crisply. She returned the salute and handed him a long strap of transparent plast. He doubled it up in his right hand, then struck it against the armored gauntlet of his left. It cracked against the plast with a sharp snap, and York suddenly understood the lash.

The marine walked around him, behind him, out of his field of view. Jarwith remained in front of him, standing at arm's length, her eyes filled with sadness. That scared York even more than had the whip crack of the lash against the marine's gauntlet.

"I'm sorry," he pleaded. "I didn't mean to do it. I won't do it again."

Jarwith shook her head and spoke without rancor. "Yes, you did, and yes, you will, though I do believe at this moment you are truly sorry. But if I let you go now, you won't learn the lesson you need to learn."

She looked over York's shoulder, nodded at the marine, and said, "You may proceed."

The metallic voice of the armored marine's helmet speaker answered her. "Aye, aye, ma'am."

There came no real warning beyond that, only a momentary delay, an infinitesimal instant during which York had enough time to hope he was mistaken about the nature of this punishment. Then he heard a loud snap, and a pencil-thin line of searing, white-hot fire etched itself with infinitely painful slowness across the back of his shoulders. His universe exploded, expanding like the fireball of a warhead in deep space, then shrinking again to that thin, narrow line of incandescent pain. He screamed and pulled violently at his restraints, had a nightmarish vision of his back splitting open to disgorge gouts of fire.

The instant ended, and the metallic voice of the marine's helmet speaker said, "One."

There came no delay now, no moment of respite. A second line of pain cut into York's back, burning its way this time across his ribs, and he disappeared for an instant into a gulf of black nothingness.

"Two," the marine barked.

The lash struck a third time and a fourth. Each time the marine voiced the count, and each time the blackness of an unknowing vacuum swallowed York for a longer and deeper moment, while between the strokes he screamed and cried and begged for mercy. For a few strokes, he screamed almost continuously, until finally he was unable to scream at all. Then the black gulf devoured him and he felt nothing more. . . .

Awareness returned slowly. He still hung by the manacles between the bulkheads, too exhausted to whimper or cry. His back was a smoldering cauldron of fire, and he could no longer distinguish the pain of the individual strokes. In front of him, the ship's doctor stood facing Jarwith, an injector in his hand. "That'll keep him conscious," the doctor said to Jarwith.

Jarwith nodded. "Any chance of permanent damage? It'd be a shame if he died."

The doctor shook his head. "He's young and strong. Probably be okay."

Again Jarwith nodded. "Thank you."

The doctor stepped out of York's field of view while Jarwith came closer and filled it completely. Her eyes were now deeply sad. "The count stands at twenty-three," she said. "I can't let you pass out. You have to feel every stroke for it to do you any good, and you have to know I'm a hard woman with a hard job to do. And I want you to understand in the depths of your soul that I will do it."

He saw lines of strain around her eyes as she looked at him, and he felt oddly sorry for her. She reached into a pocket, pulled out a length of some odd, brownish material about as big around as her thumb and a bit longer. "This is leather," she said. "Real leather, the kind you no longer see, braided strips of treated cowhide. But then you probably don't know what a cow is, do you?"

Without another word, she thrust the plug of material edge-wise into York's mouth. It tasted strangely unfamiliar. "When the lash strikes again," she said, "bite down on that. Bite down hard. It helps a little. Not much, but a little." Then she turned her back on him, walked a few paces away, turned to face him again, and called loudly, "The count stands at twenty-three. Continue the sentence."

CHAPTER 7:
THE MARINES

Lying face down on a bunk in a cell—a cell was a cell—York drifted in and out of consciousness, his back burning with the memory of the lash. When he finally came fully awake, a medical orderly stood over him, applying some sort of salve to his back.

"In case you're wondering," the orderly said, "no speed-healing for you. Captain wants you to remember the lash."

The orderly kept up a constant chatter as he worked. "Chewed your back up pretty bad. But we got you shot so full of meds there won't be any infection."

York didn't say anything. The salve—or whatever it was—cooled the burn a little.

"This stuff will help with healing, reduce scarring a little—only a little."

They let York recuperate for two days, then he went back to scrubbing decks in the cellblock. He scrubbed cells, toilets, everything. At least, in the brig, he didn't have to constantly look over his shoulder to see if Sturpik and Tomlin were coming his way.

He didn't go to the mess hall for meals with the other prisoners. He sat in his cell and choked down the unflavored, untextured protein cake, then washed it down with water. They gave him some free time each day, and he was allowed a small reader tied to *Dauntless*'s central library. He spent his time trying to improve his reading by studying the regs or the pod operations manual, though he'd probably forfeited the opportunity to become a lower-deck pod gunner.

From the regs, he learned that by committing an intentional act of violence against the NCO in charge of his station on a ship in a designated combat zone while under an elevated watch condition, he had committed a capital offense. Had the captain chosen to press charges and put the case before a formal court-martial, he would have been sentenced to death. The navy had no restrictions on age and left the means of execution up to the captain's discretion.

On the morning of the thirtieth day of tasteless food and confinement in the brig, the door to York's cell clattered open and a female marine stepped in. York didn't know much about marine rank, had glanced at it briefly in the regs, but knew enough to recognize sergeant's stripes on her sleeves, and the stencil above her shirt pocket read COCHRAN.

She tossed him khaki coveralls and said, "You ain't a prisoner no more. Put that on."

She marched him up a couple of decks, then they stepped out into a large open space. "This is Hangar Deck," she said as they walked past a shuttle craft like the one that had carried him up from Dumark to *Dauntless*. "Pretty much marine country."

She led him to an office with a marine officer seated behind a desk. He had a thin face, dark hair cut short, and piercing brown eyes that appraised York carefully as he stood there. He shook his head and said, "They didn't teach you shit, did they?"

York said, "I studied the regs."

The man continued to shake his head as he said, "I'm Cap'm Shernov. The marine rank of captain is different from the naval rank captain. It's equivalent to naval lieutenant, senior grade, but to make sure it's never confused with the captain of this ship, you never call me captain. It's cap'm. Got it?"

"Yes, sir."

"Captain Jarwith wants me to teach you manners." He looked at Cochran and said, "Show him how to do it proper."

Cochran led York out of Shernov's office, stopped there, and said, "When you enter an officer's office, you first knock politely. If the door is closed, you may open it a crack, announce your name and rank, and request permission to enter." She then walked him through an elaborate exercise. York had to repeat it several times, but eventually he learned to knock politely on the open door and wait for Shernov to say, "Enter." Then he marched into the cap'm's office following a purely square path, using parade-ground steps that were completely new to him. Two steps straight in, turn right, take one step, turn left, take one step forward, and stop facing the man squarely. York threw his shoulders back, saluted, and said, "Spacer Ballin reporting as ordered, sir."

"That's better," Shernov said. "Still not good enough, but better. At ease, Spacer."

York relaxed. Shernov and Cochran shared a look and frowned. York learned then that "at ease" meant a very specific stance. Cochran showed him how to put his hands behind his back and spread his legs slightly, but still stand squarely.

"Okay, Ballin," Shernov said. "You fucked up really bad. But us marines, we're different. You fuck up like that here, Captain Jarwith is never gonna hear about it. But you won't survive, probably just have a fatal accident. Got it?"

Bad situations frequently turned out that way on the streets. "Yes, sir."

That prompted another lesson about the difference between "Aye, aye, sir," and "Yes, sir." York also learned that while under Shernov, he was supposed to answer a question like that by screaming at the top of his lungs, "Sir, yes, sir."

Shernov leaned back in his chair and gave York an appraising look. He looked to Cochran and said, "He ain't stupid." It sounded more like a question.

York didn't look her way, but he heard Cochran say, "I'm guess-ing they just didn't pay any attention to teaching him anything."

Shernov asked York, "Did they teach you anything, Ballin?"

York screamed, "Sir, yes, sir."

Shernov grimaced and muffled his ears with his hands. "Tone it down, Ballin. What did they teach you?"

"How to work a pod, sir."

"Now we're getting somewhere," Shernov said. "Cause we need another gunner for our boats. Lost one last trip out. That's one of the reasons the captain's lending you to us."

Under the marines, York spent a little time scrubbing decks but not that much. He spent a lot of time running simulations in one of the gunboat turrets. Many of the turret's systems were iden-tical to those of a pod, and York took to it immediately. It had local systems for gravity, environmental control, targeting, and fire control. The biggest difference was that he had to wear a vac suit as a safety precaution against the turret taking a hit and losing pressure. It also had some limited external gravity control, which allowed for independent maneuvering if it was ejected from the gunboat. York didn't want to think about that.

He also had some fun doing a few runs in the gunboat pilot simulator, though Cochran told him it would be some time before he got a chance to put that to use.

The shuttles weren't *shuttles*, they were gunboats, and *Daunt-less* had three of them, named *One*, *Two,* and *Three*. Each had four gun turrets, and the gunboat's system didn't carefully allocate targets to a particular gunner. It just flagged them in his display as green for friendlies and red for foe. "If it's red," Cochran told him, "and you got a shot, you take it."

Cochran turned York over to Corporal Mike Bristow, and Bristow kept York quite busy. If he wasn't parade marching up and down Hangar Deck to Bristow's shouted commands, he was lifting weights or pumping calisthenics with some of the marines, or running simulations in a gunboat turret, or practicing weightless maneuvers in a vac suit. They taught him how to use a grav rifle and sidearm, and he spent an hour on the firing range every fourth watch rotation.

One day, after running York up and down the deck for an hour, Bristow let him take a break. York sat down on the deck near a group of marines running maintenance checks on their combat armor. "Them pod gunners give you the talk about the lowest of the low?" Bristow asked.

"Ya," York said. "Nothing lower than a pod gunner."

Bristow shouted at one of the marines working on the armor. "Hey, Cath. Is it true, nothing lower than a pod gunner?"

A small woman with short, blond hair looked up from working on the armor and grinned. "Not true at all. There's us marines." York thought she was rather pretty.

Allship blared, *Down-transition in ten minutes and counting.*

The marines all agreed that they were lower than any pod gunner, and they appeared to take pride in that. It was an odd sort of camaraderie.

Bristow said, "Ain't nobody lower than you, Cath."

She returned fire. "At least I don't have a limp dick like you, Bristow."

Down-transition in one minute and counting.

"You could make it not limp," he said. "'Course you couldn't handle it."

"Probably because it's so small I couldn't find it."

As allship started the final countdown to transition, York wondered if the two of them would come to blows. But the other marines were grinning, and York got the idea they had this conversation quite regularly.

Down-transition.

York felt that little tickle in the back of his spine, and he shivered.

Bristow frowned at him and said, "What was that, Ballin?"

"Transition," York said. "It gives me a weird feeling."

The marines stopped what they were doing and looked at him oddly. Cath frowned and said, "You *feel* transition?"

"Ya," York said. "Don't you?"

The silence grew uncomfortable, then Bristow said, "Ah, he's full of shit."

Cath quizzed York about the sensation he felt, and when he described it they all agreed he was full of shit, though apparently no one held that against him. York was relieved when Shernov marched out of his office and their attention turned away from him.

"Two boats," Shernov said. "Squads one and two, light combat harness. Milk run, going to evacuate some sort of spook team from the embassy."

He looked at York and said, "Ballin, today you get your cherry popped. You're riding side turret."

York jumped to his feet, wasn't sure if he was supposed to scramble or not. But everyone else sat or stood without moving.

Shernov said, "Calm down, Ballin. We're still outside of helio-pause."

At York's blank look, Shernov gave him a quick lesson in interstellar navigation. A ship like *Dauntless* ran blind while in transition, could only detect stellar and planetary masses, or another ship nearby if it maneuvered hard. But gravitational fields and solar wind perturbed a transition course, so when approaching a solar system, *Dauntless* down-transited just outside heliopause to take a nav fix and do a quick system map. Then they up-transited and drove in-system at ten or twenty lights, down-transiting again at a safe distance from their destination. After a bit of sub-light maneuvering, they'd be in orbit. The process usually took a couple of hours.

They ran all three boats through a thorough pre-flight check. It was determined that *Two*'s grav drive needed some maintenance, so they decided to use *One* and *Three* for the drop. York was in the bunk room closing the seals on his vac suit when three young marines, a girl and two boys, also wearing vac suits, approached him. None of them could be more than three or four years older than York. They stood there just staring at him while he finished sealing his suit. The girl stood in front of the two boys, her hands curled into fists, the fists resting on her hips, elbows out. She had a hard look about her, black hair just long enough to cover one ear on one side, shaved down to the scalp on the other side, a little too much makeup. York thought she would be pretty if she just smiled a little.

The boy behind her and on her left was a little overweight, round face, head shaved. The boy behind her on her right was medium height and rail thin, unruly brown hair sticking out in odd spiky tufts, some sort of pierced metal studs in his cheek.

Their body language said *gang*.

The girl nodded toward the fat boy and said, "This is Chunks." She nodded toward the tall, skinny one. "That's Jack and I'm Sissy. We're *Three*'s gunners, and we just want to make sure you're not going to fuck this up, because we heard about you, heard you're a fuck-up. Are you a fuck-up?"

York said, "I won't fuck up."

She dropped her fists from her hips, relaxed her hands, and stepped toward him, closing the distance between them. He wasn't sure if she was going to hit him.

"We've all fucked up at one time or another," she said. "So that don't make you no different. Just don't fuck up now."

The three of them then encircled him and carefully went over his vac suit seals, made sure he'd done it right. Chunks said, "We take care of each other."

York asked, "What happened to the last gunner? He get killed or something?"

Jack shook his head. "No, just didn't make a good gunner. Couldn't get over being exposed in the turret. He's a good marine, though."

Sissy was *Three*'s nose gunner, Chunks the portside gunner, and Jack the tail gunner. About an hour later, York climbed into *Three*'s starboard side turret, strapped in, and keyed the helmet on his vac suit. It extruded out of the stiff collar of the suit, enveloping his head in a visored helmet. He booted the pod's system and ran it through a precombat check.

When they cut gravity in *Three Bay* York's stomach rose up into his throat. He'd forgotten to activate the turret's internal gravity field, and did so now. The voice of *Three*'s pilot, Corporal Rodma, came through his headset. "It's gonna be a compensated drop all the way down, so no hi-gee necessary."

As part of York's training under the marines, Cochran had him try a dose of hi-gee a couple of tendays ago just to see how he handled it. The high-G compensation drug affected some people with a slight, euphoric high, but York had felt nothing.

One of the marines said, "Aw, you're no fun."

York recognized Cochran's voice when she said, "Shut up, Thorp."

They killed the lights as the whine of the pumps echoed through the hull, evacuating *Three Bay*. Butterflies fluttered through York's stomach when he heard a loud clatter, then the doors of the service bay parted just a crack, and a faint mist filled the bay as the vacuum of space sucked out what little air remained.

"Stay calm, Ballin," Cochran said. "Just a milk run. Nothing to worry about."

The gap in the doors of the service bay widened, and York saw the pinprick lights of a few stars on the black background of space. Then the stars slid to one side as *Dauntless* maneuvered, and the harsh glare of the nearby sun filled the widening gap between the doors. *Three Bay* had turned into a black and white world of bright glare and sharp shadows.

Because the internal gravity fields compensated for all motion, York didn't feel anything when *Three*'s service gantry telescoped the gunboat toward the open bay doors, though he got to listen to whining servos. The gantry released *Three* with a loud clang just as they reached the doors, and the gunboat floated away from its service bay. The screens in York's turret showed the massive hull of *Dauntless* as *Three* drifted away from her. Then Rodma cut in the gunboat's grav drive, and the transition ship dwindled into the distance.

"Turrets out," Rodma said.

He recognized Sissy's voice when she said, "Time to rock and roll."

York's turret slid forward on telescoping supports, putting his turret pod two meters beyond the hull of the gunboat. He now had an unobscured line of fire over far more than a hemisphere.

York put a navigation summary in the corner of one of the turret's screens. It provided a lot of information, but all he understood was that they were two thousand kilometers outside the planet's atmosphere. At that distance, it was a huge sphere that almost filled his field of view, and there wasn't much to see beyond large landmasses and several bodies of water.

"What's this place called?" one of the marines asked.

Rodma said, "It's the Thealoma system. Planet's just a number: Thealoma Two."

"No prime station," someone said. "Must be a real backwater place."

"It was in feddie hands until a year ago, and they've still got sympathizers down there."

Cochran said, "You turret gunners listen up. Intel says some of the sympathizers are hostile, might have some lightweight surface-to-air stuff, but nothing that'll reach outside atmosphere. We're still far enough out we got nothing to worry about yet, but intel's been wrong before, so stay alert."

Milk run or not, this was real, and the butterflies in York's stomach wouldn't allow him to relax. He'd promised Sissy, Jack, and Chunks he wouldn't fuck up, and he hoped dearly he could keep that promise.

The planet slowly grew larger on his screens, then filled his field of view completely. Twenty minutes later as *Three* dropped down into the outer atmosphere, he could make out large cities. He tried not to gawk, tried to stay focused on the job.

When *Three* leveled off at an altitude of ten kilometers, York turned off his internal gravity field just to feel something. When the boat hit a little turbulence, he noticed that the image in his screens didn't shake with the motion of the craft. The images were compensated as well.

"Ballin," Cochran said. "Why'd you kill your grav field?"

"Sorry, Sergeant, just experimenting."

York switched his grav field on.

One and *Three* settled down on the concrete apron of a large landing field, and Rodma said, "We're zoned."

York didn't relax until Rodma retracted his turret and Cochran said, "Ballin, shut her down, come on out and stretch your legs a bit."

York keyed his helmet to retract into the suit collar and climbed out of the turret, saw the other gunners climbing out of theirs.

"Keep the suit on," Rodma told him. "We're only going to be here a couple hours."

Sissy, Jack, and Chunks sat down to play cards.

The hatch in the side of the gunboat was an open invitation to breathe real air. "Can I step outside?"

"Sure, kid. But don't wander away from the boat."

York stepped out onto the concrete of the landing field just as two large trucks pulled away. For the first time in months, he stood on the surface of a planet beneath a blue sky—it actually had a slightly pinkish tint—with hazy clouds obscuring a sun a little too red. Cochran had deployed one squad of marines as a ring of armed guards around the two boats. York learned that the trucks were carrying the other squad as an armed escort for the spooks.

"Spooks?" York asked.

"Ya," Rodma said. "Covert ops. This place is unstable as hell.

Got every kind of faction you can imagine, all trying to kill each other off."

The war! York didn't know anything about the war. It had simply been in the background noise of his life, something far away and not of any great concern. Why think of the war when Maja's next unpalatable meal was of far greater concern? He wondered if Rodma might know a thing or two, and was trying to think of a question to ask him when the pilot suddenly glanced about, looked at York, and his eyes narrowed. "Want to have some fun?"

"Like what?" York asked.

"Come with me."

Rodma stepped through the hatch back into the boat. York followed him as he made his way to the cockpit where a woman sat dozing in the copilot's seat. "Look lively, Meg," Rodma said.

Meg opened her eyes and blinked several times. "Wah?"

"Kid's gonna get a driving lesson."

Meg had shoulder-length auburn hair tied into a utilitarian ponytail. She lifted herself out of the seat and regarded York with dark brown eyes. "He's a driver?"

"Not yet," Rodma said, dropping down into the pilot's seat. "But he scored pretty high on the sims. Let's see what he can do for real."

York's heart fluttered as he said, "Me, drive the boat?"

"Don't worry," Meg said as she pushed him down into the copilot's seat. "You can't crash this thing, especially with Rodma next to you."

Sissy, Jack, and Chunks gathered behind her, peering over her shoulder. Jack said, "You never let me drive."

"You're damn right," Rodma said. "Not with your sim scores."

York gripped the control yoke as Meg left to tell the squad guarding the boats to spread out a bit. She and Rodma seemed to think this would be a real lark, but as York's gut tightened, he didn't share their sense of adventure.

"Don't crush the yoke," Rodma said. "Relax."

York's knuckles had turned white, so he let go of the yoke and flexed his fingers.

Jack said, "Bet his dick turns white like that when he fucks."

Rodma hooked a thumb over his shoulder. "You three go back and strap down. Probably going to shake and rattle a little while the kid's learning."

He looked at York. "Okay, let's get this boat hot. You do it. I'll watch."

York heard the hatch slam shut as he brought the boat's systems up, and Meg leaned over him a moment later. "So far, so good. Seems to know what he's doing."

"Now," Rodma said, "simple lift, straight up, and hover at about a meter."

York made sure the attitude yoke was neutral, then gripped the thrust stick beside his acceleration couch. *Stay calm*, he thought, *move slowly*. He applied the tiniest bit of power to the boat's underbelly grav fields and nothing happened. He increased the power slightly and still nothing.

"He's cautious," Meg said. York glanced up at her and she added, "That's a good thing, York."

York applied more power in tiny increments until the boat lurched and lifted off the concrete. It startled him, and he cut the power. The boat settled softly back to the concrete.

Rodma and Meg had him try again, and the next time he lifted the boat and held it at one meter. The gunners cheered. The pilots made him lift and settle back down repeatedly, until he felt comfortable doing it, and he began to relax. They were hovering at one meter when Rodma said, "Now this is the tough part. This boat's so heavily gyroed and compensated, anyone can do this. Let's see how you do on full manual."

He reached out and hit a switch on the console in front of him. The computer said, *Disabling stability controls is not—*

Rodma gripped his thrust stick and control yoke as he interrupted it, "Override, override, override."

The boat canted to the right side, York compensated, overdid it, and the boat swung to the left. He overcompensated again and swung back to the right, then York's controls suddenly went dead and the boat leveled off. Rodma had taken control.

York said, "Sorry."

"No," Meg said. "You did good, kid."

They tried again, and the next time York managed to stabilize the boat and hold it hovering on full manual control.

Meg said, "Kid's a fucking natural."

York beamed with pride, lost his concentration, and the boat canted to one side.

Rodma had York doing simple attitude maneuvers with the boat hovering at about ten meters, moving the boat forward and backward, right and left, all on full manual control. They'd been at it for a couple of hours when the trucks returned from the embassy. York climbed back into his turret, and the gunboats lifted into the air to return to *Dauntless*.

He'd learned that the marines were always looking for good boat drivers, and his scores on the sims had been good enough to earn him the chance to try it for real. And he'd done well enough that Rodma and Meg were going to recommend that Shernov accelerate his pilot training.

As the boat lifted higher into Thealoma Two's atmosphere, York ignored the view and daydreamed about making a real life for himself in the navy. Maybe he could get promoted to something better than spacer apprentice. He was thinking on that when the turret's alert klaxon blared at him. *Incoming,* the computer said, and two red blips appeared on his screens, identifying two missiles arcing toward them, trailing plumes of rocket smoke behind them.

York's heart pounded up into his throat and he knew he was going to screw this up. He focused his eyes on one of the targets, and following his eye movements the computer marked it with a tracking reticle. He swung his turret toward it, locked a target designator onto it, and fired a short burst of smart rounds. *Trust the target designator and the smart rounds*, his training had told him time and again.

He swung the turret toward the other target, now ignoring the first, locked another target designator onto it, and fired another burst. The alert klaxon was still screaming at him when both targets blossomed into small suns much too soon for his second burst to have reached the target. One of the other gunners had killed the second target, and his second burst of rounds trailed off harmlessly.

The klaxon went silent, and the only sound in the turret was the pounding of his heart.

"Nice shooting, Ballin," someone said.

Sissy said, "And almost a twofer on his first time out."

Chunks said, "Ya, girl. I think he was targeted pretty good. If you hadn't taken that second one out, it would have been a twofer."

He recognized Meg's voice. "Kid's a natural."

Cath said, "Wonder if he can do a twofer when he gets his real cherry popped."

Even though he was alone and no one could see him, he blushed.

CHAPTER 8:
A THROWAWAY

York had barely stripped out of his vac suit when Cath and Bristow cornered him. They were in a festive mood as Cath said, "Come with us, kid."

They took him into the armory where they stored their combat harnesses and weapons, an area off-limits to everyone but marines. They led him through an outer room with racks of grav rifles and crates of other weapons, and into a strange space where human-shaped suits of plast hung in rows on rails suspended from the overhead deck. "We'll use mine," Cath said. "I'm only a little bigger than him."

She stopped at a row of suits, hit a switch, and the suits cycled past them.

Only once before had York seen full-combat plast armor, the day he'd received fifty strokes of the lash. He'd been too frightened then to pay much attention, had only noticed the mottled gray-black finish on the plast and the silvery glare of the helmet visor. There still wasn't much more than that to see.

Cath stopped the track at a particular suit. She muscled it off the track and said, "Here." She threw it over York's shoulder.

To his surprise, it weighed a lot less than he expected. "It's not so heavy," he said as he followed her into the outer room.

"By itself, the plast isn't much," she told him. "But when we feed power into it, it'll stop some serious firepower. It's the reactor pack and weapons that weigh us down."

Bristow and several marines were waiting for them.

York asked, "What are we doing?"

Bristow grinned. "We're going to see if you're full of shit. You better not be, cause I got some money riding on you."

They bundled York into Cath's armor undersuit, then into the armor itself, and had him sit down on a bench in the locker room with the helmet visor open.

Standing over him, with Cath beside him and the other marines looking on, Bristow said, "We're going to be up-transiting here shortly. You said you can feel that, right?"

York nodded, which didn't work too well inside the armor.

"Bristow and me, we're betting on you," Cath said. "I've put the suit in isolation mode, and I'm controlling it with an external maintenance feed. So when I close that visor, you're not going to be able to see or hear anything, including allship. It might be twenty minutes, it might be an hour, but when you feel transition, you give us a thumbs-up, or wave your arms, or something. Got it?"

"Yes, ma'am," York said.

Cath reached toward him and closed the visor. It sealed with a faint click and a huff of air. Cath had told him the visor could be set to provide an immersive projection of the outside world, or a virtual console for almost any function on ship, but it was completely opaque now. A faint red light filled the inside of the helmet, though all York saw was the visor's dark interior surface.

In the silence, the suit made strange sounds, a click here, a pop there, but York quickly grew bored, then drowsy. He struggled to stay awake, didn't want to disappoint Cath and Bristow by sleeping through transition. But his eyes grew heavy, and he slipped in and out of a light doze. Then that tickle crawled up the back of his spine, startling him into full wakefulness. He raised his arms and waved them about, but nothing happened.

He wondered if they'd forgotten him. Maybe he had slept

through transition, missed it completely, and in their disappointment they'd left him there as punishment. The marines had seemed kinder than that, and it saddened him to think that they were as callous as everyone else in his life.

The visor popped open, Bristow standing in front of him grinning, behind him Cath whooping and cheering. Bristow said, "Well, I guess you ain't full of shit, kid."

Cath leaned over his shoulder and said, "Oh, he's full of shit, all right. Just not the kind of shit we thought."

They helped him out of the armor and the undersuit, then Cath wrapped her arms around him and gave him a big kiss on each cheek. She was pretty, and that stirred something within him he'd never paid much attention to before.

She and Bristow collected quite a bit of money from the rest of the marines, though York noticed that his gunner mates hadn't done any betting. York asked Sissy, "You didn't bet?"

"No," she said, shaking her head. "But we're glad you ain't a liar."

Holding a fist full of currency, Cath looked at Bristow, nodded toward York, and said, "What do you think?"

Bristow frowned, looked at York, and said, "Ya."

The two pooled their earnings, then split it three ways and gave York a third. He'd never seen so much money before.

"That's shipboard script," Cath said. "Only good on board. You'll have to deposit it into your pay account if you want to convert it to any local currency."

"Pay account?" York asked.

She and Bristow traded a look, and Bristow said, "You do know you got a pay account, don't you, kid?"

York learned that the navy was paying him, a nice little sum every tenday, though he'd forfeited all pay while in the brig. And while Cath and Bristow considered his pay grade as a spacer apprentice downright paltry, York had never had any money before, so to him it was quite a fortune.

* * *

York didn't get to spend much time with his gunner mates, though he would have liked to because they were a little closer to his own age. Bristow continued to march him up and down the deck, drilling him in parade-ground techniques York thought were probably useless. York also spent as much time as possible training in the turret and flight simulators. He made another trip down to the surface of a planet as a turret gunner, but nothing happened going down or coming back up. While down there, he did get in a couple more hours practicing gunboat piloting with Rodma, actually took the gunboat up to an altitude of a thousand meters and brought it back down nicely. Rodma told him the marines had an attitude about skill sets: If you were old enough to wear the uniform, you were old enough to do whatever you proved you were capable of.

One afternoon, York was at the firing range practicing with a grav rifle. It had a heck of a kick and fired a round at Mach 2, which made a small sonic boom with a rather hollow sound. He heard a loud, thunderous roar boom through the firing lanes, a sound very unlike that made by the grav rifle, and a light cloud of bluish-gray smoke drifted in front of him. It smelled rather unpleasant. The thunderous roar boomed again, so out of curiosity York cleared the breech on his rifle, cut the power to it, laid the rifle down, and stepped back from it. He pressed a switch on the wall of his lane, signaling to the range marshal that his firing lane was now clear.

About three lanes over, he spotted Cath holding some sort of bluish, metallic pistol. She aimed down the lane, and when she pulled the trigger, the pistol emitted the loud boom and the bluish-gray smoke. She fired a few more times, then noticed him standing there watching her. She stepped back, hit the switch clearing her lane, did something to the pistol she held, dropping several small shells into the palm of her hand.

"Curious?" she asked him.

She handed him the bluish metal gun, which was quite heavy. "It's an old-fashioned, chemically powered slug thrower." She handed him one of the shells. "It contains a chemical explosive. When you pull the trigger, it ignites the explosive, which accelerates the bullet down the barrel. No energy signature."

"Why would you want one of these when you could have a grav gun?"

She shrugged. "They're actually pretty reliable, a good backup piece if your grav gun fails. And"—she said it again—"no energy signature. If someone does a sweep looking for energy weapons, they won't find this. You should get one for yourself, kid."

"Where would I get one?"

"Just about any place that advertises marine equipment. But be sure to register it with the master-at-arms when you board ship."

She gave him a short lesson in how to handle the gun, allowed him to fire a few rounds. It kicked even more than the grav gun.

A month later, they down-transited just outside Toellan nearspace, and a couple of hours after that they docked at Toellan Prime, a massive space station orbiting the planet. There was a sense of excitement in the air that York didn't understand until Bristow said, "Come on, kid. We got shore leave."

York asked, "We're going down to Toellan?"

Bristow shook his head. "No, but there's some great bars on Toellan Prime."

They joined Cath, who was carrying a small cloth bundle, and the three of them set out with a group of a dozen marines that included Sissy, Jack, and Chunks. York followed them as they made their way up several decks to a large open hatch in the side of the ship. Next to the hatch stood a young female officer. One by one, the marines approached her, touched the identity cards clipped to their chests, and saluted, saying, "Request permission to leave the ship, ma'am."

She raised a palm-size instrument and scanned each ID card, then saluted and said, "Permission granted."

The marine then turned to the flag of the Lunan Empire, which was draped on a bulkhead next to the hatch. He saluted it, then stepped through the hatch.

Like so many other things, no one had bothered to tell York about this little ceremony; they had probably assumed he already knew. When it was his turn, he tried to imitate the marines before him, touching his ID card, standing at rigid attention, and snapping a crisp salute. "Request permission to leave the ship, ma'am."

She scanned his ID card, returned his salute, and let him go.

York saluted the flag, then stepped through the hatch into a passageway about three meters long. He noticed it had expansion joints, and guessed it was some sort of flexible coupling to the station. At the far end, he stepped out into an avenue large enough for a couple of trucks to drive down side by side. It reminded him of a wide street filled with people in a hurry, walking toward some destination, though there were no vehicles, just pedestrians. He spotted Cath, Bristow, and the marines clustered on the far side of the street beneath a flashing sign that read JANDO'S BAR AND GRILL. York wove his way through the foot traffic to join them.

He asked Cath, "Are we going in there?"

She looked up at the sign for Jando's and said, "No, that's not for us marines."

She looked at York and frowned. "And that reminds me."

She tossed him the bundle she'd been carrying. "Put that on. Where we're going, you don't want to look navy."

York shook it out, discovered it was a marine tunic. He pulled it on over his coveralls.

York followed the marines as they wandered down the avenue. They passed a lot of bars and restaurants, some quiet and dark, with dim lights and a subdued atmosphere, some so loud that even through closed doors the noise spilled out into the street. They made their way to one of the noisier places, a bar with a bright flashing sign that read THE DROP ZONE. Beneath the bar's name, a colorful display depicted a cartoonish simulation of armored marines amidst a barrage of exploding shell bursts. And beneath that, double doors swung both ways on spring-loaded hinges. Every time a marine pushed through one of the doors, the roar from within erupted into the street like the shriek of an angry animal.

Bristow said, "There's gotta be a bar with that name in every port in the empire."

Cath said, "Bet the feddies call 'em that, too."

York followed them through the doors and into the noise. Cath threw an arm around his shoulders and said, "Food's good, booze ain't watered down, the whores are clean, and they're all legal, at least sixteen standard years old. What's your preference, kid, boy or girl?"

"Uh . . ." York said, realizing he sounded like an idiot. "I . . . uh . . ."

Cath leaned away from him to look at him carefully, her eyes narrowing. She studied him for a moment, then leaned close and whispered in his ear, "You're a virgin, aren't you?"

Bristow said, "Stop busting the kid's chops."

"Don't worry," Cath whispered. "Your secret's good with me."

They ordered a round of drinks. Back on Dumark, Cracky and Ten-Ten had introduced York to the hard stuff once, and he'd spent the night puking his guts out, had decided he didn't like alcohol. But he wanted to fit in, especially since his gunner mates ordered drinks, so he ordered a beer.

They found an empty table and commandeered it. Some of the marines broke out a deck of cards, while Cath and Bristow kept up their constant banter.

Cath suddenly pointed to a display above the bar and said, "Shit! We got a new SDO."

York asked, "SDO?"

"Ya," Bristow said, "Senior Drop Officer. Shernov's our drop officer, but the SDO's the most senior drop officer in all of Fleet, the one with the most time in uniform at any rank."

Cath said, "The feddies have a standing reward of one million imperials for whoever takes down the SDO. Makes an SDO's life interesting."

"And short," Bristow added.

The marines slammed down drinks at a rate York couldn't keep up with, so he didn't even pretend to try. Bristow wandered off with one of the female prostitutes, and Cath went upstairs with another marine. Sissy approached a male prostitute and they went upstairs, while Jack and Chunks stayed with the card game. York wandered over to the bar to get another beer, and while he waited for it, Cap'm Shernov leaned on the bar next to him.

York stiffened and straightened, but Shernov held up a hand and said, "At ease, Ballin. No saluting here. We're all on leave."

When the bartender brought York his beer, Shernov ordered one for himself. York was trying to think of a polite way of escaping the situation without just turning around and walking away, when Shernov said, "My people are saying good things about you."

York wasn't sure what to say about that.

"They say you work hard, mind your own business, do your job, and keep your mouth shut. And that doesn't add up."

"I don't know what you mean, sir."

Shernov turned toward York, leaned on the bar with one elbow, and looked directly at him. "You're supposed to be a troublemaker."

Shernov stared at him hard, waiting for him to say something. But all he could come up with was, "I took some bad advice from the wrong people."

Shernov continued to stare at him, his head nodding up and down slowly. "The lash is a hard lesson to learn. Did you learn it?"

"Yes, sir. I think so."

"Ya," he said, still nodding. "I think you did. They tell me you're a crackerjack gunner, and Rodma says you're a good pilot. Need a few hundred hours in the cockpit and a little more rank to qualify, but that can be arranged. You ever think of making a formal transfer into the marines?"

The idea of being a marine was so foreign to any of York's thinking that Shernov's question took him completely off guard. "I . . . I don't know, sir. I never thought about it. I guess I just want to be a pod gunner."

Shernov grimaced. "About that, Ballin. I gotta be honest with you. You're a throwaway. The navy doesn't want you so they threw you to us marines. And if you'd continued to be a problem, we'd have fixed the problem, but you wouldn't have survived to see the result. Sorry, kid, you're not going to get another chance with the navy. Best throw in with us marines."

Shernov took his beer and wandered away. York stood there carefully dissecting the cap'm's words, trying to find some hidden meaning, some hint that the words didn't mean what they meant. A throwaway! He'd been a throwaway all his life. And then he'd had a chance with the navy, but he'd screwed that up.

He decided to try some of the really strong alcohol the marines called 'trate. That was another mistake. He spent the night on his hands and knees with his head in the toilet.

York had no memory of returning to the ship, but the next morning he woke up in his bunk. When he stood up, his stomach churned and his knees trembled. Cath and Bristow took him to the mess hall and made him eat a full breakfast. As he choked it down, he was thankful Cath didn't broadcast the secret of his virginity to the entire squad. That evening, York stayed on the ship when the rest of the marines went on leave.

He sat down at a reader and pulled up a copy of the pod manual, then realized he was wasting his time. He spent the rest of the evening in the gunboat flight simulator, and somewhere while practicing lift-offs and landings over and over again, he decided it was time to lose his virginity.

The next day, he felt a lot better, at least physically. Mentally, he kept replaying Shernov's words: He was a throwaway. But he didn't want to be a marine; he wanted to be a pod gunner.

That evening, he accompanied Cath and Bristow to The Drop Zone. He bought a beer just to blend in, but he nursed it carefully, making it last as long as he could so he didn't have to buy another. He watched the whores working the crowd of marines. The male whores varied from almost effeminate beauty to ruggedly handsome. He wished he could be ruggedly handsome. Among the female whores, he spotted several who seemed to be only a few years older than him. He noticed a dark-haired beauty looking his way and smiling at him. He smiled back.

Cath dropped into a seat beside him and gave him an appraising look. She had light-brown eyes, wore her blond hair cut chin length, and was attractive even in marine fatigues. She grinned and said, "Don't look at me like that, kid. I'm no cradle robber. Though maybe when you're a bit older."

York's face felt uncomfortably warm and he looked away.

"It's pretty obvious what you're up to tonight."

He looked into her eyes, then glanced at the other marines around them. None of them was paying the least bit of attention to the two of them. He could probably handle it if the rest of the marines learned, but not his gunner mates.

She leaned toward him and whispered, "Don't worry, I kept your secret. You got your mind set on doing this? You absolutely sure?"

If York wanted to be completely truthful, he would have answered *Yes* to the first question, and *I don't know* to the second. He kept it simple. "Yes."

She leaned back and looked at him, her eyes narrowing. "Then if you're gonna do this, Momma Cath is going to make sure you do it right."

She stood and said, "Come with me."

York wasn't sure what she had planned, but he knew he could trust her. He stood and followed her as she wound her way between tables and figures in marine uniforms to the far end of the room. She stopped at a table where an older woman sat reading a book with pages that York thought might be made of real synth. The woman looked up from her book, and she and Cath spoke briefly, then she looked at York and said, "What's his preference, boy or girl?"

Cath glanced his way and said, "What do you think?"

The woman nodded. "Girl."

She subvocalized something, and York guessed she was equipped with implants. Then she said to Cath, "Take him up to room 203."

When they got upstairs, the most beautiful young girl York had ever seen stood leaning in the doorway of room 203. She was clearly only a few years older than him, and had blue eyes and auburn hair cut shoulder length. She wore an exotic, low-cut, floor-length gown that clung to her curves and fired York's imagination. She smiled at him and said, "You must be York. I'm Jessica."

She took his hand and led him into the room. Cath didn't say anything, but he heard the door close behind them, and he and Jessica were alone.

Much later, York learned that the girl was actually in her thirties. It didn't matter; York decided he was in love.

CHAPTER 9:
COMRADES

Dauntless spent two more nights docked on Toellan Prime. York returned to Jessica each night. He didn't have the funds to spend the entire night with her, could only afford an hour of her time each night, but it was a wonderful hour. He was in his bunk back on ship when he felt it up-transit, and he knew he'd probably never see her again.

York scrubbed decks, trained in the turret and flight simulators, practiced his reading, marched about to Bristow's parade-ground commands, spent time on the firing range, all the while trying to put Jessica out of his mind. Fifteen days after leaving Toellan, she was still there, haunting his every waking moment, when they down-transited outside the Norgaard system.

The marines all seemed nervous and on edge as they gathered on Hangar Deck to listen to Shernov's briefing. "Listen up, people," he said. "Gather round and pay attention."

Shernov held a small instrument that fit easily in the palm of his hand. He thumbed a switch on it and a projection of a greenish-brown planet appeared in front of him. Norgaard was mostly water with a few small landmasses.

"Fleet just took Norgaard from the Federals. It was a nasty fight, and now we've got to secure the system. We landed ten thousand troops twelve days ago. They've been sweeping the countryside around Dusand, Norgaard's capital, cleaning up pockets of resistance, the usual stuff. They report they're mostly running into amateurs with just a few feddie advisers among them."

Shernov touched a switch on the projector and *Dauntless*'s image appeared above the planet next to two other ships. York understood that the scale of the ships' images had been expanded, otherwise they'd just be small specks above the planet.

"We rendezvoused with *Markov*, the sleeper transport that brought in the troops, and *Avenger*, a medium cruiser. Sometime in the next three or four days, the politicos are going to arrive, and our job is to secure a large compound that's been designated as the new imperial embassy. It's on the edge of the city in a residential area, so reasonably defensible."

He paused to scan the assembled marines carefully. "All squads, full combat armor and heavy weapons, mortars, emplacements, the works. Our boats will have to make a couple of trips to get all two hundred of us and our equipment down there."

He looked at Rodma. "After the first drop, *Three* stays airborne above the compound while *One* and *Two* shuttle the rest of us down. Then I want all three boats in the air patrolling the streets around the compound. If something's going to happen, I want to know about it before it happens."

Rodma and the other pilots acknowledged the orders with a chorus of *Yes, sirs.*

Shernov added, "And go in fast and loud. I want the locals to remember who they're dealing with. Hopefully, we'll have less trouble with them that way."

While *Dauntless* maneuvered in-system, York donned his vac suit then climbed into his turret early to run it through a precombat check. The computer reported that all systems were functioning. He noticed the other turret gunners had done the same, and Rodma and Meg were likewise running *Three* through a full check. He listened carefully to the chatter in his headphones.

"My reactor pack's only at eighty percent."

"Tear it down and do an overhaul. We got time."

The usual banter had completely disappeared.

"I'm getting a minor leak in my left gauntlet. I guess I could ignore it since we're not doing any vac work."

"Don't take any chances. We got spares. Change it out."

York considered what he was hearing, then said, "Computer, detailed diagnostic scan of all turret functions, verbose output."

He rarely ran such a full analysis since it took more than an hour, but he had the time, and the way the marines were behaving told him to be extra cautious. He flagged a couple of minor concerns for later review, no more than maintenance issues, nothing that would affect performance during the coming drop. He finished the diagnostic scan about ten minutes before launch, and heard the clatter and clang of the marines boarding the gunboat in the bulky, full-combat armor. The marine com channel remained silent.

York switched to the gunboat's intership channel.

"Launch in five minutes and counting."

The marines had finished strapping in and *Three* now clung to an unnerving silence.

They cut gravity in *Three Bay*, killed the lights, and the whine of the vacuum pumps echoed through the boat's hull. The large doors of the service bay opened, and the docking gantry shoved *Three* out into the blackness of space. York caught a momentary glimpse of *One* and *Two*, then Rodma kicked in *Three*'s drive.

"We're not going in fast enough for hi-gee," Rodma said. "But we are going in fast, less of a target that way."

York tapped into the gunboat's telemetry feed, saw that Rodma was accelerating at thirty G's, the maximum at which the boat could compensate for an internal field of one G.

"Turrets out," Rodma said, and York's turret telescoped out from the hull.

After a little more than a hundred seconds at thirty G's, Rodma reversed the drive and decelerated. They hit atmosphere at Mach

40, the air screaming past *Three*'s hull. York's screens blanked for an instant, then recovered as the computer processed images so he could see through the burning reentry plasma.

At Mach 3, Rodma launched the boat's drones.

The gunboat had twenty small combat drones, and York heard the *chug-chug-chug* as *Three* spit them out. On his screens, the computer flagged them as friendlies with a green reticle. He spotted another green blip about two hundred meters out which the computer identified as *One*.

At three hundred meters, they dropped below Mach 2 and leveled off. York now understood what Shernov meant by ". . . go in fast and loud." It must have been an impressive sight from the ground to see the three boats scream by overhead, sonic booms blasting the entire city.

York spotted quite a few damaged buildings below them. Some had walls missing, exposing the interior of several floors, and some were mostly rubble with no more than a portion of one wall still standing. All appeared badly burned.

As they approached the outskirts of the city, there were fewer multistory buildings, and the streets opened out into broad, multi-lane avenues. *Three* slowed considerably and banked to York's side, and his stomach lurched as the ground rushed toward him. Rodma leveled off at a hundred meters and circled a large compound with several buildings protected inside a masonry wall. York saw the blip of *Two* also circling as *One* settled down lazily on the ground inside the wall, then dislodged its marines, many of them lugging heavy equipment. After *One* lifted into the air *Two* took its turn unloading its marines, then it was *Three*'s turn.

York swallowed hard as again the ground rushed toward him. He felt no physical sensation, since all motion was fully compensated by the boat's internal gravity fields. But something primal inside him cringed, his mouth filled with saliva and he gulped back nausea.

"Gunners," Rodma said as he settled the boat toward the ground, kicking up a cloud of dust, "stay alert."

While they were still three meters off the ground, the main hatch slammed open with a clang that echoed through the hull. At one meter, Rodma said, "Zoned for drop."

York heard the marines clambering out of the boat. He sat in his turret scanning the wall of the compound, not sure what he was supposed to be alert for. Then Rodma lifted the boat straight up in a gut-wrenching vertical elevator climb.

Rodma leveled off at an altitude of a hundred meters above the compound wall. "Gunners," he said, "watch the streets below. If you see any movement, flag it with a targeting reticle so the combat grid can analyze it."

York heard a bunch of chatter back and forth between the pilots of the boats as all three circled the compound. The majority of the buildings in the vicinity were only one or two stories, and with wide streets separating them he now understood Shernov's comment about *"reasonably defensible."*

He kept his eyes on the streets below, was surprised at the complete lack of activity on the outskirts of such a large city. He guessed the civilian population must be huddled in their homes, awaiting the outcome of the transition in power.

When all three pilots were satisfied there was nothing going on within a hundred meters of the compound wall, *One* and *Two* accelerated in a vertical climb back to *Dauntless.*

Rodma lifted *Three* to five hundred meters and slowly circled the compound about two hundred meters outside the wall. York's turret was on the side that faced out into the city proper. He thought he saw something moving, flagged it with a targeting reticle, but the computer told him it was a false alarm.

Rodma said, "Calm down, Ballin. You're jumping at shadows."

"Better to jump at shadows that aren't there than miss one that is," Sissy said.

Meg said, "Good point. Stay jumpy, Ballin."

They flagged several more false alarms, then York spotted

something and flagged it. In a fraction of a second, the computer showed him an enhanced image of a young boy standing in the doorway of a residential structure. It flagged him as yellow, meaning it was up to York whether or not to take a kill shot. The kid wasn't more than six or seven years old, and York couldn't imagine him menacing the heavily armed gunboat. Then an adult woman swooped into the picture, swept the boy up in her arms, and closed the door.

"I got a live one," Sissy shouted. The alert signal started bleating at him, telling him they had incoming, but York had no targets on his screens. York heard Sissy fire three bursts, then she said, "Got him. But that asshole was no local insurgent. He was in full combat armor, with a shoulder-fired RPG."

Rodma said, "I'm relaying that info up to—"

The alert system blared a warning, but York didn't have any targets on his screens. He heard the other turrets firing burst after burst.

"Taking evasive action," Meg shouted.

The boat slewed heavily to starboard as Rodma swung it into a sharp turn. York's turret swung downward as the boat banked and a target came into his range of fire. He didn't have time to do anything but swing the turret around and fire a burst. Then the boat lurched so violently York actually felt the motion, and his helmet speakers cut out to deaden the sound of an explosion.

Below him, buildings raced past as his telemetry feed showed him Rodma trying to gain speed and altitude, and failing. It also showed him that his turret supports were damaged.

"We're going down," Rodma shouted.

"York," Meg said. "I can't retract you, and you don't want to be there when we bury the starboard side in dirt. I got to cut you loose. Listen to your onboard computer."

His internal gravity died, then explosive bolts on his turret supports fired, pressing him into the acceleration couch and ejecting his turret from the boat.

Rodma had managed to gain some altitude, but from eight hundred meters up the ground rushed at him all too quickly.

His computer said, "*Cutting feed to all nonessential systems to conserve local power reserves. Recommend you initiate manual operation of external gravity fields for a controlled landing.*"

York was going to die. His turret would slam into the street and splatter bits and pieces of him all over the place, and there was nothing he could do about it. Then the computer's words hit him. . . . *manual operation . . . controlled landing.*

His training kicked in; hundreds of hours in the simulator produced a strange sort of autonomic response, as if he were a robot controlled by some exterior mind.

"Computer," he said, his voice trembling, his gut tightened with fear. He gripped the crude control yoke and attitude stick, nothing as sophisticated as the gunboat's. "Activate external gravity fields and manual flight controls."

"*Controls activated. To conserve power, it is recommended that you maintain freefall for another six seconds . . . five . . . four . . . three . . . two . . . one . . .*"

York powered up the external gravity field, decelerating the turret at a uncomfortable three G's, only then realizing that while his hands were calmly controlling his descent, his mouth was screaming, "Ahhhh!"

The ground rushed toward him, closer and closer, then the turret came to a stop, floating about two meters above the street.

He sat there for several seconds, gulping, trying to calm his racing heart.

"*Hovering without purpose is depleting power reserves.*"

York settled the turret gently onto the street.

"Hang in there, *Three*. We're on our way, thirty minutes out, hi-gee drop."

A blip on his screens showed him that *Three* had gone down about four hundred meters west of him, but he noticed another friendly blip a hundred meters north. He switched to visual, saw an oblong object canted to one side in the middle of the street. A hatch in the side popped open and Chunks climbed out. They must have ejected the portside turret as well.

Fifty meters beyond Chunks, he spotted a soldier in mottled green combat armor, carrying a rifle and jogging toward Chunks, followed by a half dozen other soldiers in similar garb. York wanted to believe the marines from the compound had come out to rescue them, but that was more than a kilometer away, and there was something different about the armor the soldier wore, something not imperial. York's fears were confirmed when the soldier stopped about ten paces short of Chunks and aimed his rifle at him. Chunks raised his hands high above his head.

On ejection from the gunboat, the computer had automatically put a display of his power reserves in the corner of one of his screens. He could sustain flight at a little more than one G with no internal gravity compensation for about ten minutes. Or he could fire twelve three-round bursts, but not both.

Another soldier jogged up to the one holding the gun on Chunks, and the two conferred for a moment.

"Computer," York said as he gripped the control yoke and attitude stick. "Turret weaponry on visual tracking control." The computer would now control aiming of the turret's guns by tracking York's eyes, leaving him free to control the turret's flight with his hands. He could fly in one direction and shoot in another. He scanned his readouts; the turret was hot and ready to go.

The two soldiers finished conferring. The first turned to Chunks, and without warning swatted him in the face with the butt of his rifle. Chunks crumpled into a heap on the street. The second soldier stood over Chunks and lowered the muzzle of his rifle toward the gunner's head.

York applied power to the external grav fields and his turret sprang up off the street. He focused his eyes on the street to one side of Chunks and fired a burst. It tore up the tarmac and both soldiers looked his way. He slammed the attitude stick forward, screaming toward the enemy troopers, fired another burst that caught one of them in his chest plates.

Compared to the weapons a marine could carry and power with a reactor pack, the guns on a turret were seriously heavy firepower. The three-round burst splintered the feddie's armor and slammed him to the ground. As York drove toward them, the remaining soldiers turned and sprinted up the street away from him. York followed, dropped two more of them, but each burst of rounds reduced his energy reserves by a minute. With rifle rounds pinging off his turret, he chased them about three hundred meters beyond Chunks's turret, where they took cover in the rubble of a damaged building. York had just more than a minute of power reserves left. He spun the turret about and retreated back toward Chunks. His turret ran out of power two meters up and twenty short of his comrade. The turret dropped like a rock and slammed into the street, jolting York in his acceleration couch. It rolled and ended up on its side. York popped the hatch and climbed out ten paces from Chunks, who lay unmoving.

Hopefully, the enemy marines would move cautiously against the firepower of a turret. It would take them a little time to cover the distance, moving cautiously forward. He figured he had two or three minutes at most.

Chunks was still breathing, but out cold. York gripped him by the heels and dragged him toward his turret, grunting and sweating, thinking if they survived this, Chunks needed to lose a few kilos. He leaned through the hatch in Chunks's turret and checked the reserves. He had about twenty minutes. Chunks had apparently not wasted any time hovering above the ground in shock.

There was no possible way he could get them both into the turret; there wasn't enough room, and York wasn't foolish enough to believe he could lift Chunks. But all vac suits had a retractable, plast utility line, most often used as a tether in EVA vac work. York reeled out a couple of meters from Chunks's suit, locked the reel in place, then tied the end of it around one of the turret's gun barrels.

He climbed into the turret, flopped into Chunks's acceleration couch and was thankful Chunks hadn't shut the turret down completely. He lifted off the tarmac, Chunks dangling beneath him, turned the turret toward the spot where *Three* had gone down, and applied power to the external gravity fields. He stayed low, didn't want to give the feddies an easy target.

He found the gunboat at the edge of a large, empty parking lot situated at the end of a wide avenue. Its nose was crumpled against the ground, with its tail leaning against the wall of a building. He lowered Chunks gently to the tarmac, then set the turret down beside him. He had eighteen minutes of reserve power left.

He left Chunks there and sprinted to the gunboat. The main hatch was still open so he climbed inside, found Meg and Rodma still seated in the cockpit. Meg's head lolled to one side, her eyes staring vacantly at nothing, a trickle of blood running down her face. Rodma was conscious, but groaning in pain. The nose of the craft had crumpled, pinning his leg in a mess of twisted plast and broken steel.

"First-aid kit," he said through gritted teeth, pointing at the kit clipped to the back bulkhead of the cockpit. "Get me a kikker."

York ripped the kit off the bulkhead and tore it open. Combat kikkers! He'd heard of them, a mixture of drugs to kill pain and jack up alertness at the same time. As he fumbled one out of the kit, Rodma said, "Give it to me. You go check on Jack and Sissy."

York handed him the kikker, then scrambled toward the aft of the gunboat.

There wasn't much left of Jack. When the boat's tail had clipped the side of the building while coming down, it had crushed his turret and him with it. York found a hand in the twisted wreckage, but when he pulled on it lightly, it came away without an arm attached to it. When he spotted the gunner's head, leaking gray matter, he emptied his stomach down the front of his vac suit.

He found Sissy still alive, but trapped in her turret. She had blood smeared across her face, which frightened him, especially since her systems were down and they could only communicate by shouting at the top of their lungs through the plast and steel of the turret armor. She assured him she wasn't hurt badly. But the crumpled nose of the boat had damaged the turret's hatch. They'd need more than a wrench to get her out.

The gunboat's computer said, *Enemy combatants approaching, two hundred meters out. They appear to be Federation regular troops, numbering approximately fifty.*

Fifty feddie marines. York recalled the way they had tried to execute Chunks, no taking prisoners. He asked Rodma, "How far out are *One* and *Two*?"

Rodma looked a little better. The kikker must have helped him. He grimaced as he spoke, "More 'n twenty minutes."

York tried to calm his breathing, tried to think of what to do. The feddie marines would be there in under five minutes, and they'd all be dead before help arrived. He could grab a rifle from the weapons locker, try to slow them down. But one rifle against fifty . . . no, Chunks's turret was their only chance.

York scrambled out of the boat, untied Chunks's plast tether from the turret gun barrel, and dragged him back to the boat. Then he climbed into the turret, sealed the hatch, and strapped in. He ran a quick check on the systems, changed a few settings on the turret to configure it more to his liking.

His screens showed a cluster of red target blips approaching the boat. They were leapfrogging, the rear elements running forward and taking a position behind whatever cover they could find. The nearest were about a hundred meters out. He let them come, waited until they were at fifty meters, then slammed power into the external grav fields, lifted straight up off the tarmac, firing three-round bursts as he climbed to about twenty meters. He caught the enemy marines off guard, dropped four of them in those first few seconds.

Every time he fired a burst, his estimated reserve power dropped by a minute. He zigzagged side to side as they fired back, tried to hold off on expending the power too quickly, the turret ringing with the clatter of dozens of rounds pinging off its armor.

The computer said, *"Power reserves at ten minutes."*

York shot up then down, right then left, then fired a burst. One of the feddies stepped into the open with a shoulder-mounted RPG. York drove straight toward the rocket plume, then pulled up at the last instant and the missile shot past him. He fired a burst, took out the feddie with the RPG.

"Critical hazard warning, power reserves at three minutes, and altitude too high."

York shot downward, feeding excessive amounts of power into the external grav fields.

"Critical hazard warning, power reserves at one minute—"

York fired his last three-round burst.

His grav fields sputtered erratically, and down below he saw another feddie with a shoulder-mounted RPG. The feddie fired the rocket just as York's turret went into freefall. His screens told him he was at forty meters. He watched the rocket streak his way as he tumbled toward the ground. The rocket got to him first.

CHAPTER 10:
REPRIEVE

". . . crushed pelvis and spine . . ."

  ". . . lose both legs and an arm . . ."

  ". . . skull fracture . . ."

"He's waking up."

"No, don't let him come to, not in the shape he's in."

There was only pain for a while, and then the pain dissipated and the dreams came. He dreamed of a strange landscape where he walked on legs that didn't exist, used an arm that ended in a jagged stump, and saw through an eyeless socket.

Then came oblivion.

York slammed awake, gasped, tried to sit up, but restraints held him pinned down. He lay on his back looking up at a sterile white ceiling—*deck*, he reminded himself. He tried to turn his head, to move in some way, but his muscles wouldn't respond. He could blink his eyes, and that was about all.

"Easy there, Spacer."

Sissy leaned into his field of view on his right side. Marko leaned over him on the left.

He found he could speak. "Am I paralyzed?"

"No," Marko said. "You're fine. They've just got you on a central nervous system block—don't want you moving too quickly yet."

Sissy grinned. "But you were really fucked up, York."

Even with a blocked nervous system, fear clutched at York's gut. "I . . . I didn't mean to fuck up."

Sissy looked stricken. "No, no, you didn't fuck up. What you did took guts, but when we recovered you, you were a fucked-up mess."

A man in a white coat looking very doctorish leaned over him. "Well, Spacer Ballin," he said, "glad to have you back among the living."

There was a cluster of instruments attached to the headboard of York's bed. The doctor looked at them for a moment and nodded. "Vitals are good, and everything's progressing nicely."

He held up a small instrument. "I'm going to slowly turn off the nerve block. You won't get any prickly sensation, like when you've slept on your arm or something, but you might spasm a little, especially in the new limbs we grew for you. That's not unusual, so don't let it frighten you, and we've got you restrained so you can't do any damage."

As his nervous system returned to normal functioning, his right leg twitched a bit, but then it calmed. Then he got a sudden and very demanding erection. Sissy looked at the growing bulge in the sheets and said, "Well, it looks like he's pretty healthy to me."

The doctor said, "That's also not unusual."

Sissy grinned, leaned down, and whispered in his ear, "I may have to help you get rid of that bad boy, in a fun kind of way."

The erection disappeared instantly.

They removed the restraints and reconfigured the bed so York could sit comfortably. Now that he could turn his head and look about, he saw that he was in a ward with ten beds, only two of them occupied.

The doctor said, "We'll have you out of here before dinner."

York asked, "What happened to me?"

The doctor consulted a small reader. "You lost your left leg above the knee, the right below the knee. We grew you new ones. You lost your right arm almost at the shoulder. We grew you a new one. You're going to experience a little weakness in them until your system fully integrates them, so we're putting you on an exercise regimen."

The doctor looked at the instruments above York's bed. "We reconstructed the orbit of your right eye, had to grow you a new eye. You shouldn't have any vision issues, but if you do, I want to know about them right away.

"The skull fracture was worrisome, but the speed healing took nicely. You may experience a little memory loss, but nothing going forward."

Sissy said, "Like I said, kid, you were really fucked up."

York learned that the firefight on Norgaard had happened only three days before, was amazed at how quickly they'd fixed him up.

The doctor said, "Listen carefully to me, Spacer. We subjected you to quite a bit of accelerated regrowth and speed healing. Too much of that and you can start experiencing systemic rejection, so we don't want any further injuries for at least a couple of ten-days. You're going to be on light, strictly nonhazardous duty for a while."

In a matter of minutes, they had York out of bed and walking on his new legs, Sissy and Marko walking beside him in case he stumbled or fell. Interestingly, Marko was more motherly than Sissy. Inside of an hour, York returned to the marine barracks, where a marine medic took charge of him, took him to the gym, and started him on a carefully planned exercise program.

The gathering was a small one. There wasn't that much room in the aft maintenance bay on Hangar Deck. Jarwith, Thorow, Shernov, Cochran, Sissy, Rodma, and the rest of *Three*'s crew, four flag-draped bodies, and a couple marines and a few crew members.

Jarwith looked at York, and he quailed under her gaze. She

kept her eyes on him as she spoke, though he knew she wasn't speaking merely to him. "I delayed this for a few days so their injured comrades could recover and be present."

The way she looked at him bothered him, for he didn't see any of the anger he expected. Instead, she seemed more curious, as if she had a question she wanted him to answer. She still didn't look away from him when she said, "Sergeant."

Cochran bellowed, "Atteeuun'shuuuuun."

York and everyone but Jarwith and Thorow snapped to rigid attention. Jarwith finally stopped looking at York when she said, "Sergeant, call the roll."

"Yes, ma'am." Cochran stepped forward carrying a list of names on an old-fashioned piece of paper. But as she called out the first name, the paper stayed locked in her fist, unopened. "Private First Class Jack McCaw."

Jack, York thought. She'd spoken the name of a dead man.

"Here, ma'am," one of the marines bellowed loudly.

Cochran continued. "Corporal Megan Danoski."

"Here, ma'am," another marine called out loudly.

Jack and Megan! York hadn't known their last names, hadn't known Meg's full first name, and his eyes teared up a bit.

"Private First Class Dugan Stanner."

"Here, ma'am."

"Private Shella Gomstak."

"Here, ma'am."

York didn't know the last two, but it still saddened him that they were dead. The marines had been good to him.

Jarwith's gaze had returned to York. Looking at him she nodded, and the marines of the grave detail began stacking the body bags into the maintenance hatch. A crew member passed out small plast cups filled with a clear fluid. As they sealed the hatch, York looked at the liquid in his cup: slightly diluted 'trate, very strong.

Jarwith lifted her cup to her lips. York and the others followed her example. He'd been told to take only one sip, and when he did the 'trate burned its way down his throat.

Jarwith then held the cup out in front of her and said, "For them, it's over. For us, it goes on." She tipped the cup slowly and poured the rest of the 'trate onto the metal and plast of the deck where it spattered and splashed all over her boots. York and everyone else did the same, then Jarwith called out, "Release them," and the hull echoed with the emergency blow-down cycle of the aft maintenance hatch.

York was in the gunboat flight simulator when Cochran interrupted him. "Ballin, shut that thing down and get out here."

"Be right there, Sarge."

He shut down the simulator's system, unstrapped, and climbed out onto the deck, where he found Cochran and Cap'm Shernov waiting for him. York snapped to attention, saluted, and said, "Sir."

Shernov looked at him in a curious way, then said, "XO wants to see you. Come with us."

York's gut tightened with fear, but he tried not to show anything as they led him up several decks. He'd never been in officer's country before, though it didn't look any different from NCO country.

Shernov stopped at an open hatch and stepped inside, leaving Cochran and York in the corridor. York heard him say, "Cap'm Shernov, Master Sergeant Cochran, and Spacer Apprentice Ballin reporting as ordered, sir."

A male voice said, "Bring the kid in."

Cochran nodded to the hatch, so York stepped through it, caught a momentary glimpse of Captain Jarwith seated casually on a couch to one side. York guessed he should ignore the captain, that he should address himself to the man seated behind a desk in front of him.

York recognized the fellow immediately. He'd been the sharp-eyed officer seated next to Jarwith at captain's mast the day he'd gotten the lash. Trying not to shake with fear, York marched forward two steps, stopped in front of the desk, snapped to attention, and saluted. "Spacer Ballin reporting as ordered, sir."

The man had a narrow face and salt-and-pepper hair neatly trimmed in a military cut. He wore commander's pips on the collar of his carefully pressed uniform, and didn't return York's salute right away, just sat there staring at him with dark brown eyes. York wasn't sure if he saw disapproval in the man's face, or simply a question.

After several seconds, the man raised his hand and threw a casual salute at York. "At ease, Spacer Ballin."

York carefully moved the way Bristow and Cochran had taught him. He lifted his right foot, snapped it down to the deck at shoulder width, and gripped his hands behind his back, his stomach fluttering with dread. He could only wonder what he'd done wrong, and his thoughts locked onto his memories of the lash.

The man behind the desk leaned back in his chair, cupped his hands in front of him, and regarded York with narrow, piercing eyes. "I'm Commander Thorow, executive officer of this ship."

It felt like a test. A civilian would have returned some sort of comment to the commander, would have said something like, *Nice to meet you, sir.* But the man hadn't given York an order, nor asked him a question, so York guessed he should keep his mouth shut.

Thorow nodded and said, "You're a bit of an enigma."

York didn't know what *enigma* meant, but Thorow's next words gave him a good idea.

"You're supposed to be one of our screw-ups, a problem child. So why is it you're not a problem?"

York answered him honestly. "I don't know, sir."

"No," Thorow said. "I bet you don't."

The lash, all York could think of was the lash. He wanted to run from the room and hide.

Jarwith stood and approached him. He wasn't sure if he should snap back to attention, or remain at ease, so he didn't move at all.

Beside him, she leaned down and said, "Why are you trembling, Spacer?"

The words burst out of him. "The lash. Whatever I did wrong, I didn't mean it. I'm sorry."

Jarwith straightened and said, "Ah, shit."

Thorow closed his eyes and rubbed his temples for a moment. Then he opened his eyes, leaned forward, and placed his hands flat on the desk in front of him. "You're not going to get the lash, Spacer. You didn't do anything wrong this time. In fact, you did something pretty right."

He looked to Jarwith. "That's why I hate the lash."

Jarwith's voice hardened as she said, "I hate it, too, but it's sometimes a necessary evil. It might have even saved this kid's life."

Thorow shrugged and took a deep breath. "Possibly. I confess I'm surprised he's still with us."

All York really heard was that he wasn't going to get the lash again, and only when his knees stopped shaking did he realize how visibly he'd been trembling.

Jarwith said, "We downloaded the telemetry packs from Chunks's turret and yours, and from the gunboat. You suicided Chunks's turret to save your comrades. Why did you do that?"

Again, York tried to be honest. "I don't know, ma'am. I just couldn't let the feddies kill them."

Shernov said, "May I say something, ma'am?"

She waved a hand dismissively. "By all means." She looked at Cochran. "And you too, Master Sergeant. Drop the formalities. I want frank and open discussion here."

Shernov said, "My people tell me that when he came to us, he had some pod training, but nothing else. No military etiquette, no naval customs, and he'd been with us for over four months. Sergeant Cochran turned him over to Corporal Bristow with orders to rectify that, and he responded nicely. We've had no problems with him."

Jarwith considered his words for a moment, then turned toward York, folded her arms and rubbed her chin, looking at him with narrowed eyes. "You're a drug runner, and yet you're clean, no sign of any use. Why?"

With the knowledge that he wasn't going to receive another fifty strokes, York had relaxed inwardly, hadn't tried to follow their argument. It took a second to play back Jarwith's question. "I didn't want the drugs, didn't want to take them."

"Didn't take them voluntarily?" Jarwith asked. "Then who forced you to take them?"

"I don't know," York blurted out, then realized how stupid that sounded.

Jarwith leaned forward so she stood nose-to-nose with him. "You don't know?"

"I . . ." It occurred to York that while he hadn't done anything wrong yet, he just might still get the lash if he did something wrong now. "I . . . uh . . ."

"Ma'am," Cochran said. "I think the kid's scared."

"Ya," Shernov agreed. "Someone's got him running real scared."

"Sarah," Thorow said, and York realized he'd just heard the captain's first name, "let's focus on the fact that the kid's now doing a good job, let the past go."

Jarwith straightened, leaned back, and rocked on her heels. "Spacer Ballin, with an act of conspicuous gallantry, you saved the lives of three members of my crew, at considerable risk to yourself. But more importantly, you've been trouble-free for some time now."

She glanced at Shernov for a moment. "Cap'm Shernov tells me you aspire to be a pod gunner. I hope someday you aspire to something more than that, but for the time being, that'll do, so I'm going to give you another chance."

She turned to Thorow. "Promote him to spacer third class, and reassign him to Straight's gunner crew."

York couldn't believe his ears, tried to resist the urge, but a broad grin formed on his face.

Jarwith turned back to him and growled, "Wipe that grin off your face, Spacer."

York stiffened, and she smiled. "You're dismissed."

The marines threw a little going-away party for York, which surprised him, because no one before had ever cared one way or the other. It wasn't much: Sissy, Chunks, Rodma, Cath, Bristow, Cochran, and a few others, a beer or two, and Cochran somehow got a small cake from the mess. York regretted leaving them, but he didn't want to be a throwaway.

After the party, he bundled up his few possessions and made his way down to the lower decks. As he followed the curve of the hull past the pod stations, he spotted Sturpik and Tomlin seated at a console playing cards. When he tried to pass them without acknowledging them, Tomlin stood and stepped in his way.

York stopped and Tomlin said, "Hi, kid."

Still seated at the console, Sturpik said, "Heard you were coming back. Heard you *wanted* to come back. Imagine that, Tomlin, kid actually wants to be a pod gunner."

Tomlin took a step forward and leaned uncomfortably close to York. "I think he's just an honest kid, wants to live up to his obligations, wants to pay us back the money he owes us."

York stepped back. "I don't owe you—"

"With interest," Sturpik said, interrupting him.

Tomlin stepped forward again, leaned down, and hissed, "You try to welch on us, you'll be in such deep shit you won't even see the rim of the asshole we stuff you in."

Somehow York needed to get them off his back, and he'd gladly give up what little he had in his pay account. "What do I owe you?"

Tomlin grinned, straightened and looked at Sturpik. "You see, I told you he just wants to live up to his obligations."

York asked again, "How much?"

Sturpik said, "Five hundred imperials."

They'd chosen a sum so astronomically high, York could never hope to pay them off. "I don't have that kind of money."

Sturpik leaned back in his chair. "No, I don't suppose you do." His eyes widened and he straightened. "But wait, I have an idea. You could earn it from us, pay it off with just a favor or two."

"York."

Tomlin turned around at the sound of Marko's voice. York looked past him at the older man walking down the deck toward them.

"Heard you were back," Marko said as he joined York and Tomlin. "Glad to have you, kid." He hooked a thumb over his shoulder. "Come with me. Your old coffin is waiting for you."

York stepped around Tomlin and joined Marko. The older man turned and, walking side-by-side, the two of them headed toward their bunk room. They'd gone about twenty paces when, without looking York's way, Marko said, "You got some sort of problem with those two?"

York would have dearly loved Marko's help, and considered asking the older man to intervene. But he glanced over his shoulder and looked Sturpik's way, saw him standing in the middle of the deck with his fists on his hips, staring at York angrily and shaking his head from side to side as if he could read York's mind. Beside him, Tomlin simply grinned unpleasantly, both threat and warning quite clear. They must have overheard, or at least guessed at the gist of Marko's question. "No," he said. "They just wanted to welcome me back."

CHAPTER 11:
GUNNER'S BLOOD

Straight gave Marko the job of overseeing York's training, which the older man didn't seem to mind. But York quickly learned that Straight still intended to make sure he got much more training in scrubbing decks than in pod gunning. At least being assigned to Marko meant they shared the same watch rotation.

The first time Marko and York were on graveyard watch, as York reached for his bucket, Marko said, "Belay that, Spacer."

York gave the older man a questioning look. Marko glanced over his shoulder, then grinned at York. "Straight's asleep," he said. "She won't know you didn't spend all night scrubbing decks."

He nodded toward one of the pod hatches. "Get in that pod. Let's see how badly the marines screwed up your gunner skills."

Marko ran him through the basics, which York had long ago mastered. "Good enough," Marko's voice said in York's headset. "Nothing lost there. Let's try multiple targets, some allocated, some not. You won't know when a target is going to be allocated to you, but you'll have to respond quickly when it is."

York tried to stay calm, wanted to score well on the sims, if for no other reason than to at least impress Marko. His screens showed three incoming targets, one allocated. He had no trouble with that kill, and none with the next and the next.

"Let's escalate this," Marko said. "We're part of a fleet of twenty ships in a big battle with a large feddie fleet. You're going to have shit all over your screens, which is distracting as all hell. Stay focused on your targets and ignore everything else."

Marko took him through a full simulation; the tedious wait for battle to begin, then a few, sporadic targets, then all hell broke loose. York did well up to a certain point, then the sheer number of targets overwhelmed him. After two hours of that, he climbed out of the pod, dark sweat stains coloring his armpits. As his feet hit the deck, he braced himself, ready for Marko to give him hell.

Seated behind the command console, Marko smiled at him and said, "You did pretty good, kid."

"But I lost," York said. "They got past me. If it had been real, we'd all be dead."

Marko leaned back in the console chair. "That's not the point. I wanted to see how much you could handle, so I kept throwing more and more at you. I wasn't going to let you out of that pod until I swamped you with targets. And you did as good as just about any gunner on this ship."

York couldn't hide his surprise. "Really?"

"Yes, really. Though I shouldn't be surprised. The best gunners are always young. It was almost like you kept practicing all those months with the marines."

York said, "But I did."

Marko frowned and said, "They don't have any pods in marine country."

York thought it was obvious. He shrugged. "I configured the gunboat turret simulator like a pod so I could keep practicing at both."

Marko smiled and nodded his approval. "Good for you, kid."

A couple of tendays later, Sissy, Chunks, and Cath showed up in the lower deck bunk room late on third shift. As they walked into the room, Zamekis said, "Well, to what honor do we owe the privilege of a visit by three of the meanest, toughest marines I know?"

Cath looked at York and said, "Just came to wish the kid a happy birthday."

Zamekis frowned and turned to York. "It's your birthday, and you didn't tell us."

York was as surprised as her. "I . . . forgot."

Zamekis shook her head and they all got a good laugh out of the fact that York had completely forgotten his own thirteenth birthday.

Late one night on fourth watch, while Marko and York were seated at the command console reviewing York's simulation scores, Marko cocked his head at an odd angle and went silent, a sure sign he was receiving some message through his implants. He listened for a moment, then said, "Yes, sir. I'm with him now."

Again the silence while he listened, then he said, "I'll be right up."

Marko looked at York. "Yesterday I showed your sim scores to Pallaver." The older man grinned conspiratorially. "He wants to see me now, wants to look at your scores again." He stood. "I won't be long. Practice your reading while I'm gone."

As Marko headed up to officer's country, York pulled up a copy of the regs on a screen and began reading. But only a few minutes later, Sturpik and Tomlin came sauntering down the deck toward him. Both men walked with a wise-guy swagger York had seen too many times on the streets, and he knew it was no coincidence the two men had shown up shortly after Marko had left him alone. While sharing Marko's watch rotation, York didn't have to constantly look over his shoulder for Sturpik or Tomlin, and he realized now he'd grown complacent, didn't have his wrench with him.

As the two men approached, York stood and backstepped away from them. He'd learned the hard way not to let them put him between them.

Sturpik glanced at Tomlin, grinned, and said to York, "What's wrong, kid?"

"Nothing," York said, backing slowly away from them. "Just need to stretch my legs."

York had grown in the year he'd been on *Dauntless*, and now stood almost eye-to-eye with Tomlin, though both of them were shorter than Sturpik. But he had no illusions about being able to beat either man in a fight, let alone the two of them together. He backed up against a bulkhead and stopped. The two men stopped just out of reach.

Tomlin said, "Thought about what we told you?"

York shrugged, tried to think of some way to stall. "No. I haven't had time. Been too busy."

Sturpik's eyes narrowed. "This is important shit, kid. You need to make time." He stepped forward and York tensed.

Tomlin laughed. "The kid just ain't too smart. Maybe we need to smarten him up a bit."

Tomlin stepped forward, but as he did so Marko came into view, weaving his way between the instrument clusters and command consoles.

"Marko," York said.

Tomlin and Sturpik both stiffened, glanced over their shoulders, and took a step back. Sturpik turned and said, "Marko, old buddy. How's the kid doing in his sims?"

Marko stopped a few paces away, his eyes narrowing. He spoke slowly, cautiously. "He's doing just fine."

Tomlin said, "Nice that he got a promotion out of that marine firefight." He looked at York. "Apprentice pay grade is just shit, ain't it?"

Still frowning at Sturpik, Marko said, "Kid's got to come with me. Pallaver wants to see him."

Sturpik stepped aside and said, "By all means. We were just about to leave anyway." He and Tomlin walked away together, with no sign of their wise-guy swagger.

Marko watched in silence as they left, and once they were gone he turned that same appraising look on York for several seconds. Then he cocked his head and said, "Pallaver wants to see you, going to assign you to a real battle station."

York was on his hands and knees scrubbing the deck when the alert klaxon started blaring, and a voice on allship said, "*Watch Condition Red. All hands, this is not a drill. Repeat: This is not a drill. Battle stations.*"

He jumped to his feet, grabbed his bucket, and rushed to the maintenance closet, emptied it, and stowed it. He jogged down the deck to the empty console seat, almost sat down and strapped in, but at the last instant remembered that was no longer his battle station.

Pod G-26!

He spun around, hoping Straight hadn't seen his hesitation, ran back up the deck to the pod hatch. Less than a minute later, he strapped in and booted the pod's system. He let out a sigh of relief when he saw he wasn't the last crew member on station. He couldn't shake the fear that he'd screw up somehow and get demoted, though he tried not to obsess on that as he waited for something to happen.

The captain addressed them on allship. "We're down-transiting blind outside a system with suspected Federal activity. We don't know if we're going to run into any trouble or not, so stay alert."

York waited, his screens blank. Ten minutes later, he felt that tickle up his spine as they down-transited, and his screens lit up, though he had nothing to look at but a few stars on a black background.

York recognized Zamekis's voice when she said, "Looks like the feddies are a no-show."

Marko said, "Better a no-show than a firefight."

Ten minutes later, they dropped back to Watch Condition Yellow. York listened to the chatter in his headset for an hour, then the captain took the ship off alert, and York climbed out of his pod exhausted.

During the next month, York went through that same sequence twice more. Both times the ship down-transited at the edge of a system and nothing happened. But the next time, actually growing a bit bored as he waited in his pod for them to down-transit, York felt that tickle at the back of his spine, and as his screens lit up, *Dauntless*'s hull shrieked.

"Heavy damage amidships, starboard."

As *Dauntless*'s hull thrummed with the deep, bass sound of its main batteries spitting transition shells at some enemy, York tried to ignore the desperate voices in his headset and scanned his screens. But there was nothing there, no friendlies, no bogies.

"Helm, protect starboard."

Dauntless spun, and York's screens filled with yellow targets, nothing allocated to him. Reflexively, he wanted to fire at everything, but he forced himself to hold to discipline, not to fire at unallocated targets. An incoming transition torpedo allocated to Zamekis caught his eye, ranged at a hundred million kilometers and streaking toward them. She fired, missed, fired again, and as the bogie drew closer, targeting allocated it to more pods, but still nothing for York. He tracked it anyway, locked a target designator on it but held to discipline as his crewmates fired and missed. Then only twenty million kilometers out, it flashed a bright red on his screens and he fired. He thought his own shot went wide, but someone hit it and it blossomed into a ball of thermonuclear fire.

After that, they gave him targets on a regular basis. He was pretty certain he deflected several, but no kills. His gunner mates had told him that was the life of a gunner. Rarely did they actually hit incoming fire with a pod round, just deflected it most of the time, which was good enough. That was the reason it took years as a gunner to accumulate an arm full of chevrons, and why spacers like Straight, who'd served only a few years in a pod, never got any.

There came a moment in the battle when the number of targets on his screens threatened to overwhelm him. Then they grew fewer, and in just a few short minutes, it all stopped as abruptly as it had started, no more targets. *Dauntless*'s main batteries fired a few more rounds, but after that all York heard was a frightening silence.

The silence lasted for well over a minute, and then Zamekis said, "Wish I'd worn my brown pants."

One of the male gunners York didn't know said, "Sweetheart, if you need help changing your pants, I'll be happy to give you a hand, or two."

Zamekis countered, "If I didn't know your hands spent so much time in your own pants—"

Straight said, "Cut the chatter."

An hour later, York climbed out his pod hatch onto the lower deck, feeling a little weak in the knees. Straight's gunner crew had gathered around her console, so York joined them.

"Hey, hot shot," Stark said. "You look a little shaky."

Zamekis said, "Don't worry about it, York. It's tough to have your first firefight in really deep shit like that."

York felt he owed someone an apology. "Sorry I didn't do better."

She frowned and looked at Marko. Marko grinned. "I told you he's a natural." He turned the grin on York and said, "Kid, you got three kills. We'll see you at gunner's blood tonight."

In the lower deck bunk room Straight's entire gunner crew— Marko, Durlling, Stark, and Zamekis—surrounded York and examined him carefully. All four had changed into coveralls with cut-off sleeves.

Looking York up and down, Marko said, "This won't do," and they all shook their heads sadly.

Zamekis and Durlling each grabbed one of York's arms. He'd rolled the sleeves of his coveralls up past his elbows, and the two women carefully unrolled them. The butterflies in York's stomach churned.

"That's better," Marko said.

Durlling said, "You're going to make us proud tonight, York Ballin."

Marko said, "Let's go." He led the way.

Durlling and Zamekis each took one of York's arms and followed him with York walking between them, almost as if they thought he might try to escape. Stark laughed and took up the rear. Several times, the passage was too narrow for the two women and York to pass walking three abreast. Durlling always led the way, followed by York, Zamekis, and Stark.

When they stopped at the closed hatch in the aft of the ship, all York could think about was that he wanted to get this over with as soon as possible. He knew it would hurt when they cut into his arm.

Marko knocked; they were admitted. York's four companions rolled up the sleeves of their cut-off coveralls to expose their gunner's rank. Zamekis grinned, leaned close to York's ear, and said, "Before this is done, you're going to outrank me, you little shithead."

York looked at the scar on her arm, and realized she only had a single half-chevron. She'd gotten another kill that day, so that night she'd get another to complete the chevron, but York would have a chevron and a half before the night was over. His nerves ratcheted up a notch, and then she slapped him on the back with no hint of resentment or jealousy.

The chief who'd admitted them announced the name and gunner's rank of the four, then turned to York. He stuck his hand out and York didn't know what he was supposed to do, then realized the fellow wanted to shake his hand. He reached out and clasped the older man's hand, which completely engulfed his. The chief nodded and said, "Fucking good shooting today, Ballin."

He released York's hand, turned, and shouted, "Spacer Third Class York Ballin, no chevrons, but he's drawing blood tonight, and the asshole gets a threefer."

Everyone cheered, and the butterflies in York's stomach fluttered up into his throat as someone slapped a mug of beer in his hand, spilling it on his arm. He'd lost his friends in the crowd. Spacers kept slapping him on the back, and he didn't know how to respond.

Zamekis rescued him. "You look more scared than I was my first time in combat."

She grabbed his sleeve and guided him to the others. They jostled him about in a friendly way, made crude jokes about his manhood, and called him all sorts of names. York chugged at his beer, was halfway through it when the ranking chief called, "Spacer Third Class York Ballin, front 'n' center."

Him alone! York asked Marko, "Am I the only one who's drawing first blood?"

Marko shook his head. "They call the newbies up in groups based on number of kills, and you're the only virgin got three today."

Marko took York's beer. "Get out there, kid."

York had trouble making it out to the ranking chief in the middle of the deck. Spacers nudged him and called him the foulest names, always with a laugh or a smile. When he stopped in front of the chief, the noise was deafening. Using an old-fashioned steel knife, the chief cut away York's sleeves at the elbow, then carefully rolled them up to expose his upper arms. Then he raised his hands, and the cheers and shouts slowly died.

The chief said, "This virgin got a threefer today."

More cheers and shouts erupted from the gunners. The chief raised his hands again to silence them. "That means he's drawing blood on both arms, a full chevron on one and a half on the other."

Marko stepped forward and expounded on York's prowess as a gunner. York learned he had capabilities beyond anything human. Then the chief gripped York's elbow, raised the steel knife, and sliced into York's arm. It hurt; York's knees felt week, and the deck swayed crazily.

Marko grabbed his other arm and steadied him. He whispered into York's ear, "Don't worry, kid. You wouldn't be the first newbie to faint."

The chief made another slice, and York prayed desperately that he didn't faint in front of everyone. Marko raised a beer to York's lips and said, "Take a gulp, a big one."

York sucked at the beer, and in some way it did seem to help. Then the chief cut the third half-chevron into his other arm, and York almost emptied his stomach. Again, Marko had him take a big gulp of beer.

They let the blood drip all the way down his arms to his fingers, where it dripped onto the deck of the ship. Then they washed the blood away with dark beer. York watched it puddle on the deck, an odd mixture of brown beer and red blood, and he knew he'd never forget that sight.

CHAPTER 12:
SISSY

York kept his eyes open for Sturpik and Tomlin as he slopped water out of the bucket and onto the deck of the mess hall. He'd thought that as a blooded gunner he wouldn't have to scrub decks anymore, but apparently Straight didn't see it that way. It was first shift and there was no one else around, not even Marko. As he moved down the deck, he pushed the bucket in front of him and dragged the duffel filled with cleaning supplies behind. His wrench was in there, and he wanted it close at hand. The mess hall was a large room with several entrances, and he tried to keep an eye on all of them.

He had about an hour left in first shift, and was hoping he might be in the clear, when Tomlin stepped through a hatch into view. He was accompanied by a spacer York didn't know. A noise in the other direction drew his attention, and he looked that way, saw Sturpik walking his way with another spacer he didn't know. York reached into the duffel, retrieved the wrench, stood, and put his back to a bulkhead. He couldn't stop them from cornering him, but at least they couldn't surround him.

Sturpik, Tomlin, and their two companions stopped well out of reach of the wrench. "Well, Ballin," Sturpik said. "Got up a little early today, never thought I'd run into you."

"Ya," Tomlin said. "Pure coincidence. But now that we're

here, I guess we can take care of that unfinished business we got. You ready to pay up?"

York said, "You know I don't owe you anything. You made me take that stuff. You tricked me. And you told me I was supposed to hit Straight back, stand up for myself like on the streets."

Sturpik closed his eyes and shook his head sadly. York saw that they weren't going to walk away this time. "What I told you don't matter, and it don't matter how or why you got the stuff. It was our stuff, and you lost it, so you owe us five hundred imperials."

York said, "I told you I don't have that kind of money."

"And I told you that you can make it up by helping us out."

"No," York said. "I'm not going to help you."

Tomlin grinned, and York realized he'd wanted to hear that answer, that he was enjoying this. "Then we're going to take payment in another way."

He reached into his tunic and pulled out a wrench even bigger than York's. Sturpik and the other two produced plast bars about as long as their forearms. They spread out and the two strangers edged forward cautiously, coming at York from the sides, while Sturpik and Tomlin clearly intended to take him head on. Fear clutched at York's stomach as he realized he might not survive this.

Motion at the far end of the mess hall near one of the entrances caught his eye. Sissy and Chunks stepped through the hatch there. Sissy started when she saw York, waved her hand, and said rather loudly, "York, what a coincidence finding you here."

Sturpik, Tomlin, and their two friends turned, saw the two marines walking toward them, and quickly hid their weapons in their clothes.

Sissy spoke as she walked. "Chunks and me thought we'd catch an early breakfast."

The two marines stopped about three paces from Sturpik. "What are you doing here?" he demanded.

Sissy smiled at him, not a friendly smile. "Like I said, me and Chunks are looking for a little early breakfast."

Tomlin stepped toward her. "Mess hall doesn't open for another hour. Come back then."

She made a point of looking carefully at each of the four men, one at a time. "Well then, we'll just have a little caff to kill the time. But what are you doing here?"

Sturpik said, "We got business with the kid."

"What kind of business?"

"None-of-your-business kind of business."

Marko and Cochran stepped through another entrance chatting amiably. Marko didn't seem to be surprised at the small crowd he found there. "The sarge and me," he said, "we're going to have a little caff."

Cath and three large marines stepped through another entrance. She announced, "Me and the boys here are in the mood for a little caff." They sat down at a mess table, all of them on the same side, all pointedly watching Sturpik and his friends.

Stark, Durlling, and Zamekis stepped through the same hatch Sissy and Chunks had used. Zamekis announced, "I feel like a little caff." They sat down at a table, and like the marines, they all sat down on one side watching Sturpik and his friends.

Sturpik leaned toward York and whispered, "We're not done here."

He and his friends walked out of the mess hall together.

Cochran said, "Ballin."

Only then did York realize he was standing in a crouch holding the wrench. He straightened and tried to hide the wrench behind his back. "Yes, Sergeant."

"Aren't you supposed to be scrubbing the deck?"

"Yes, Sergeant."

"You sure don't look like you're scrubbing the deck."

"Sorry, Sergeant."

York stowed the wrench back in the duffel, got down on his

hands and knees, and returned to scrubbing the deck. Interestingly enough, no one ever got any caff, and they all stayed until the shift ended, only leaving the mess hall when York did.

The next day, York passed Tomlin in a corridor going the other way and almost didn't recognize him. He walked with a limp, one arm in a sling, and his face was covered in puffy, bluish-black bruises, one eye swollen completely shut. His nose looked like it had been mashed completely, then swollen to twice its normal size. Whatever had happened to him, York thought it strange that he hadn't been patched up with all the miraculous medical treatment they had on ship.

The day after that, he saw one of Sturpik and Tomlin's two friends, and the fellow was worse off than Tomlin. Again, he wondered why the fellow hadn't received better medical treatment. Then he recalled that when he got the lash, they had refused to patch his back up, wanted him to live with his punishment.

York hunted down Marko, found him seated at a command console. He didn't beat around the bush, but asked him straight out, "What happened to Tomlin?"

Marko frowned, considered York for a moment, then said, "This ain't the streets, kid, no matter what you've been told. There's people here got your back, so you make sure you got theirs."

York said, "You didn't answer my question."

Again, Marko considered him carefully, as if trying to decide something. "I had a suspicion you got suckered, and then I began to suspect who did the suckering. Pure coincidence me and Cochran were standing just outside the mess hall, heard every word you and them lowlifes said. And them marines got a pretty simple idea of justice."

"But Sturpik," York said. "He won't just walk away."

Marko leaned back in his seat, folded his hands, and looked at York for a long, hard moment. "No, he won't. He's a hard case, been a problem for a long time. Maybe it's early enough for his friends to learn a valuable lesson, but not Sturpik. Funny thing about Sturpik, though, he's been AWOL since that night, probably slipped and fell right out through an air lock."

After that, York didn't have to scrub any more decks. He suspected that Marko had arranged for him to be scrubbing the mess hall that night, by himself, on first watch. The older man had used York as bait to get Sturpik to reveal his hand. Interestingly enough, York never saw Sturpik again.

York managed to stay out of trouble for the next year. He continued to practice in the pod and flight simulators, frequently configuring the pod simulator like a gunboat turret so he could stay in practice. That turned out to be a wise move, because once they got a replacement for *Three*, the marines were still short a gunner whenever they needed a full complement, so the captain loaned York to them quite regularly.

Rodma continued his flight training whenever they had some slack time down on the surface of a planet. And when he joined the marines, York got to see more of Sissy, another benefit of being loaned out to them, though he had to be careful about that. The marines were casual about their bodies, and both men and women shared the same showers. Once, after a simple mission to supply an outpost down on an airless, nameless planet, York made use of the marine showers. He was just finishing up when Sissy stepped into the showers and began soaping down with chem wash. At the sight of her bare body, her round hips, small breasts, and dark brown nipples, York felt an erection coming on and he exited quickly, covering his crotch with a towel. He liked seeing Sissy, though she would never think of him as anything but *the kid*. She probably already had a boyfriend, likely one of the marines.

York also kept scoring pod kills, though the only time he again scored three in a single battle was at Arman'Tigh. But that was a massive encounter that involved more than a hundred ships, with multiple engagements over a period of two days. By his four-teenth birthday, he had four full chevrons on each arm and got a promotion to spacer second class, and two days after that he scored another kill.

At gunner's blood, Zamekis looked at the new half chevron cut into his arm and said, "Quite the hotshot, aren't you?"

Marko slapped her on the back and handed her a beer. "I tell you, Meleen, it's always the young ones who are the best. I've seen it before. Don't know what it is, but sometimes a kid like York turns out to be a natural. Couple more years, he'll lose the edge. He'll still be good, but never again as good as now."

York had grown another ten centimeters in that year, and now looked most of the adult men straight in the eye. He even stood taller than some, but he was lanky and thin.

"Don't worry about it," Stark told him. Several gunners were seated in the barracks playing cards. "My younger brother did that, grew straight up first, then filled out later."

Stark frowned and a sad look crossed his face. He lowered his eyes to the deck and said, "He was killed in a firefight somewhere in Ganymede sector last year."

"Sorry," York said.

Stark shook off his melancholy. "Don't worry about it, kid. For him, it's over. For us, it goes on."

They were only a few hours out of Cathan, a major imperial holding, and everyone was looking forward to a few days' shore leave.

"Ballin," Straight said as she walked into the barracks. "The marines need you down on Hangar Deck for a drop."

York looked at his cards. They weren't worth playing.

Straight said, "You got time to finish the hand."

"No," York said, tossing the cards onto the table. "I fold."

Zamekis asked, "What do they need a gunner for? There aren't any feddies within thirty light-years of Cathan."

Straight shrugged. "Beats me. But orders are orders."

When York stood, she took his place at the table.

Down on Hangar Deck, he retrieved his vac suit from his marine locker and was in the process of running a quick check on its seals when Rodma approached him and said, "Hold on there, Ballin. You won't need that." He had a conspiratorial grin on his face.

"What's up?" York asked.

"Put that thing away," Rodma said. "You're riding in the cockpit."

York frowned and Rodma added, "XO gave me permission to let you ride shotgun. You're the copilot this drop."

York spluttered, "Why?"

"Part of the training. Got to pick up some heavy equipment in the Cathan Navy Yard. Ideal place for you to get some real cockpit time. No problems for light-years, nothing to go wrong."

York found it exhilarating to sit in *Three*'s cockpit and watch the large doors of the service bay open directly in front of him. Then the docking gantry shoved *Three* out into the blackness of space and they drifted away from the ship's hull.

"It's all yours," Rodma said.

"Mine?" York asked.

"Ya, you're going to pilot her."

"But I'm just the copilot."

"Copilot's got to be able to fly just as good as the pilot, so she's all yours."

York hesitated for an instant as they drifted farther away from *Dauntless*. But his gut didn't clench with fear, and while his stomach fluttered with butterflies at first, they disappeared quickly as his training took over.

He brought up a nav summary on his screens, dialed in the coordinates of the navy yard, was about to kick in the drive when Rodma said, "No."

York took his hands off the control yoke, wondering what he'd done wrong.

"You're taking us down on manual all the way. It's the only way to learn."

Behind them Sissy said, "Glad I don't have to be a pilot."

She, Chunks, and Meg's replacement were seated in the aft cabin.

Chunks said, "Don't you get our asses killed, Ballin."

Interestingly enough, the friendly teasing calmed York. Piloting the gunboat turned out to be quite similar to piloting a gunboat turret, though this was his first time in the vacuum of space with none of the aerodynamic surfaces active, and he needed to consciously think in three dimensions. But once they hit atmosphere and the reentry plasma dissipated, the only difference from previous descents was that he was bringing the boat down from twenty kilometers, not just one.

When he had the boat parked on the tarmac of the navy yard, Rodma said, "You're on leave. Just be back here at oh five hundred in three days. You're flying this bucket back up once we've got her loaded."

Sissy had come prepared with a spare marine tunic that fit York reasonably well. "You're coming with us, Ballin," she said. "You haven't partied with the marines for months."

She and Chunks led York to a marine bar called—York was not surprised to learn—The Drop Zone. By the time they got there, it was already quite late. They joined a group of *Dauntless*'s marines at a cluster of tables, drank, and played cards.

One of the female prostitutes caught York's eye and gave him an inviting look. She was quite beautiful, very voluptuous, but for some reason she just didn't appeal to him. He caught himself looking across the table at Sissy. The first time York had met her, he'd thought she had a hard look about her, but at some point that impression had disappeared. He liked the way she wore her hair in a buzz cut on one side, and over the ear on the other.

He suddenly realized she was watching him look at her. He looked away quickly, stood, and carried his beer to the bar. It was still half full, but he needed an excuse to get away from the table. He leaned against the bar and tried to muster some excitement for the prostitute.

"Ballin," Sissy said as she came up and leaned against the bar next to him. "Why were you staring at me?"

"I wasn't staring at you," he lied. "I was just thinking."

The place was crowded and noisy, and they were oddly alone in the middle of a lot of marines. She took her elbows off the bar and turned to face him. "Look at me."

He turned to face her, and for the first time realized he was now taller by several centimeters.

"Have you ever been with a real girl?" she asked.

He stumbled over his words, "Well . . . ya . . . of course—"

"No," she said, stepping forward, standing uncomfortably close to him. "A real girl. A *girl* girl, not a *prostitute* girl. Someone who expects to have as good a time as you."

"I . . . uh . . . well—"

"That's what I thought." She closed the gap between them, wrapped her arms around his neck, and kissed him. He wrapped his arms around her waist and enjoyed every second as their tongues fought a very pleasant little war. It wasn't like any kiss he'd ever had before. It was hot and passionate, but it also meant something.

When they separated, she looked him in the eyes and said, "I'm no whore."

It hurt that she assumed he might think that. "I never thought of you that way."

Her eyes narrowed. "I just had to be sure. Anyway, I have to do something to get you to stop staring at my ass and my tits."

He shrugged. "I like your ass and your tits."

Her eyes narrowed. "You'd better. Come with me."

She led him up to the second floor. At the top of the stairs, they paid an attendant for a private room. York thoroughly enjoyed taking her clothes off little by little, and they spent the next three days in bed. Sissy was quite instructive.

CHAPTER 13:
HOMEWORK?

York learned that the navy was quite tolerant about relationships between spacers, recognizing that they couldn't send people out among the stars for months at a time and expect them to remain celibate. There was even a clause in the regs stating that *healthy relationships were not discouraged*. The powers that be disapproved only if there was a serious discrepancy in rank and one party was subordinate to the other in the chain of command. Sissy's and York's watch rotations frequently kept them apart, but they spent every moment they could find together, and York learned that there was so much more to the act of sex than what he got from a whore. York took a little ribbing from Zamekis, Stark, and Durlling, but it was all in fun, and they seemed to be happy for him.

He started taking an interest in the ship as a whole. He'd spent his first year just trying to survive Sturpik and Tomlin, his second trying to become the best lower-deck pod gunner he could, hadn't really considered anything beyond the next meal and a place to sleep. But now he wondered why they had gone to Cathan, and before that Arman'Tigh. And he also wondered about the why of it all. When he asked Marko a few questions, the older man glanced around nervously and said, "Be careful, York. Every ship has a couple Admiralty Intelligence agents working under cover. And you don't want anyone from AI reporting back that you're questioning why we're fighting this war. Mess with AI and they'll charge you with treason. That's a convenient way for them assholes to get rid of someone asking questions they don't want asked."

Surprised that Marko had taken that meaning from his questions, York said, "No, I didn't mean that."

Marko's paranoia did make York wonder why the older man was so fearful of AI. And it occurred to him that he never had heard a reason for the war itself. No one had ever claimed that the Federals were fundamentally evil, or that they intended to conquer the empire and enslave its citizens. But while he wondered about that, he took Marko's warning to heart and kept his thoughts to himself.

"I meant, why did we go to Cathan?" he said. "And why did we go to Arman'Tigh? And where are we going now, and what's the purpose of the mission?"

Marko turned to a terminal and pulled up *shipnet*, which was available from just about any screen. He showed York where the bridge crew regularly posted unclassified information about the ship's course, heading, and next destination. At the moment, they were on the way to a destination on the front lines to rendezvous with the rest of the Seventh Fleet, though the details of the mission were classified.

"You mean this has been here all along?" York asked.

Marko smiled and nodded. "It's about time you got your head out of your ass."

York looked at their destination, which was listed as nothing more than a meaningless string of numbers and symbols. "What's that mean?"

"Those are interstellar coordinates."

"How do I figure that stuff out?"

Marko pointed him to a couple of books on interstellar navigation in the ship's library, and others that gave information on basic ship's systems and operations. The books on ship's systems were interesting, but York struggled with the navigation books, understood nothing, and finally gave up. A few days later, Marko asked, "How'd you like the books?"

York grimaced. "The navigation stuff is way over my head."

"Over my head, too," Marko said. "But I'll talk to Pallaver. Maybe he can give you a few pointers."

Pallaver took a keen interest in York's curiosity, sat him down, and helped him wade through several pages of one of the navigation texts—then, to York's horror, gave him a homework assignment. York didn't want to do homework; he wanted to spend his spare time with Sissy. But Pallaver's mind was set: York had shown an interest in interstellar navigation, and Pallaver was damn well going to make sure he learned it.

"I don't get it," he told Sissy, lying beside her in his coffin, tracing a finger along the curve of her bare hip. When they'd come back from that first shore leave together, they'd both tried to squeeze into York's gunner's coffin to get a little privacy, and they'd discovered that the coffin automatically adjusted to the size of its occupant—or in their case, occupants. The coffin did not restrict their activities in the least.

"Don't get what?" she asked.

"Why Pallaver's so interested in teaching me navigation."

She rolled toward him, and looking at her breasts he almost forgot the question he'd asked. "They do it to all of us," she said. "Look at me. I just turned sixteen so I'm an adult, and they're still making me take lessons."

"I am looking at you," he said, leering at her breasts.

She whacked him in the side of the head. "Talk to me, not my tits."

He reluctantly looked her in the eyes. "Okay, they still make you take lessons. But my first year they didn't make me do anything but scrub decks and drill in the simulators."

"That's because we thought you weren't going to make it, what with your record and a couple of bad mistakes you made after you joined us." With her finger, she traced one of the lash scars on his shoulder. "And then you shaped up, and we learned that maybe your mistakes were because of a certain bad influence on ship, and now you've been trouble-free and done your job for more than a year."

"Exactly," he said. "I do my job, so why does Pallaver need to teach me all this crap?"

"It's in the regs," she said. "Something about encouraging our continuing education. I think all ship's officers are stuck with it—NCOs included."

York wasn't that interested in the topic of conversation, and using extremely unfair means, he managed to distract Sissy and focus her on other activities. But later he did look it up in the regs, which stated clearly that it was the responsibility of all senior personnel to continue the education of the junior members of the crew. During their next session, Pallaver even admitted that somehow Jarwith had heard of York's interest, and the lieutenant's enthusiasm for York's training had come directly from her.

They rendezvoused with the Seventh Fleet near Turnham's Cluster, a heavily disputed group of stars all within a few light-years of one another and possessing several occupied planets. Pallaver gathered all his gunner crews together in the main mess, where Jarwith and Thorow briefed them on the coming mission—though Thorow did most of the talking with Jarwith looking on.

"This is going to be a big one," he said. "We've been quietly assembling all of Seventh Fleet, and in the next day or two, we'll number over two hundred. We think we'll have the Federals outnumbered, but don't get overconfident. Captain Jarwith and I both think this is going to be a nasty one."

York noticed that Jarwith's eyes had settled on him with an almost vacant stare, and that made him uncomfortable. He looked away from her and focused on Thorow's words.

"With this many ships involved, friendly-fire casualties are inevitable, but try to keep that to a minimum. Stay calm, listen to your station commanders, don't shoot without an allocated target, and shoot straight."

As the briefing broke up, York glanced Jarwith's way. Her eyes followed him as he left the mess hall.

For the first engagement at Turnham's Cluster, there was no sudden screech from the alert klaxon, no blaring voice from allship, and no scramble to battle stations. The Imperial Seventh Fleet had assembled one light-year from the opposing force. They could detect transition wakes to a distance of about five light-years, so there'd be no surprises on either side. That morning, York and the gunners took their rotation in the mess hall and ate a leisurely but tense breakfast, with none of the usual teasing and banter. Then they climbed into their pods to wait.

Jarwith gave a little speech on allship, spoke of loyalty to the grand empire and the need for a decisive victory. Shortly after that, they up-transited, driving hard toward the enemy fleet.

York put a navigation summary in the corner of one of his screens. Because of Pallaver's tutelage, he now knew how to interpret it properly. At two thousand lights, they'd traverse the distance to the opposing fleet in just under four hours. On his screen, he saw the green blips of a dozen ships they'd left behind in sublight, spread out over a tenth of a light-year to give them a large baseline for their transition scanners. With the fleet blind while in transition, their comrades who remained behind could upfeed targeting information. Every tenth light-year, a dozen ships down-transited to provide more accurate data in the upfeed, while those farther behind, who were no longer needed for that, up-transited to catch up with the main body.

At a half light-year, they still hadn't encountered any opposition, and even with nothing happening, the stress wore on them all. Straight's voice came over York's headset. "Per section's orders, we're administering a low-dose kikker to all of you."

As the drugs flowed through his system, York felt a rush of adrenaline that did nothing to calm his fear.

At a quarter light-year, one of the imperial ships on York's screens blossomed into a white-hot ball of thermonuclear fire. A tense voice on allship said, "*We've run into a cluster of seeker mines, so stay alert.*"

York tensed and waited. An enemy blip appeared on his screens, allocated to Zamekis and Stark. They both fired, didn't get a kill but diverted it.

Another imperial ship exploded, the gunners took out a few more targets, then allship announced, "*We're clear of the mine-field.*" York saw it on his navigational summary from the upfeed a second before allship said, "*Approaching enemy pickets. Gunners watch for transition rounds from their main batteries.*"

The upfeed gave *Dauntless* a targeting solution on one of the pickets, and the ship's hull thrummed with the boom of its main batteries. Unallocated targets appeared on York's screens, nothing close to *Dauntless*. He tracked the pod gunner rounds from other ships in the fleet. One zinged close to *Dauntless*, flashed red as it was allocated to York. He locked a target designator on it and fired. His round killed it, but it wouldn't count for a chevron at gunner's blood since it was friendly fire. By then, most of *Dauntless*'s gunners were occupied with targets and York had another bogie to worry about.

They down-transited at a hundred million kilometers from the enemy fleet, split into five strike forces with one going straight at the Federals, while the other four fanned out in an attempt to flank and englobe them. *Dauntless* was assigned to one of the flanking flotillas. They swung wide, but as they approached the enemy ships, York's screens filled with targets, with one or two always allocated to him.

His gut tightened with fear, and his jaw hurt from clenching his teeth so hard. He examined that fear as he fired another round—missed the target, but Stark took it out. *What did he fear?*

he wondered. *Was it death?* He thought about that while he locked a designator on another incoming round. Death didn't hold much sway over him, and he realized the thing he dreaded most was letting down his comrades. And there was a piece of him that found the constant threat of death exhilarating, that found the next incoming transition torpedo a thrilling challenge.

A stronger dose of kikker washed through his system—someone must have decided he needed it. It put his nerves on edge, and he clenched his teeth even harder, but it helped him focus.

The day turned into a grueling test of endurance, *Dauntless's* hull pinging regularly with the sound of smaller rounds that made it in to her plast shields, her main batteries thrumming like large drums. There seemed no end to the targets on his screens. Then the fleet withdrew and a strange calm settled over the ship.

When York climbed out of his pod, he learned that Stark had been killed. A fragment from a round had punched a hole in his pod shielding, took off most of his head.

After four days of on-and-off fighting, Turnham's Cluster was declared a grand victory for the imperial forces. They'd lost thirty ships with all hands, while they estimated the enemy fleet had lost more than seventy. When York asked about survivors from the ships that had been destroyed, Straight shook her head and said, "Ten-megatonne transition torpedo blows just off a ship's bow, there ain't no survivors."

They withdrew a few light-years, then down-transited in the middle of interstellar space. The most seriously wounded were transferred to a hospital ship, while those *Dauntless's* medical staff could handle remained to be treated in her sick bay.

Since the gunners didn't have anything to do, they were assigned to assist engineering on damage control. There was quite a bit of minor damage that needed repairing, and York spent several days crawling over *Dauntless's* outer hull in a vac suit, became quite adept at moving about in zero-G.

Three days after the last engagement at Turnham's Cluster, they buried the dead in space. *For them, it's over. For us, it goes on.* York noticed that Durlling's eyes were red and puffy, and when it was time to bury Stark, her eyes teared up. He asked Zamekis about it, and she told him that Durlling and Stark had been an item. Luckily, York and Sissy were on the same watch rotation, so they spent the nights together in York's coffin.

That night they up-transited, headed back toward the central empire. York had gotten two kills at Turnham's Cluster, and they cut another full chevron into his arm.

CHAPTER 14: PARTY TIME

"Did you hear?" Marko said as he strode into the lower deck bunk room.

Seated at a table, York, Zamekis, Sissy, and Durlling looked up from their card game. They'd all noticed the note of excitement in the older man's voice.

"Hear what?" Zamekis asked.

Marko paused in the middle of the room as if he were about to make a momentous announcement. "I just heard our new orders."

For some reason, Marko wanted to stretch out the delivery of his message dramatically.

"Out with it," Sissy said.

Marko grinned. "We're to head to Muirendan."

"That's inner empire," Zamekis said.

Even York understood there must be more to it than that.

Durlling prompted Marko. "And . . ."

Marko's grin broadened. "For an indefinite period of time, for repairs and major refitting."

The three women jumped to their feet, whooped and shouted and slapped one another on the back. York asked, "What's going on?"

Sissy turned toward him, closed the distance between them, wrapped her arms around his neck, and gave him a kiss that curled his toes. When they came up for air, she said, "We've been rotated back."

York heard the muted sounds of other spacers elsewhere on the deck whooping and cheering. Apparently, going for refitting was good news that spread quickly.

"What's that mean?"

Zamekis said, "When they use that wording, it means only one thing: We're being taken off combat status."

Marko said, "And they sent us to a nice, plush inner-empire world."

Durlling slapped York's back so hard he staggered. "We'll be there for at least a year or two, maybe more. Light duty, no combat. While *Dauntless* is in orbit around Muirendan getting refitted, she'll only need a skeleton crew."

Sissy leaned close to York's ear and whispered, "Let's get an apartment off base. We'll only have to come up to the ship for a day or two out of every ten, just to log some time in the sims to keep our skills up. We'll have all the time in the world to just kick back and enjoy."

"Everyone gets their turn," Marko said. "That's the way it's always been, kid. We've been out here for close to five years. Now we get a couple off to relax and enjoy ourselves. It's fair payback."

Nothing on *Dauntless* changed immediately; they were too close to the front lines to ignore the ever-present danger of a feddie hunter-killer lying in wait, ready to put a big transition torpedo into the ship's gut. But as they put more distance between them and that possibility, the entire crew grew almost festive. They still got up each watch and did their work, but after four days at two thousand lights they'd covered a little more than twenty light-years, and York noticed a decided difference in the collective mood of the crew.

Seated at a workbench in the lower deck supply room, York was assisting Marko and Straight at inventorying spare pod parts.

They'd been at it for several hours: a necessary task, but tedious at best. They had about an hour left in the watch when he came up with a small discrepancy in the count of target designators.

York glanced over his shoulder, saw Marko standing at an open parts locker looking at a hand terminal. "Marko," he said, standing. "I'm short one target designator." He started toward the cabinet where the designators were stored. "I'll have to do a physical count."

York had only gone two paces when Marko said, "Hold on a moment, kid."

York halted and turned toward the older man. Marko shouted, "Straight, can you come in here?"

Straight appeared in the door to the supply room's inner office. "What do you need?"

"We came up short one designator. Kid's going to have to do a physical count."

"Shit," she said, glancing at the clock above the hatch. "That'll take a couple hours, and we've less than an hour left." She looked at York, then at the clock again, considered it for a moment, then said to York, "Forget it, Ballin. We'll do the count next watch."

York couldn't believe his ears. It was so out of character for Straight to show such flexibility. Under any other circumstance, she'd not care in the least that they'd have to work well beyond the end of their watch.

"Better yet," Marko said. "It's just one designator. Let's just forget it, let the engineers handle it during refitting. They'll write it off on a discrepancy report, and we'll have a fully reconciled inventory when we have to go out again."

York tensed, appalled that Marko would make such a suggestion. He waited for Straight to explode. But she shrugged and said, "That works for me." She turned and disappeared through the door.

York noticed a lot of little things like that, and the deeper into the empire they traveled, the more frequently such small lapses in discipline occurred. Five nights later, the petty officer in charge of another gunner crew found two of his team quite drunk on contraband 'trate, a horrible breach of discipline while on ship. But instead of turning them over to Zhako to be tossed in the brig, they spent one watch scrubbing decks.

York had long ago learned to adjust to the situation and not fight the inevitable. In any case, he'd never been so happy. He had friends, and his crewmates respected him for his skills as a gunner. He was one of the best, and somehow he'd found a future in this strange world he'd been dropped into. He had a simple set of rules to live by, regular food, and a comfortable place to sleep. And above all, there was Sissy; the two of them had such plans for the coming year.

After eighteen days under full drive, and a little more than a hundred light-years, *Dauntless* down-transited outside Muirendan's nearspace.

As the sound of Muirendan Prime's docking gantries coupling to *Dauntless* echoed through the ship's hull, York examined his small bundle of meager possessions. Unlike the other spacers, he didn't have any souvenirs or sentimental keepsakes; he'd come aboard with nothing but the clothes on his back and the manacles on his hands and legs. Now all he had was a couple of uniforms, a small personal reader he'd purchased from ship's stores, and a few toiletries. He considered carefully what to take for his year on Muirendan, and decided to take it all. He didn't make any attempt to fold the uniforms as he tossed them into a small duffel.

"Ballin."

He recognized Straight's voice, turned, and found her standing in the hatch to the bunk room. She hooked a thumb over her shoulder. "Report to the captain's office."

His heart skipped a beat. "Did I do something wrong?"

She shook her head. "Not that I know of."

York stopped by the marine barracks. "Here," he said, handing Sissy his duffel.

She eyed him warily. "Where are you going?"

"I'm supposed to report to the captain's office."

"You do something wrong?"

York shrugged. "Straight doesn't think so. I'll meet you down here as soon as I'm done. Hang on to my duffel."

York climbed up the ship's ladders deck after deck. There were grav lifts, but those were reserved for personnel on important business. The hatch to the captain's office was open, but York stood outside and knocked politely.

"Enter."

As York stepped through the hatch, he saw the captain seated behind a small desk, while Thorow stood over her looking at a hand terminal. York went through the ritual of marching squarely up to the captain's desk, stopping a pace away from it, saluting, and saying, "Spacer Ballin reporting as ordered, ma'am."

Jarwith looked at him carefully while Thorow continued to look at the screen of the small reader, frowning and shaking his head slightly from side to side, as if something he saw there seemed out of place, or incorrect.

Jarwith returned the salute and said, "At ease, Spacer."

York spread his feet and clasped his hands behind his back. He'd never been in the captain's office before, though that didn't intimidate him half as much as Thorow's disturbed look. The executive officer said, "This isn't right."

Jarwith stared at York as she said, "No, it isn't. But I told you the rather unusual circumstances under which he came to us."

"Ya," Thorow said. "With a suit giving orders to civilian and military authorities alike. But this"—he wagged the small terminal at her—"doesn't fit anything."

For the first time, Thorow looked at York. There was no anger in the man's look. "You've been a good spacer, Ballin, even though you had a rough start."

York decided that the mystery of the moment allowed him to break discipline just a little. "I don't understand, sir."

Jarwith leaned forward and put her hands flat on the desk in

front of her. "We've received new orders for you. You're being transferred to the destroyer *Relentless*. You're to report there immediately. They're headed outbound to the front lines tomorrow."

York had to replay her words carefully in his mind to understand their meaning, and a lump formed in the pit of his stomach.
"Immediately?"

"God dammit," Thorow said, "it's just not right."

Jarwith ignored him and said to York, "This is very unusual—
just not done. Not when someone's paid their dues out there."

York's thoughts raced as he tried to come up with some ratio-
nal explanation. "Maybe it's because I was with you for less than
three years. Maybe they figure I haven't earned it yet."

Jarwith shook her head, her brows furrowed not with anger,
but with obvious pain. "No, Mr. Ballin, that's not it. This is very
unusual. You've earned better. If it's any consolation, I'm promot-
ing you to spacer first class. And you'll be welcome on *Relentless*.
They're quite happy to get a top-notch gunner with a good record."

Thorow added, "We've cleaned up your record, no references
to your past, nor to the mistakes you made here at the beginning.
It's the least we can do."

During the entire climb back down to the marine barracks, York
hoped that if he moved slowly enough, Thorow and Jarwith
would have time to learn there'd been some mistake, a glitch in
Fleet's computers. But that miracle never came.

When he stepped into the marine barracks, he spotted Sissy
seated at a terminal with her back to him. She heard him approach,
glanced over her shoulder for only an instant, then turned back to
the screen. "I've found a little beach cabin. We're going to share it
with Chunks and a couple of gunners."

She turned around to look him in the face, saying, "It's expensive but we . . ." When she saw the look on his face, her words
slowly trailed off. ". . . can just . . . afford . . . it. What's wrong?"

"I've been transferred to *Relentless*."

She frowned and her nose wrinkled. "How much time do we have?"

"None. I'm to report there immediately."

"No," she shouted, standing. "There's no fucking way. You got it wrong."

York couldn't find any anger, just sadness. "I got it straight from Jarwith and Thorow."

Sissy's eyes flashed with anger. She turned and marched across the deck, shouting, "Sarge, somebody fucked up big-time."

When Cochran heard the news, she was as perplexed as Jarwith and Thorow. She got Shernov involved, and they made a call to the captain. But after much discussion, they reluctantly agreed there was nothing they could do about it.

"No," Sissy said, tears brimming in her eyes. "It's not right. It can't be."

Cochran shook her head. "But it is what it is, Sis."

Sissy stomped her foot and shouted again. "No." She threw her arms around York. "I won't let you go."

As she held on to him, York felt her tears soaking into the shoulder of his tunic. He wanted to cry himself, but his soul felt just plain numb. Cochran and Shernov had to peel Sissy off him, and as Sissy collapsed in Cochran's arms, Shernov said, "Sorry, kid."

York's orders stated that he was to report to *Relentless* without delay, a military phrase that meant *now*.

"I'll transfer to *Relentless* with you," Sissy said.

York glanced at Shernov, who shook his head silently, telling York that would never happen.

York kissed Sissy on the cheek and tasted the salt of her tears, mixed with a bit of girlish perfume, and the scent he would always remember as uniquely her. He grabbed his duffel and left her there still sobbing. He climbed up several decks to the main personnel hatch, went through the ritual of requesting permission to leave the ship then saluting the flag of the Lunan Empire.

He stepped out onto a busy concourse that ran the length of

the docks on Muirendan Prime. He paused for a moment and stood there as people walked past him, feeling empty and alone. An odd thought occurred to him. *What if he turned around, got Sissy, and the two of them deserted?* He looked up and down the docks and wondered where they would go, realized the MPs would scoop them up in rather short order.

On his way to his new ship, he passed a shop that advertised marine gear. On a whim, he stepped through the door and walked inside. A fellow standing behind a counter smiled and said, "What can I do for you, kid?"

The shop offered all sorts of equipment, only some of it weaponry. "I'm looking for a type of sidearm that uses chemical explosives to fire a bullet."

The fellow's eyes narrowed, and as York tried to describe the bluish-metal gun Cath had let him try out on the firing range, his eyes narrowed further.

"What do you want with a gun like that?"

York didn't really have an answer to that, so he said, "A marine friend, a good friend, recommended I carry one as a backup piece in case my energy weapon fails."

The fellow stared at York for several seconds, then nodded and went into the back of the store. When he returned, he laid several bluish-metal weapons on the counter in front of York. York chose a small one that looked like that Cath had used. It had a short barrel and a revolving cylinder that held the bullets. He bought it and a box of shells, paid for it with the money he would have used to pay for the cabin on the beach with Sissy.

He found *Relentless* easily, stepped through its main personnel hatch, saluted the flag, touched the identity card clipped to his chest, then saluted the young male officer on duty there. Holding the salute he said, "Spacer"—he hesitated as he recalled his new rank—"First Class York Ballin requesting permission to board ship, sir."

The officer scanned his ID with a small instrument. "Welcome aboard, Mr. Ballin. I'm Lieutenant Crispin. A good gunner is always welcome on *Relentless*. You'll want to report immediately to Lieutenant Mercer."

York said, "I'll also need to register a personal weapon with the master-at-arms."

Crispin gave York directions, and a few minutes later he knocked on the hatch to a small office. Mercer turned out to be a tall woman with plain features. "Good to have you aboard, Mr. Ballin. Your record says you're a top-notch gunner. We can use you. Recently promoted to first class, I see. I'll arrange to have your implants installed."

Seated behind her desk, she gave him an appraising look. "I see you were in a lower-deck crew on *Dauntless*. You're welcome to an upper-deck posting here."

"No," York said. "I'd prefer to stay on the lower decks."

She frowned at that and cocked her head. "As you wish. It doesn't matter to me, as long as you burn feddie incoming."

She sent him to Chief Stolkov, an older man with a lined face and a crew of eight gunners reporting to him. He introduced York to three of them who happened to be present at the moment, though York felt detached from his surroundings and didn't really catch their names. He stowed his gear and spent a couple of hours checking out his new pod—identified a few maintenance issues and flagged them for review. Then he climbed into his new coffin, said, "Computer, lights out."

He lay in the dark and thought he could still smell a hint of Sissy. He wiped the side of his cheek with his finger, then touched it to his tongue, tasted the dried remnants of her salty tears, and there was still a trace of that scent she'd worn. As he lay there trying to find sleep, a piece of him knew he would never see her again.

CHAPTER 15:
TANK DREAMS

Shortly after *Relentless* departed Muirendan Prime, York was ordered to report to the senior medical officer. He climbed up several decks to sick bay, and when he checked in, was greeted by a medical corpsman. "Ballin," the fellow said, looking at a screen at his desk. "Implants, is it?"

No one had told York what to expect, so he said, "I guess so."

York waited for about an hour, then a female corpsman appeared in the waiting room holding a small terminal. She had brown hair cut chin length, didn't wear any makeup, was a little overweight in an attractive way, and couldn't be more than a year or two older than York. The stencil on her chest read PLEMIN. "Ballin," she announced. York was the only one waiting there, but she said it as if the room was filled with people waiting to be seen and she had to call out his name so he could identify himself.

He stood and towered over her. He'd grown a bit more, which had him standing just a little taller than most men, but he'd also started to fill out in the shoulders.

Plemin led him into a small room where she sat him in a powered medical chair. As she lowered a strange helmet with spiky protrusions over his head, she said, "We cultured an organic polymer to match your DNA. I'm going to punch six holes in your skull and inject the polymer. It's genetically triggered to grow circuits among your synapses. It's all minor outpatient stuff. You won't feel a thing."

Beyond her statement that he wouldn't feel anything, he didn't understand much of what she said. She adjusted some sort of controls on the helmet, did something at a terminal nearby, then said, "Here we go."

York braced for some sort of pain as the contraption punched or drilled or bored holes in his head, but she immediately lifted the helmet off his head. "How do you feel, York?"

"What?" he said. "You didn't do anything."

She grinned and said, "Typical reaction. You've been out for more than an hour. Only takes a couple of minutes for the drilling and injections, but a good hour for the speed healing to take."

She hustled him out of the chair. He didn't feel weak or sore—or anything.

As she walked him out to the waiting room, she said, "We haven't activated anything yet, need to let the circuitry grow for a bit. Report back here in a tenday and we'll run some initial tests."

During the next few days, Stolkov put him through some simulated firefights. York scored well and everyone was quite impressed. He tried not to think how much he missed Chunks and Zamekis and all the rest, but he missed Sissy horribly.

After a tenday, they partially activated his implants. Apparently, the circuits still had a little growing to do, and he had to learn how to use them. With a lot of practice, he mastered certain thought sequences that were trigger keys for specific functions, but he quickly learned that the most important was the trigger that shut everything down. Otherwise, he had this constant background din running through his thoughts.

"You'll get used to that," Plemin said. She smiled at him, and he thought he saw a bit of invitation in the look she gave him. He liked her, and she was pretty, but he could only think of Sissy. So he smiled back at her and kept any flirtatiousness out of the look. Then he turned and left.

York was hoping he'd left the lessons behind, but someone had told Mercer he'd shown an interest in navigation. She was all too happy to help further his education. He now regretted that he'd asked that one simple question of Marko.

During the next year, York fought in several smaller engagements, earned a gunner's chevron here and there. But at the massive battle at Trefallin, which lasted for more than a tenday, he earned six half-chevrons, and by his fifteenth birthday he had eight full chevrons on each arm. Only two crew members outranked him as a gunner: the chief gunner, and an older woman of very slight stature who'd been a gunner for years. Her eyes had a haunted look to them, and York didn't want to outrank her that way.

He and Plemin became lovers, but it didn't mean as much to him as it had with Sissy. *Relentless* hadn't been back for a full refit for more than four years when he joined her crew, and he sometimes wondered if it was he who held back with Plemin, he who kept their relationship more a matter of convenience for both of them. Sometimes she seemed to want to break through that, but when he was with her, he always thought of Sissy.

About a year and a half after York had joined *Relentless*, he got some mail from Cath, the female marine on *Dauntless*.

York:

I'm sorry to have to tell you this. We had a nasty little firefight on a bush-league planet in Aldebaran sector. *Three* took a big shell, went out with all hands. Chunks, Rodma, Sissy, they're all dead. I knew you'd want to know.

Cath

York cried himself to sleep that night, alone in his coffin. A month later, they docked at Cathan Prime. *Relentless* got orders to report to an inner-empire planet *for an indefinite period of time, for repairs and major refitting.* York got orders to report for duty aboard the heavy cruiser *Africa*, outbound for the front lines.

*   *   *

Africa saw a lot of action and York picked up more gunner's chevrons. About six months after York had joined her crew, they were ordered to rendezvous with the Ninth Imperial Fleet at Sirius Night Star, a cluster of uninhabitable planets and planetoids orbiting a large red dwarf with a mass about half that of a standard solar. The three planets in the system were just large enough to avoid the designation *planetoid*, and the low gravity on each was ideal for heavy maintenance on warships. Over the years, they'd evolved into an important naval base that supplied and repaired ships close to the front lines. But the Federals were amassing a large fleet nearby, so it appeared they wanted to take, or destroy, Sirius Night Star. The Admiralty had tasked the Ninth Fleet with ensuring that that did not happen.

By the time they assembled, the Ninth had a complement of more than a hundred warships, and based on the intelligence at hand her commanders were confident they could repel anything the feddies threw at them. In the first engagement, the Federal forces came in using a classic swift-strike approach, down-transiting a few ships to upfeed targeting data to their main force of about eighty ships. York had developed his navigational skills to the point where he could handle any targets allocated to his pod but still follow developments in the overall battle with an occasional glance to a scan summary in the corner of one of his screens. The attacking force was always at a disadvantage, so he thought it foolhardy that the feddies would come at them without overwhelming odds.

He was surprised when *Africa* and twenty other ships were ordered to redeploy to their flank about two hours after the battle began. When York's scan summary updated, he saw the reason: Their intelligence data had been incomplete. The feddies had two additional forces of seventy ships each coming in from opposite sides of the system. York didn't need an officer to tell him that they were badly outnumbered and outflanked, and cut off from any help or reinforcements.

For days, they fought a running battle that the Federals were winning by a tactic of slow attrition, and by the end of the sixth day, York had four more confirmed kills. With an extended lull in the fighting, they held gunner's blood.

York stood silently as the chief cut a new chevron into each of his arms, let the blood run down his arms and drip from his fingertips onto the deck. He now had twelve full chevrons on one arm, twelve and a half on the other, and if the battle continued for another day or two, he'd outrank the chief, would be elevated to chief gunner. But he didn't think they'd last long. From a complement of more than a hundred ships, the Ninth had been whittled down to a count of about twenty operational warships. The festivities at gunner's blood that night were muted.

When York slammed awake in his coffin to the sound of the alert klaxon, his implants told him he'd had only about an hour's sleep. His coffin determined that he needed a little ant-alc, and he felt the pinch in his neck as it gave him the injection. When the coffin cycled open, he hit the deck running with the practiced ease of an experienced gunner.

He heard the thrum of *Africa*'s main batteries echoing through her hull even before he had the power up in his pod, a bad sign. As soon as the pod signaled to the central combat computer that it was online, it immediately allocated two targets to him, another bad sign. He deflected one, but by that time he had another allocated, managed to kill one while someone else deflected the other.

The next two hours turned into a frantic scramble, with shell fragments pinging off *Africa*'s hull, the occasional screech of tearing plast and metal as something bigger penetrated her defenses. His implants allowed him to erect virtual screens, so he monitored damage control closely while taking care of his targets. Fear crawled up his gut as one of the power plants went off-line when a big shell hit it. His own power feed redlined, then dropped to 80 percent, finally leveling off at 70 percent.

With limited power, he barely managed to deflect the next target, and the next. Then he had three targets allocated, then four, then—

"Easy there, Spacer."

York drifted back and forth between oblivion and pain. He tried to focus on the words of the medical corpsman.

". . . have to tank you . . . hospital ship . . . bad shape . . ."

He eventually found a strange state of lethargy where nothing mattered. More by reflex than anything else, one of the thought-trigger keys for his implants rolled through his mind, but nothing happened.

He went away for a while to a place with no concept of self, didn't really sleep, but surfaced now and then to a slightly elevated state of consciousness. When that happened, he wondered where he was, and again that thought trigger tried to key his implants. He thought he might have been successful, but then he went away again.

Mathias! Why did that name come to mind?

An older man appeared in front of York in a hazy shimmer of a dream. He was missing a leg and an arm, but somehow he stood on one barely visible ghost of a leg. The man screamed and tore at his own face, then charged, his hands extended to tear at York, one nothing more than a phantom visible by a vague, shimmering outline. York screamed, turned, and ran.

The man returned again and again, and there were others like him, men and women. One of them finally cornered him, a woman he wanted to call Sharfa. In desperation, he fought back as she tore at his eyes, found himself kneeling on her lifeless body pounding on her face, her eyes open and unseeing. The next time Mathias came after him, he did the same to him.

CHAPTER 16:
RECOVERY

"Stand by all hands," allship blared. *"Down-transition in twenty minutes and counting."*

Commander Valerie Chechkova scanned her fire control console one last time to reassure herself that all was in order. She glanced sideways at Ensign Tomura, who was hunched over his own screens, tense and fearful. He looked her way, and attempting to sound casual and at ease, she said, "Relax." She gave him a reassuring smile and tried not to let her own fear show. The imperial heavy cruiser *Defiant*, with all hands at battle stations, was about to down-transit blindly into what might be a very hot situation, and she didn't like having an unblooded trainee assisting her at Fire Control.

She glanced down at the outboard scan summary she'd loaded into the corner of one of her screens. Still in transition, *Defiant*'s own scan systems were useless as the ship screamed toward Orion 1341, an unnamed system that had been in enemy hands for two years.

Captain Turcott had five ships under his command. One hour ago, three-tenths light-year out, *Talent's Pride* had down-transited, launched its combat drones, and began broadcasting detailed scan data to the rest of the strike force, all still in transition and driving into 1341's nearspace. In that way, they weren't completely blind while attempting a close approach. But the *Pride* was still too far out to give them any detailed information.

On her screen, she saw the destroyer *Harbinger* down-transit behind them. It started feeding them scan data immediately, and she was relieved to see no sign of enemy activity, so they weren't in imminent danger of taking a torpedo. Now that *Harbinger* was providing better scan data from closer in, *Talent's Pride* up-transited to rejoin the strike force.

"Down-transition in ten minutes and counting."

Captain Turcott's voice spoke softly through Val's implants. "Helm, let's start dumping some of that speed."

After a series of heavy losses in this quadrant, the feddies had retreated several light-years, withdrawing from quite a few systems in the area. Most of them were much like 1341: no real strategic resources like habitable planets, but as imperial forces moved in to consolidate the new front line, it was a great place for a nasty little ambush.

As a cautionary move, they were coming in on a classic swift-strike approach. At full drive, in excess of two thousand lights, they knew their transition wakes were easily visible and could be targeted by pickets properly positioned along their course. The classic approach should allow the strike force to drive deep into 1341's nearspace with minimum probability of blindly taking warheads. If an enemy vessel threw anything at the strike force, the ship that had down-transited would lock onto the transition launch and provide accurate targeting data to the main force.

Orion 1341? That number sounded oddly familiar, so Val ran a quick search, was surprised at how rapidly results showed on her screen. "Shit!" she said as she read the first entry.

She keyed her implants into the command circuit. "Captain, I just checked, and the last engagement of Sirius Night Star took place in this system."

"Holy shit!" She recognized the com officer's voice.

"That's a gloomy thought," Turcott said. "Got to be a lot of ghosts in this system."

Ensign Tomura leaned toward her and asked, "What's Sirius Night Star?"

"Two years ago," Val said, "the imperial Ninth Fleet was wiped out at the battle of Sirius Night Star. Not a single imperial spacer came back."

Tomura's eyes widened and he looked fearfully at his console.

"Down-transition in one minute and counting."

Val ran her systems through one last pre-combat check, then leaned over and said softly to Tomura, "Remember, while there may be trouble waiting for us, we don't know that for certain, so be very careful to wait for orders from me or the captain before firing on anything."

He nodded. "Aye, ma'am."

"Down-transition minus ten seconds and counting, Nine . . . Eight . . . Seven . . . Six . . . Five . . . Four . . . Three . . . Two . . . One . . ."

Val's screens fluttered as the helm-officer said, "Sublight."

The bridge went silent. Fresh out of transition, *Defiant* was a blind target with only long-range information from *Harbinger*'s scans, and no idea of what they'd down-transited into until Scan got them data.

"We're clear to a hundred thousand kilometers and expanding, sir."

Val let out a breath she hadn't realized she'd been holding, heard others doing the same.

"Thank you," Turcott said easily. "No surprises then. Now let's see what's on long range. Drones out, Commander. Hold them at the limit of your short-range scan."

A distant, ghostly clang sounded through the hull of the ship as six drones shot out of their launch bays. "Drones out, sir," Scan said.

Val's scan summary compressed as the drones shot outward

from *Defiant's* hull and their effective scan baseline broadened. At fifty thousand kilometers, the drones shifted into a complex circular orbit about *Defiant*, and the scan summary compressed even faster.

With one ear tuned to the bridge circuit, Val focused on the main batteries. If they got into a firefight now, it would at least be at a reasonable distance.

"Parasitic demand from the drones is smooth. Response is strong. Clear to one million klicks and expanding."

"Excellent," Turcott said happily. "Good job. Hold the drones at fifty thousand klicks. Go to extreme long range and start scanning. I want a full system map soonest."

Over the next half hour, the tension on the bridge slowly dissipated. And while they remained at battle stations, everyone relaxed a bit. After two hours, they had a full system map, though if there were any feddie hunter-killers running silent, their scans wouldn't spot them, so they still had to move cautiously.

"Captain," Val's implants said in the com officer's voice. "I'm getting a computer-generated imperial distress signal. It's on an old, out-of-date encryption key, but it appears to be authentic."

"Computer-generated?" Turcott asked.

"Yes, sir. I've asked the ship's computer to connect me with a live operator, but it says there are none. It's identified itself as *Andor Vincent*, a hospital ship, and it's apparently unescorted."

"What the hell is an unescorted hospital ship doing out here?"

"Don't know, sir, but I'm accessing its registry details now. Based out of Dumark, it was . . . Oh my God!"

All the tension that had dissipated from the bridge suddenly returned, and when the com officer again spoke, there was no mistaking the awe in his voice. "It was last assigned to the Ninth Fleet, is listed as having gone out with all hands at Sirius Night Star."

Defiant's bridge was silent for several seconds, then Turcott said, "No live crew left?"

"No, sir."

"Tell the *Vincent* to stand by. We're busy right now. We'll get to it in a couple of days."

"Aye, aye, sir."

Like her fellow crew members, Val's thoughts immediately shifted back to the more important task of ferreting out any possible dangers in the system. But a few seconds later, the com officer spoke again in that awestruck tone. "Captain, the *Vincent*'s computer wants to know if we want to take possession of its . . . patients."

"Patients?"

"Yes, sir. Apparently, it has more than a hundred critically wounded survivors of Sirius Night Star. The *Vincent*'s been running silent and keeping them alive in her medical life-support tanks for the last two years."

When York awoke, he immediately recognized the trappings of a sick bay ward on a large man-of-war. He assumed he was still on *Africa*, but he felt strangely different. He tried to move, but his muscles didn't respond. Moments later, a medical corpsman walked into the room, looking into a hand terminal and vocalizing into his implants. "Yes, he's awake."

He stopped beside York's bed and said, "Well, young man, welcome back to the living. How do you feel?"

"I can't move," York said.

The corpsman shook his head. "Don't worry about that. We've got you on a central nerve block. Don't want you overreacting or seizing after two years in the tanks."

"Two years?" he asked.

An older man marched into the room wearing an officer's uniform, rank of full commander. "How is he?"

The corpsman looked again at his hand terminal. "Looks pretty good. The regrowth took nicely. Let's turn off the block."

The older man nodded. "Sounds good. Do it."

The corpsman did something on his hand terminal, saying, "We're going to bring your nervous system back online slowly. Don't worry about feeling partially numb. That will pass quickly."

York had been through this once before, but not after being out for two years. He expected to feel the kind of prickly sensation like that when circulation returned to an arm on which he'd slept. His fingertips tingled a little, but over a period of several seconds, he regained the use of his hands and legs without any real discomfort. They helped him sit up, then stand up, and he felt surprisingly strong. He learned they were on the heavy cruiser *Defiant* and that the older man was her senior medical officer, Commander Platkin, and the corpsman was Petty Officer Checkman. The corpsman told him that soon he'd be sent back to a hospital at a large naval base, though no one was quite certain where.

Platkin said, "We're not sure what to do with you, young man."

They showed York a vid of his naked body and it surprised him. He was more muscular than he remembered.

"You must've filled out," Platkin said. "Sixteen to eighteen, that's an important growth age. And the *Vincent* kept up your muscular stimulus treatments, so we expect you'll recover rather quickly."

They asked York hundreds of questions, most of which he couldn't answer. At one point, they read a list of names to him, wanted to know if he recognized any of them. Among them were Mathias and Sharfa, but he cautiously denied ever hearing of them.

"We think some of the tanks failed," Checkman told him one day while York was exercising in a physical therapy rig. "Some of the older spacers died of trauma that wasn't on their admitting report, so it must have happened after they were tanked, a lot of bruising about the face and shoulders."

York recalled the visions of beating Mathias and Sharfa to death, and was glad he hadn't admitted to ever hearing of them.

They were quite interested in the dreams he'd had while tanked. He admitted to the nightmares, but didn't tell them about fighting Mathias and Sharfa.

"When we tank someone," Checkman told him, "we always shut down their implants. But all of you shared similar dreams, so we think there was some sort of leakage going on, something we don't understand yet. We're guessing that's why you had those nightmares."

York learned that the older spacers in the *Vincent*'s tanks had died during that two-year stretch, and that among the younger ones, they were seeing signs of mental instability for which they could find no record of prior symptoms. "It's interesting," Checkman told him. "The older the spacer, the more instability we see. You were the youngest, and you're the only one who appears to have come out of it mentally unscathed."

York decided to never speak of his experiences on the *Vincent*. And he swore that he would never allow them to tank him again.

Carson stood in front of the news kiosk on Luna Prime looking through the display window, pretending interest in a vid showing a local sporting event, while really watching the reflection in the window of the people moving back and forth behind him. He spotted his contact across the busy concourse walking his way, couldn't recall the fellow's name, wanted to call him Tolliver, but he wasn't the same young fellow he'd met before, though he appeared cut from the same mold. Again, Carson suspected an attaché of some sort working for someone very high in the Admiralty. And again, there was no question that the fellow was regular navy, not AI.

He stopped next to Carson, pretended to be interested in the same sporting event on the same vid. "Any difficulties?" he asked softly without looking Carson's way.

"The commandant was a little reluctant," Carson said. "But I pointed out that it would be detrimental to his career to . . .

resist. And the identity codes you gave me ensured his cooperation, though he was actually insulted when I offered him the compensation you provided. I was unable to assuage his bruised sense of duty."

"Will that be a problem?"

"No, he'll cooperate."

"Then keep the extra compensation for yourself," the young man said. "Consider it a bonus. I'm glad to be done with the Ballinov brat." He turned to leave, and as he did so he dropped a small comp card on the floor beside Carson's shoe. Carson lifted his shoe and stepped on it, hiding it from anyone nearby. He let the fellow disappear in the crowd before reaching down and picking up his payment.

He wandered down the concourse, had a couple of hours to wait before he could board his ship. He found a bar, sat down at a small table with his back to a wall. An attractive young waitress came his way and he ordered a drink. Then he pulled up a small hand terminal and let his curiosity get the best of him. The young fellow had said, ". . . the Ballinov brat."

That name sounded familiar, but he couldn't place it, so he ran a quick search. When he got the answer, his heart went cold.

He shut down the hand terminal, threw some cash on the table, and didn't wait for his drink. He walked quickly out of the place then down the concourse, conscious of any vid that might be recording him. He used the moment just as he turned a corner to switch his visual distortion field to a different image. On one camera, a distinguished man in a business suit would appear to walk out of sight around the corner; on another camera, a merchant spacer would appear to step into view. He changed appearances four more times, threw the payment chit in one trash bin, the hand terminal in another, and in a third he completely discarded the identity of the Carson persona. He would never use that again.

He didn't dare board the ship for his scheduled departure,

instead took the first berth he could find on an outbound ship. He'd go out a dozen light-years and obscure his trail before returning to his base of operations. It was a horrible waste of time, and he'd miss an appointment or two, but better that than the alternative.

What a fool he'd been! *Never be curious*, he reminded himself.

CHAPTER 17:
THE ACADEMY

York healed quickly, though they'd taken care of the real healing before allowing him to reawaken. He did ask Checkman
about his injuries, learned that he'd lost a leg at the hip and a
good-size chunk of his lower torso. His lungs had also suffered
some serious decompression damage. The medical staff guessed
his pod had been punctured by a shell fragment that had taken
off the leg and decompressed the pod. But the pod's damage-
control systems had managed to reseal it before he suffered too
much brain damage, though there had been some neurological
impairment they'd patched up. The pod's medical systems had
kept him alive until his comrades aboard *Africa* had retrieved
him. Then the *Vincent*'s tanks had kept him alive until *Defiant*
came along. Checkman said, "If you're alive when we get to you,
and still retain some reasonable level of cognitive ability, we can
probably fix you."

York asked to transfer to *Defiant*'s crew, but apparently they
had standing orders that all survivors of the *Vincent* were to
remain on noncombat status until the powers-that-be decided
what to do with them. Once they'd offloaded the survivors from
the *Vincent*, they'd split them up among the five ships under Captain Turcott's command. There were a little over twenty on *Defiant*, but York never saw them. Checkman told him the others had

all suffered at least one psychotic episode and were in isolation under psychiatric observation.

With no active-duty responsibilities, York spent his time reading, exercising, and studying, because Mercer would give him absolute hell if he didn't do his homework properly. He reminded himself that Mercer was long gone, probably no longer alive. And while he hated to admit it, he was slowly coming to understand the interstellar navigation calculations. Out of sheer boredom, he asked them to let him do something, so they assigned him to light duty in engineering.

York followed the reconsolidation of nearby interstellar space like a drama on the vids. Imperial ships of all kinds arrived in Orion 1341's nearspace almost daily. At first, the new arrivals were just warships to augment Turcott's strike force. But as they swept the surrounding space of all feddie resistance, all sorts of vessels arrived: merchantmen to resupply the bases, engineering teams to repair the damage caused by bombardment, even a few tramp freighters hoping to take advantage of the need for supplies. A little more than a month after they'd pulled York from the tanks, he received orders to transfer to INR-681, an imperial supply ship scheduled to go back for more supplies. INR-681 could only push about nine hundred lights, so forty days and a little more than one hundred light-years later, he stepped onto the decking of Aagerbanne Prime, a large naval base and sector headquarters. He reported to the assignments desk there, and was given one-way tickets to Cathan on a merchant freighter named *Chelsie's Delight*.

At Cathan, he boarded an imperial destroyer headed for Muirendan for refitting and rotation back. Muirendan was the closest he'd ever come to the heart of the empire, and like his first time, he only spent a few hours there. His new orders assigned him to a berth on a passenger liner destined for somewhere deep within the inner empire. They assigned him to a cot in a large bunk room occupied by about thirty members of the liner's crew, and there he learned that they were headed for Luna. He wondered why Fleet would send him to Luna, which was not merely close to the heart of the empire, but the heart itself.

York had never been on a passenger liner, so out of curiosity, he explored the civilian ship. He wandered down to the engine room, asked if he could look around. The chief engineer was retired navy, and after warning York not to touch anything, turned him over to a young crewman. The engineering crew proved to be quite tolerant of his inquisitiveness. He spent a couple of days down there looking over their shoulders, though he was careful not to get in the way. He learned from a couple of the civilian spacers that there were different classes of accommodation on the liner, so he wandered up to first class to see what it was like to travel in luxury. He passed an open doorway—they didn't call them hatches on a liner—to a room in which a maid was hard at work cleaning the place. He glanced in, and at her frown he said, "Just wondering about first class."

She smiled and said, "You and me, we ain't never gonna live like this, are we?"

She let him look around, but told him to be quick about it. The place was a suite of rooms, enormous by any shipboard standards in his experience. There'd been no effort to conserve space the way they did on military vessels.

When he stepped out into the corridor to return to the lower decks, he ran into one of the ship's officers. The man stopped him and demanded, "What are you doing up here?"

York stood several centimeters taller than the fellow. "Just curious," he said.

"Don't come up here again," the man said, his eyes narrowing. "I don't want your kind bothering important people."

"Sorry," he said, then stepped around the man and left.

He explored one of the second-class decks, noticed that the rooms were still more spacious than on a man-of-war, but nothing like first class. Third class was only a little better than the bunk room he shared with the liner's crew members.

A few days later, while exploring the upper decks, York wandered into a passenger lounge. The place was quite luxurious, with chandeliers hanging from the ceiling, drapes covering the walls, a long bar running the length of one wall, and small tables with white tablecloths carefully placed about the floor. It was midafternoon and with the exception of a half-dozen people, the place was empty. He gripped the back of a chair and slid it across the deck a few centimeters; as he suspected, nothing was bolted down.

"Can I help you?"

York started at the sound of the voice, turned to find a bartender standing behind the bar regarding him. The fellow wore a uniform with a high stiff collar and looked more like a waiter than a crew member. York stepped over to the bar and said, "Just curious. Just looking around."

The bartender looked York over carefully, then glanced about the room. "Ya, the rich just get richer. Want anything to drink?"

York said, "I can't afford it."

The bartender frowned. "You traveling on orders, or personal business?"

"Orders."

"Then you've got a per diem. What's your name?"

York gave him his name and the fellow looked him up on a terminal behind the bar. "Ya, it's not a lot, but it looks like you haven't spent it on anything but meals, so it's building up nicely. You can afford it."

York didn't really want anything to drink, but out of sheer boredom he ordered a beer. He'd been signing for his meals and hadn't realized there'd be anything beyond that. The bartender brought his beer, he signed for it, and he had just taken the first sip when he heard laughter behind him, a young woman's voice. He turned around and saw a man crossing the room toward him with an attractive woman on his arm. The fellow couldn't be much older than York but he wore a naval uniform, rank of full commander. The uniform had odd little non-regulation embellishments all over it, including epaulettes on the shoulders; no one wore epaulettes.

The fellow noticed York and stopped short, a look of distaste on his face. York snapped to attention and raised his hand in a salute. The fellow didn't return the salute, which forced York to stand there holding it. He frowned at York, released the woman's arm, and stepped forward to stand uncomfortably close to him. "What are you doing in here, Spacer?" the fellow demanded.

York still held the salute. "Just having a drink, sir."

The man looked slowly around the room, then back at York. "Isn't it obvious to you that your kind doesn't belong in here?"

"It is now, sir."

The fellow's frown deepened. "Don't be impertinent."

"Sorry, sir."

He finally returned York's salute with a sloppy wave of his hand and said, "Please leave."

York left the beer unfinished. Out in the corridor, he recalled the words of the ship's officer he'd encountered in first class a few days before. They had both used the same words: *your kind.* He was beginning to realize they found people like York and "his kind" rather distasteful. It was something he would be reminded of again, many times.

York tried not to gawk like a bumpkin as he stepped off the passenger liner onto the docks at Luna Prime, still wondering why they'd sent him there. The docks there looked just like docks anywhere, but when he stepped out into the main concourse of the massive space station, the sights and sounds that assaulted him were overwhelming.

His implants automatically connected to Naval Operations Command, and he received orders to report to a shuttle bay. He keyed up a map of the station, and his implants projected a virtual overlay with directions for the most direct route there. He knew it was unlikely he'd have this chance again, so he decided to take a less direct route. He'd still get there, but he might learn a little on the way.

He was walking past a store when an advertisement flashed onto the virtual overlay in front of him, offering him the best jewelry that money could buy at discount prices. The advertisement claimed that it would please his girlfriend immensely, and she'd have no idea he'd bought it at a reduced rate. He quickly learned to set up a reception filter in his implants to shut out most of the advertising.

Up ahead, he spotted a couple of barboys standing on the sidewalk outside an establishment that catered to spacers. As he walked past them, one of them gave him an inviting look, but he ignored it. He was surprised at the complete lack of advertising for the resident male and female prostitutes. Apparently, in the heart of the empire, such pursuits were not openly promoted. They probably found it distasteful to be reminded of the recreational activities of *his kind*. It occurred to him *their kind* probably enjoyed the same sort of activities, just at a more expensive place.

He waited an hour for the shuttle, but a large observation screen in the lounge gave an impressive view of Luna's primary, the planet Terr, a sparkling blue-green orb, mostly water with wisps of clouds in the upper atmosphere. He'd read that only about 30 percent of its surface was habitable landmass, though the word *habitable* had to be used cautiously. The surface of the planet was covered with the ruins of a large civilization that had been burned off by some fairly extensive bombardment about two or three thousand years ago. There were large areas of land in which survival was dependent upon a shielded radiation suit or habitat.

The ride down to the surface of Luna took all of twenty minutes. His orders directed him to an address in Mare Crisia, so he hopped onto a subsurface transport, took a seat, and sat patiently wondering what he'd find at the other end. He left Mare Crisia Station on foot headed for an address that meant nothing to him.

On an airless moon like Luna, York expected the enclosed city to resemble the interior of a ship or space station, all plast and steel, corridors and tight spaces. But the architects of the Lunan habitat had done their best to imitate a green and verdant world. York stepped out of a broad avenue into a wide, domed enclosure and walked through an open park filled with trees and all sorts of plant life. He followed his directions through the park, out the other side, then down a wide avenue, and finally to a gate guarded by naval MPs. Above the gate, a rather elaborate sign read IMPERIAL NAVAL ACADEMY. He hesitated, wondering what they had planned for him, guessed he'd just end up scrubbing floors.

One of the MPs turned his way, a bored look on his face. York said, "I have orders to report here."

The fellow waved a small hand terminal at him and his implants got an ID request. York keyed the proper response and the MP yawned as he waited for his terminal to authenticate York's orders. Looking at it, he frowned and said, "You're cleared for entry with fourth-class midshipman privileges."

"Midshipman?" York asked.

"A cadet," the fellow said. He gave York's uniform an odd look. "It also says you're to report to the commandant immediately upon arrival."

"The commandant?"

"Captain Martinson. He's in charge of all this."

They uploaded directions into York's implants, and he followed them to a building with a sign out front that said ADMINISTRATION. A receptionist in the front lobby directed him to an office near the back, where a secretary seated behind a desk told him to sit down and wait. He sat down, wondering what this was all about. It must be some sort of administrative screw-up, or maybe just a glitch in the computer. Martinson would tell him the error in his orders had been corrected, and in short order he'd be shipping out to the front on another ship. He sat there for more than an hour.

"Commandant Martinson will see you now."

The secretary's words startled him. He stood, and she pointed to a door. "Go right in."

He stepped through the door, carefully recalling every bit of discipline the marines on *Dauntless* had taught him. The room was dominated by a man seated behind the largest desk York had ever seen, his eyes focused downward, reading something on a small terminal in front of him. He had dark hair, gray at the temples, wore a crisp white uniform with not a wrinkle visible, and he sat there with posture so rigid he seemed to vibrate with tension. York followed the standard formula, marched into the room, raised his hand in a salute and said, "Spacer First Class York Ballin reporting as ordered, sir."

Martinson didn't look up, didn't move, and except for that invisible vibration that seemed to emanate from him, he remained as still as a statue. Still looking at the terminal resting on the desk in front of him, he said, "It's no longer Spacer York Ballin, it's now Midshipman Fourth Class York Ballin."

"Sorry, sir," York said. "Midshipman Fourth Class York Ballin reporting as ordered, sir."

Martinson lifted his chin slowly, looked up, and York was struck by the paleness of his green eyes. The commandant returned the salute, snapping it with no less rigidity than his seated posture. York finished his salute, trying to imitate the commandant's unyielding discipline.

Martinson stared at him for a long moment, then bellowed, "Chief."

York heard the door behind him open, someone step into the room, then the door closed. He was careful not to react in any way.

Martinson said, "It upset me when they told me we had to take you on. I don't care that you were on *Andor Vincent*. I don't care that they want to keep an eye on you. Your kind doesn't belong here."

Hearing those words again angered York, though it occurred to him that might be exactly what the commandant wanted.

Martinson rose up out of his seat, walked around the desk slowly like a predator sizing up its prey. York kept his eyes locked on a diploma on the wall as Martinson approached him, walked slowly around him, then stopped directly in front of him at an uncomfortably close distance. The two of them were of a similar height.

"Then I took a look at your record: four years in combat, three commendations for meritorious service, apparently a very skilled gunner. How many chevrons have you got?"

"Twenty-four and a half, sir," York said.

"We don't like that custom here," Martinson said.

York probably should have left it at that, but he was tired of hearing about *his kind.* "It should be twenty-five and a half, but they tanked me before I could go to another gunner's blood. If I ever get the opportunity, I may get that corrected." He purposefully allowed a short delay before adding, "Sir."

Martinson looked past him at whoever had entered the room a moment ago. "He thinks he'll irritate me by being a smart-ass. Hopefully, he'll learn better."

Martinson's eyes returned to York. "Nothing in your record about why you joined the navy."

There was an implied question in that, but since he'd made it a statement, York was not required to answer, so he held his silence.

"Why did you join the navy, Mr. Ballin?"

York had seen a couple of recruiting brochures, so he stole a line from them. "They said I'd get to see the galaxy, sir."

Martinson gave him a predatory grin. "And you signed up for a lifetime enlistment."

"I didn't have anything else to do, sir."

"No, I suppose you didn't. And there's nothing negative at all in your record. Have you never made any mistakes, Mr. Ballin?"

"I've made a mistake or two, sir." Again, York knew he should keep his mouth shut but couldn't resist. "And I've got the scars on my back to prove it."

One of Martinson's eyebrows shot up, and he glanced past York again. It was the only reaction York had seen from him. "Well then, Mr. Ballin, it appears you did learn a lesson or two. As I said, I was upset that they forced you upon us, and the fact that you have a good record doesn't change that. But since I'm stuck with you, I'm going to see to it that you learn this lesson, too. The next four years are going to be the hardest of your life, but if you slack off, I'm going to make them even harder. I will not allow you to make us look bad. Is that clear?"

York gave him a marine response at the top of his lungs. "Sir, yes, sir."

Martinson's lips slowly turned upward, not a pleasant smile. He said, "Mr. Ballin, please turn and face Command Master Chief Petty Officer Parker, Retired."

York pivoted with parade ground precision and turned to face an older man, shorter by several centimeters. Behind him, Martinson said, "Chief, show Mr. Ballin his quarters. And get him out of that spacer's uniform."

CHAPTER 18:
PLEBE MONTH

York followed Parker out of the Administration building in silence. As they walked across a large parade ground, Parker said, "Martinson's not a bad man."

York growled, "He's an asshole."

"He's just frustrated by the midshipmen they send him."

"Lowlifes like me, huh?"

"Not really. He meant what he said. You work hard and do well, and you won't get any trouble from him. No, he's frustrated by the spoiled snots they admit, kids with parents who got money and titles, frequently more money than brains. They don't have to work hard to get a commission because their parents already bought it for them. A good chunk of the graduating class each year isn't qualified to command a lifeboat, let alone a man-of-war."

He stopped in front of a four-story building. "This is Baskers Hall, the plebe barracks. Most just call it Plebe Hall. You get a locker, uniforms, equipment, and a bunk."

Parker led him into the building and up a stairway to the second floor, then into a bunk room with two rows of old-fashioned double-decker bunks, lockers behind each one. "Forty of you share a bunk room. These will be your platoon mates for the next four years. Your new pay grade is better than it was as a spacer, but you won't see much of it. Most of it goes to pay for the uniforms and equipment."

Parker showed him his locker, which was filled with uniforms. "Martinson's going to push you to be in that part of the graduating class that is qualified to command. You're either going to make the grade, or die trying."

Parker pulled a set of fatigues out of the locker and handed them to York. "Change into this right away. Don't let anyone see you in that." He nodded toward York's spacer's uniform. "In fact, just throw the damn thing away. They don't like our kind here."

York stripped down quickly and pulled on the new uniform.

"We've got a tenday," Parker said. "A tenday before the rest of the plebes show up. A tenday to show you how to act like a midshipman."

Parker took York to dinner at an inexpensive restaurant. After they ordered, they sat in an uncomfortable silence while they waited for the food. York was hungry, and when it arrived, he picked up his fork and started eating without saying anything. Parker didn't touch his own food and watched York eat for a few minutes. Then he said, "No, this won't do."

Dinner turned into a lesson in good table manners, and over the next tenday, York learned about the proper use of a number of eating utensils he hadn't known existed. Apparently, that was going to be important.

The next morning, Parker led him out to the parade ground and marched him around for an hour. "Not bad," he said. "Who taught you that?"

"The marines on *Dauntless*," York said. He wondered if he'd ever be able to find Bristow and thank him.

"*Dauntless*, eh? Is that where you tasted the lash?"

York nodded.

"We can get the scars removed before the rest show up. And you'd be wise to get rid of the gunner's chevrons. They'll mark you."

York considered it for a moment, but every time he saw the scars on his back, he was reminded of the lessons he'd had to learn. And the chevrons were the only real status he'd ever had. "No thanks," he said. "I'll keep them as is."

Parker shrugged, then he smiled and appeared to approve of York's decision. "Have it your way."

Parker drilled York carefully on the proper way to address titled cadets, officers, and civilians, tutored him extensively on the nine members of the Admiralty Council and their heirs and offspring. York found it interesting that the chief never commented on any of them, never expressed even the slightest opinion about them, no gossip, no rumor, nothing. He simply stated the facts, like the number of warships each could amass, the fleets they controlled, and their wealth. There was something missing, something the chief wasn't saying. One day, York asked him about that.

Parker paused, his eyes narrowed, and he regarded York with a hard look. "People who get too close to the Nine, or get involved in their affairs, or work directly for one of them . . . well . . . they just don't seem to live as long as the rest of us."

York could see that Parker had become exceedingly uncomfortable, but he continued nevertheless. "Over the next four years—if you make it through the next four years—remember that if certain opportunities come your way . . . many things here are not as they appear." The old chief refused to discuss the matter further, and York wondered what he had meant by such a cryptic statement.

York had grown accustomed to being the only resident of Plebe Hall, but eight days after arriving, as he walked up the stairs, he heard other voices present. When he walked past one of the bunk rooms, he spotted a few young men and women unpacking their gear. At his own bunk room, he stopped in the doorway, saw a young fellow with dark hair and features lying on a bunk with his hands behind his head, watching a young woman with brown, shoulder-length hair at the other end of the room. She stood at a locker with her back to York, sorting through the uniforms it contained. She retrieved one and held it up in front of her. "It looks like they got it right this time. They never get it right."

The fellow lying on the bunk said, "That's why I brought my own, had them tailored properly. I'm throwing out the junk they provide."

The young woman turned around, and when she spotted York, her hazel eyes widened. "You must be the mystery man."

York asked, "Mystery man?"

She hooked a thumb toward his bunk. "That bunk is so neatly made we knew someone checked in before us."

She marched across the room toward York, and as she came closer he realized she was almost as tall as he. He had only a few centimeters on her.

Draping the uniform over an arm, she stuck out a hand. "I'm Karinina Toletskva. You can call me Karin."

York shook her hand, and when he released it, she nodded toward the fellow on the bunk. "That's Anton Simma."

From Parker's tutoring, York recognized the name immediately: oldest son of Marko Simma, the duke de Jupttar, and heir to the ducal seat. Karin confirmed it when she said, "I suppose we have to call him *Lord* Simma and kiss his ass."

Simma sat up and threw his legs off the edge of the bunk. "You've never kissed my ass before, Karin." He made a point of leering at her butt. "Though I wouldn't mind kissing that nice little ass of yours."

"Not on your life," she said. She winked at York. "Though I may have to let him since he's going to be a duke, and he'll have all that power."

Simma stood up. "You know as well as I that all the real power is held by de Maris, de Vena, and de Satarna." He looked at York and nodded toward Karin. "She's got all the money, could buy and sell me in a minute."

He stuck out his hand and York shook it. "I'm told we drop all titles here at the academy, so you can just call me Tony."

Before York could introduce himself, a short fellow with blond hair stepped into the room. Slight of build with a duffel thrown over his shoulder, he spoke softly. "Hi. I think I'm supposed to report here, not sure I'm in the right place."

Simma and Toletskva forgot York and turned their gregarious banter on the poor fellow. They determined that he was in the right place, Delta Company, Second Platoon. He introduced himself as Muldoon Tagresh.

"Tagresh!" Simma said. "Is your mother Senator Indreena Tagresh?"

"Yes," he said, and seemed almost embarrassed about it. "That's her."

Simma turned back to York. "What is your name again?"

"Ballin," he said. "York Ballin."

"Ballin!" Karin said. "Haven't heard that name before." She nodded to Simma. "He's power." She nodded toward Tagresh. "He's influence, and I'm money. What are you, Ballin?"

"I'm really nothing," York said.

"Okay, Mr. Nothing," she said. "We know who we are. Who are you?"

He gave them the story Parker had concocted for him: that his father had been a high-ranking noncom, killed in combat a few years ago, and awarded an Imperial Cross, and that got him his appointment to the academy.

By the next morning, Plebe Hall had filled up, and that afternoon, the upperclassmen arrived. They lined up all the first-year midshipmen and shaved their heads, though it was customary to use old-fashioned clippers, which the upperclassmen wielded with considerable zeal, leaving all of the plebes with spikey, uneven stubble on their heads. Karin actually looked kind of sexy that way, though she thought the custom barbaric.

"No sense of fashion," she said.

They followed that with basic training in the proper technique for saluting. York watched the other plebes struggle with the unfamiliar and tried to imitate them. He knew better than to let on that he'd long ago mastered such basic military techniques.

The day after that, they were all sworn in, and then they began plebe month, forty days of grueling exercises and training, primarily focused on familiarizing them with the navy's way of doing things. York had been through it all before under the marines on *Dauntless*, and like saluting, as they learned to march around the parade ground, he stumbled about with all the rest and imitated their clumsiness. He carefully paced his own learning curve with that of his peers. Tony Simma had a lot of trouble with the marching techniques, while both tall, lithe Karin and shy little Tagresh took to it naturally. York, Karin, and Tagresh spent what little spare time they had helping Tony improve his technique.

Their platoon was divided into four squads of ten plebes each. It pleased York that he and Karin were assigned to the same squad, though not because of any sexual attraction between them; they were just friends, and it was good to pair up with a friend on some of the more demanding drills.

Their cadet company commander was Madeen Schessa, a third-year middy and one of the daughters of Andralla Schessa, the duchess de Vena. "She's like fourth in line to inherit," Karin told York. "So she's got no prospects there. Her best bet is a military career."

One day, they went through a simulated marine combat exercise, a hi-gee drop down to the surface of Terr, then a forced march in full combat kit through rough terrain. They were not allowed the assistance of powered armor, so it was all muscle and sweat.

"Ten-minute break," Schessa shouted. "Conserve your water because there won't be any refills until we make camp tonight."

Karin sat down on a rock, and York dropped down onto the

dirt beside her, crossed his legs, pulled out his canteen, and took a sip of water. Schessa walked down the line of plebes and stopped at Karin, standing over her. Karin started to rise, but Schessa waved her back down, saying, "No, stay seated. I just want to tell you to pick up the pace. You're slowing the whole company down."

Karin said, "Yes, ma'am," and Schessa moved on.

Karin leaned close to York. "She doesn't like me."

"Why?" York asked. "What did you ever do to her?"

She gave York the kind of look a parent might throw at a stupid child. "Too much money. My family is just a bunch of upstarts, as far as she's concerned. I think she's afraid we'll start thinking we're her kind or something."

There it was again, those words: *her kind*, *their kind*, *our kind*, *your kind*.

At the end of plebe month, they all returned to the academy. Where previously there'd only been a few upperclassmen around—those providing training during plebe month—with the beginning of the academic year, all four classes of midshipmen were in attendance in their entirety. They assembled in a massive formation on the parade ground, were introduced to the brigade commander, Midshipman Captain Tellan Soladin, heir to the de Satarna ducal seat. He gave a short speech, then each plebe platoon was absorbed into one of the six battalions of the brigade. Second Platoon Delta was assigned to Eighth Company, Second Battalion. Their battalion officers were introduced and each said a few words. Commander Lord Nathan Abraxa, heir to the de Maris ducal seat, commanded Second Battalion. York recognized him immediately: Abraxa was the officer on the passenger liner who'd thrown him out of the upper-class lounge with the words *Isn't it obvious to you that your kind doesn't belong in here?*

York was thankful for the anonymity of being just one face among thousands on the parade ground that day.

CHAPTER 19:
EXPOSED

After swearing-in, they had five days before classes actually began. All the plebes were required to meet with their academic advisers to review their course schedule, and York's appointment was set for the following day. But he had no free time. With thousands of upperclassmen present, merely walking from one building to the next frequently proved to be an ordeal. During those first few days, even the slightest infraction earned a verbal whiplash from an upperclassman: a hat not square, a name tag slightly tilted. York was a bit luckier than most. After spending four years as the lowest of the low, sometimes under the watchful eyes of an obsessively strict officer, York knew to be obsessive about appearance, demeanor, and all the little rules required of him. He still earned his share of snipes from upperclassmen, but maybe just a few less than the others.

He'd been assigned Commander Laski as his academic adviser. He was careful to arrive early for his appointment, though that proved to be a bit of a mistake. He had to wait in a line of plebes in the hall outside Laski's office while three upperclassmen harassed them unmercifully, making them recite or sing everything from memorized regulations to silly little songs. When York's turn to see Laski finally came, he removed his cap, tucked it under his arm, knocked on Laski's door, entered, saluted, and presented himself with the standard formula.

"At ease, Midshipman," Laski said.

Seated behind his desk, Laski was somewhat overweight, with a receding hairline, a couple of chins, and prominent jowls. Laski let him stand there without saying anything while he read something in front of him. More than five minutes passed before he looked up at York. "I've been reviewing your background, Midshipman Ballin."

York's gut clenched. It hadn't occurred to him that anyone in a position of authority could easily look up his service record, and he realized what a fool he'd been to fail to anticipate that. At least Jarwith and Thorow had expunged any references to his criminal past when he left *Dauntless*. But still, York knew exactly what kind of reaction he'd get from Laski at the knowledge that the midshipman who stood before him was actually a lower-deck pod gunner spacer first class.

Laski said, "Don't worry, Midshipman. I won't hold your background against you. Your father, Command Master Chief Thomas Ballin, died valiantly in the service of the empire. It's only right that we allow a few of your kind into the academy each year."

To cover up his utter surprise, York said, "Thank you, sir."

"Think nothing of it, Mr. Ballin. We owe a debt to the lower strata who serve us well. And here you have an excellent opportunity to rise above your station."

Could it have been Martinson and Parker? Could they have faked up his background? York realized it was imperative that he play his part. "I'm quite grateful for that, sir."

"And you should be," Laski said. "I doubt you'll be able to keep up with the academic rigors of life here at the academy. But I'll do what I can to help you, and if you have any trouble with your coursework, let me know and I'll try to intervene. There's nothing I can do about the physical demands, nor the verbal abuse you'll have to put up with from upperclassmen the first year, but you appear to be a strapping young man, so I'm sure you can handle that."

Inside, York seethed at the assumption that *his kind* lacked the mental acuity needed to make the grade. But he knew better than to let it show. "Again, sir, I am quite grateful."

"I see you and Lord Simma are bunkmates. I'll ask him to help you out with the academics. He may not be willing to do so, but it never hurts to ask."

When York left Laski's office, he vowed that he would do well at every challenge the academy offered him.

In some of the academic subjects, York had a little head start because of two years of tutoring aboard ship. That helped in subjects like navigation and engineering, but in fundamentals such as mathematics, he still struggled. Each day started early and ended late, and when not in class, every moment of his time was carefully dictated by other scheduled activities, or the whims of an upperclassman.

Interestingly enough, Tony Simma had trouble with the academic subjects. He was by no means stupid or slow, but he showed no drive to excel, and York wondered if perhaps he was accustomed to having everything handed to him. York found it fascinating that Tony, who'd grown up at the pinnacle of imperial status, was less of a snob than Laski, who was completely untitled and could make no claim to nobility.

As midterms approached, Tony grew a little desperate, fearful that he'd fail and have to face his father, so he and York studied together. It actually helped York to help Tony.

"You know," Tony said, "Laski thinks I'm tutoring you. That snob is the worst wannabe I've ever met, thanked *me* for helping you out. Sorry about that."

When the midterm results were announced, Tony passed with flying colors and received a small ribbon for doing so well. York never said anything, but he wondered at that, thought it likely Tony would graduate at the top of the class no matter what, but be one of those officers Chief Parker said was not qualified to command a lifeboat, let alone a man-of-war.

Laski called York to his office to review his results.

"Very good, Mr. Ballin," he said, as York stood at ease in front of his desk. "You won't graduate at the top of the class, but you're certainly in the top half, and if you keep this up, you might make it into the top thirty percent. I hope you appreciate the benefits of Lord Simma's tutoring."

York nodded and said, "I have expressed my thanks to Lord Simma most sincerely, sir."

"Excellent, Mr. Ballin, excellent! We'll make an officer of you yet."

At random intervals, the barracks was subjected to a surprise, white-glove, black-sock inspection in which even the tiniest speck of dust earned demerits, or some sort of creative punishment. And they all learned that the entire platoon suffered the fate of the most slovenly among them. Most often an upperclassman or two conducted the inspection on an informal basis, while the plebes stood at attention at the end of their bunks listening to the upper-class midshipmen shout at them. The plebes came to look upon it as part of the general harassment meted out by their student superiors, though they were told the true purpose was to prepare them for a real inspection. York noticed that when the white glove came away from Tony Simma's bunk with a dark smear on it, nothing was ever said about it, while if any of the rest of them proved less than perfect, there was all hell to pay.

Formal inspections were conducted much less frequently by their cadet company commander, Madeen Schessa, with their company officer, Commander Murtaugh, looking silently on. Just after first-semester midterms, Schessa and Murtaugh showed up unannounced with Commander Abraxa in tow, which was unusual, but not unheard of. After all the plebes had snapped to attention at the end of their bunks, Abraxa announced, "Don't think for a moment that your battalion officer isn't personally interested in the discipline of even the lowest plebe."

Standing at the end of his bunk, York tucked his chin in just a little bit tighter, hoping the bill of his cap would hide his face that much more.

The inspection didn't go badly, a little dirt here and there, but nothing that warranted a severe reprimand. Abraxa took it upon himself to do the shouting for Schessa. And when they were done, Abraxa walked one last time down the aisle in the middle of the bunk room. As he walked, he glanced briefly at each cadet, left then right, left then right, though he never looked for more than an instant before moving on, never even slowed his pace. But when he looked at York, he hesitated, looked a second time, and his pace faltered for a fraction of a step. He recovered with only that slight hesitation, continued on, and left the room. York breathed a sigh of relief.

Two days later, Schessa was about to conduct a formal inspection of her company, all lined up in ranks at attention on the parade ground, when Abraxa approached and spoke briefly with her. She turned from him and announced, "Commander Abraxa would like to inspect Eighth Company, a rare honor indeed."

As Abraxa walked down the lines of men and women with Schessa beside him, looking at each, York again tucked his chin tightly to his chest. Abraxa didn't seem particularly interested in upbraiding anyone that day, he simply made a comment or recommendation here and there. When he got to York, he said, "Midshipman, your chin is a little low. Don't tuck it so tightly into your chest."

York raised his chin, lifting the bill of his cap and exposing more of his face. Abraxa frowned and squinted. "Midshipman"—he glanced down at the name tag on York's chest—"Midshipman . . . Ballin, have we met before?"

"Sir, no, sir," York said. "I don't believe I've had the honor, sir."

Abraxa stared at him for a long moment, then continued on down the line, finishing the inspection without further incident.

York asked Tony about Abraxa.

"Oh, he graduated last year," Tony said. "Top of his class."

"Last year?" York asked. Something didn't add up. "That means he left here an ensign and came back a few months later a full commander."

Tony shrugged. "He was probably assigned to one of his father's ships in Home Fleet, served a few tendays, got a promotion, and came home to complain that full commander wasn't enough."

"But aren't all graduates supposed to serve a half-year evaluation tour on a ship-of-the-line?"

Tony laughed and shook his head sadly. "Don't be naive, York. His father wrote his evaluation, probably wrote it before he graduated. Even better, he probably wrote it before he was born."

After midterms, there were a few empty bunks in Plebe Hall, but York was happy to see Tony, Karin, and Muldoon still present. Tony continued to demonstrate a complete lack of motivation for anything like studying, and once it became clear he would graduate at the top of his class, he decided all the stuff they were trying to learn must be quite easy. At that point, he began studying even less. Muldoon couldn't overcome his painful shyness, and York and Karin grew to be close friends. York would have been happy to allow their relationship to go beyond mere friendship had Karin shown any interest, but it was not meant to be.

Every month, Plebe Hall had another empty bed or two, and York could see that Karin and Muldoon shared his fear that one day their bunks would be prematurely vacant. For the three of them, life at the academy turned into a simple struggle for survival, while Tony just coasted.

During the second half of the first semester, they were introduced to the pilot simulator for small craft like gunboats. York recalled his lessons with Rodma, and to make sure he didn't give away his past, he carefully repeated all the mistakes of his first time in the cockpit. It turned out Karin had learned to pilot small craft at an early age on her father's estate, and was appointed as an assistant instructor. After their first few lessons, she pulled York aside and quietly said, "Why are you faking it, Ballin?"

He stuttered and said, "Uh . . . what do you mean?"

"I mean you clearly know how to fly, and are very carefully pretending that it's all new to you."

"Please," he said. "Don't say anything."

She frowned and gave him an appraising look. "Okay. . . . But someday you have to tell me the truth."

He nodded. "Before we graduate, I will."

York sweated his way through the semester finals and was certain he'd flunked out. But when the results were announced, he learned he'd just squeezed his way into the top 30 percent of the plebe class. Again, Laski called him into his office and congratulated him for doing so well, with the unwritten message that Laski was pleased he wasn't as stupid as *his kind.*

With the stress of first-semester finals behind them, Commandant Martinson issued an invitation to all cadets, a semicasual reception to congratulate the plebes who'd made it that far. They were instructed that proper attire was service dress whites, and that attendance was mandatory for plebes, and all battalion, company, and cadet officers. Attendance was optional for upperclassmen, and for that one evening the sniping of plebes would be suspended. The invitation finished with, *Alcohol will be served, though moderation is required of all attendees.*

"A party!" Karin said. "With no upperclassmen harassing us."

Muldoon said, "I bet we still better not have anything wrong with our uniforms."

Even Tony took that seriously, and when the four of them were ready to leave for the event, they carefully inspected one another, doffed their hats, and walked as a group to the reception. Tony and Karin seemed at home, holding a drink, standing and casually chatting with other cadets and officers. York's experience was limited to dockside bars and brothels, so for the most part he just kept his mouth shut and listened. When Abraxa approached him, he almost snapped to attention out of pure reflex.

"Ballin, are you sure we haven't met somewhere?"

"Perhaps just in passing, sir," York said, hoping desperately to get away from that subject. "But I don't believe we've actually truly met or spoken."

When Tony and Karin joined them, York was glad to see Abraxa turn his attention on them. "Tony, old boy, how long has it been since we last met, a year or more? And how's your father?"

"He's doing well," Tony said. "Probably outlive us both."

Abraxa turned to Karin. "And I know I've not been introduced to this lovely creature."

Tony introduced Karin. Abraxa took her hand and kissed it with a flourish. "It is a pleasure to meet you, my dear."

Karin said, "The pleasure is mine, Your Lordship."

"Perhaps the next time Tony and I get together, you might join him."

Karin smiled. "That would be wonderful, Your Lordship."

York now knew Karin well enough to see that her smile was forced. A few moments later, with Tony and Abraxa occupied catching up on the past year, York leaned close to Karin and whispered, "What's wrong?"

She whispered, "When he talks to me, he talks to my boobs. He never looks me in the eye, and it gives me the creeps."

"Mr. Ballin. Miss Toletskva."

Both York and Karin stiffened and turned at the sound of Commandant Martinson's voice. "Sir," they said in unison.

Martinson was no less rigid standing than sitting, and York wondered if he had a plast girder clamped to his back. "Are you enjoying yourselves?"

"Yes, sir," they said.

Abraxa and Tony joined them at that moment. Martinson said, "Good. You deserve it. You've both done well. But . . ."

Martinson carefully looked York over from head to foot. "Mr. Ballin, I believe you're out of uniform."

"Sir," York said, trying not to stammer. He'd done all he could to make sure his uniform would pass the most meticulous inspection. "I don't understand, sir."

Martinson gave York a predatory smile. "Your service ribbons. You're not wearing a single one, and I know you have quite a few."

York couldn't believe what he was hearing. Both Karin's and Tony's mouths dropped open, their jaws slack. Muldoon stood behind them looking unsure of himself. Abraxa frowned and looked closely at York, as if by doing so he might recognize him.

"Mr. Ballin," Martinson said. "Please return to your barracks immediately and correct the matter, then report back here to me."

York snapped to attention. "Sir, yes, sir."

As York left the reception hall, all eyes were on him. But what bothered him most was the frown on Abraxa's face. All the way back to Plebe Hall, he wondered if he could simply not return, but that might make it even worse. At his locker, he considered putting on only a few of his ribbons, the least of them, simple good conduct, stuff like that. But he realized Martinson wasn't going to let him get away with that.

Why had Martinson done this? He'd promised that if York worked hard and did well, he'd not add to his difficulties. Surely, he knew that this would be catastrophic.

He pulled off his coat and carefully attached all of his ribbons, paying close attention to the order of precedence. Only after everything was exactly correct did he slip the coat back on and walk back to the reception. When he entered the hall, he walked straight to Martinson, and he noticed that he wore more chest candy than some of the commissioned officers present. He stopped and saluted, saying simply, "Sir."

Abraxa joined them immediately. Tony, Karin, Muldoon, and some of the other cadets gathered around.

"That's better, Mr. Ballin," Martinson said. "And please relax. This is supposed to be a casual affair."

Tony asked, "Where'd you get all the ribbons?"

Muldoon pointed at one and said, "That's a combat commendation. What are all the others?"

Karin grinned. York came to the slow realization he really had no choice, so he pointed at one and said, "Arman'Tigh." He pointed to another. "Turnham's Cluster." And another. "Trefallin."

Tony said, "Holy shit!"

Martinson said, "Mr. Simma, watch your language."

Karin pointed at a ribbon and said, "What's the dead black one?"

Martinson said, "That would be Sirius Night Star."

Abraxa frowned. "No one came back from that."

Martinson grinned. "A few did." He glanced down at the service ribbons on Abraxa's chest. "Do I see a ribbon there for the Aquila Campaign?"

Abraxa seemed at a loss for words. "Why . . . I . . ."

"No," Martinson said. "It couldn't be. I must be wrong. Aquila was before you were born." He turned and walked away.

Abraxa looked at York, his eyes narrowed, and his mouth hardened into a flat, straight line. "Well, Mr. Ballin—or should I say Spacer Ballin? Spacer First Class, as I recall." He spun about and walked in the opposite direction of Martinson.

Tony looked about conspiratorially and whispered, "I'll say it again: Holy shit."

Karin said, "So, Ballin, you're not Mr. Nothing. Tony is power, Muldoon is influence, I'm money, and you . . . you're experience. We have a hardened combat veteran among us."

CHAPTER 20:
KARIN

York would not have believed that life at the academy could ever be worse than his first semester, but as the second semester dawned, he quickly learned how wrong he could be. His first clue was a surprise white-glove, black-sock inspection of the entire Eighth Company, upperclassmen included, and personally conducted by Abraxa. His Lordship let nothing slip past him and made life miserable for the entire company that day. York also suspected that he planted some infractions. When Abraxa ran a white glove underneath York's bunk, it came up with a heavily discolored brown stain. York would be the first to admit that his bunk and locker might not always be perfect, but he was much too meticulous for it to have ever been that bad. As Abraxa ripped into York, even Tony looked doubtfully at the stain on the glove.

It wasn't just Abraxa. York learned that when the man in charge made it clear he was not happy with an individual, even if done subtly, it filtered down through the entire organization. Certain cadets just avoided him, even some who had been friendly before, possibly worried about guilt by association. Many joined in the harassment but seemed to do so reluctantly, perhaps worried that if they didn't contribute something to York's torment, Abraxa might assume they sympathized with York. And then there were those members of the company who were angry that York had brought the wrath of the battalion officer down upon them all. But the worst were the few who participated actively and enjoyed doing so, taking some strange satisfaction from seeing another person under their thumb. At least Tony, Muldoon, and Karin stood by York and seemed immune to Abraxa's influence.

York was now certain Martinson had purposefully played the service-ribbon gambit at the reception to expose him to Abraxa, but why had the commandant done that?

"Hey, Mr. Experience."

York looked up from his reader as Karin sauntered across the main reading hall in the library. With just a locker and bunk, plebes were forced to use the tables in the library to study. He looked again at the face of the reader to recall what he'd supposedly been reading, when in fact he'd been musing on the new difficulties facing him.

Karin sat down opposite him, leaned close, and whispered, "Abraxa *was* wearing the Aquila Campaign ribbon at the reception. I looked it up. And it *was* before he was born, so he couldn't have earned it. And from the look on his face, I don't think he even knew what ribbon it was, probably just purchased a handful of chest candy and plastered them on his coat. That pretentious phony!"

York said, "You really don't like him, do you?"

"He's creepy," she said. "I don't think he's ever looked into my face. Yesterday, when he did that inspection, he didn't inspect anything but my boobs."

York knew nothing would ever happen between them, but he couldn't resist the temptation. "Well, Toletskva, in his defense, you're really not bad to look at."

Her nose wrinkled up and she snapped, "I've seen you look at me and I don't mind that. And I guess I wouldn't mind it if he looked at *me*, and not just my boobs. I tell you what, I'll give them each separate names, then you and he can have individual conversations with them and leave me out of it."

That had backfired badly. "Sorry."

She frowned, leaned back, and looked at York carefully. "Why so glum?"

He sighed and said, "He's making it harder every day."

"Ya, he is making your life kind of hellish."

"Kind of?" York asked.

She stood. "Come on, I want to show you something."

She didn't wait for him to answer, but turned and walked away. He shut down the reader, stood, and followed her. The library had quite a large collection of real books printed on synthetic paper. She led him down to the lower floors where they were stored in row after row of shelves. She said, "There's an old text I want you to see. I think you'll find it quite interesting."

She turned down an aisle between shelves and walked to the end of it, then stopped and pointed upward. "Up there."

He stopped next to her and looked where she was pointing, squinting, seeing a lot of book spines, with nothing to distinguish any one from the others. He turned around to face her. "Which one?"

She stepped forward, reaching for a book over his head, closed the distance between them completely, and her breasts pressed against his chest. They both froze that way and she looked into his eyes.

After a few seconds, she said, "You know, Ballin, when a girl is leaning this close to you with an inviting smile on her face, and purposefully pressing her breasts against your chest, you do realize it's an invitation to kiss her, don't you?"

Somewhere York had heard that these empty rows of bookshelves were sometimes used as a place for couples to meet for a few minutes alone, though not for anything extreme. "Same company," he said, "same platoon, even same squad; that would be against regulations."

She put her arms around his neck. "I know you've always wanted to, and now I'm throwing myself at you. Not very gentlemanly of you to make me do that."

"Oh, fuck it," he said, and he kissed her. She pressed the entire length of her body against him, and the kiss lasted until they both were forced to come up for air.

"Whoa," she said. "That was much better than I thought it would be." She ran a finger along the line of his jaw. "We've both got town liberty at the end of the tenday. Let's get off this campus and continue this then."

"Why now?" he asked. "After all this time?"

She brushed her lips against his cheek and whispered, "I just have a kinky fetish for you men of action, you experienced combat types."

It occurred to him that Karin thought she was joking, but she'd never shown that much interest in him before, so it was quite possible she was attracted to him because of his background and just didn't realize it. Or perhaps she was slumming. He thought about that for a moment, and he didn't care. He kissed her again, and they both started to enjoy it a bit too much. When the kiss ended, she pressed her hand to the middle of his chest and pushed herself away from him. Breathlessly, she said, "We'd better stop this now, or we're going to end up violating all sorts of regulations." As York followed her out of the tall shelves of books, his legs felt a little unsteady.

His relationship with her was the only bright spot in his life that semester. They agreed that nothing could ever come of it, that neither of them was interested in falling in love, so there was no danger of that. But, for both of them, it did cut through the loneliness a bit.

Even with all the added pressure from Abraxa, York thought he did reasonably well on his second-semester midterms. As always, Laski called him to his office to review his results, but this time Abraxa was present, standing to one side and slightly behind Laski's desk.

York followed the traditional formula, stood at attention, and saluted Laski. The commander returned the salute, but this time did not tell York to stand at ease. York stood there rigid as a post for a good ten minutes, sweat dripping down his back inside his shirt, before Laski finally acknowledged him.

"So, Mr. Ballin, you falsified your record."

York said, "No, sir, I—"

"Don't speak," Laski shouted, rising up out of his chair, his hands flat on the desk in front of him, "unless you're invited to."

Laski took a deep breath to calm himself, then sat down. "Nathan tells me . . ." He glanced over his shoulder and smiled at Abraxa, who smiled back at him. "Nathan tells me he encountered you on a passenger liner on your way here, tells me you were wearing a spacer's uniform. Is that true?"

York opened his mouth, but Laski didn't let him speak.

"Of course it's true, since His Lordship says it is. So you're a liar and a cheat. You've been cheating all along, haven't you?"

York had to say something in his defense. "No, sir, I haven't."

"You expect me to believe you got these scores on your own?"

"Yes, sir."

"Impossible."

"Why is that impossible, sir?"

Laski shook his head, turned slightly and said to Abraxa, "He just doesn't understand, does he?"

Abraxa said, "I suppose that's to be expected."

Laski looked at York as if he were something distasteful that had been scraped off the bottom of someone's boot. "It's impossible because your kind is just not capable of performing at the level required by the academy. Again, with the benefit of your cheating, it appears that you scored in the upper thirty percent of the class on these midterms. But we know better, don't we, Mr. Ballin?"

"And how do you know that, sir?"

"As I told you, you're just not capable of scoring well on these tests. So I'm lowering your score to what I'm certain you would have done had you not cheated."

"But I—"

"Don't speak, Mr. Ballin. If it were up to me, we'd expel you immediately. But Commandant Martinson won't allow it, says I must have hard evidence, doesn't realize that you yourself are the only hard evidence we need. But then he's fundamentally one of you anyway."

The new scores Laski applied to York's midterm results put him in the bottom 10 percent of the class, which meant York's enrollment would come under review and he might possibly flunk out.

At the end of his plebe year, after finals, Laski called York into his office to tell him what a piece of shit he was. Again Laski was certain York had cheated because his exam scores were higher than possible for *his kind*, so Laski adjusted his scores accordingly. York finished the year in the lowest 10 percent of the class, and was called before an academic review board. At the appointed hour, he knocked on the door to a conference room in the Administration Building, popped the door a crack, and said, "Midshipman Ballin reporting as ordered."

Someone inside said, "Enter."

He opened the door, stepped through, closed it, and marched forward to stand before a table behind which sat Martinson, Abraxa, Murtaugh, and two other company officers he vaguely recognized. York glanced briefly at the two men's name tags: Storch and Prescott. Laski sat in a chair to one side, and York wondered if that meant he wasn't part of the review board.

York squared his shoulders and saluted. Martinson returned the salute with a crisp snap of his hand and said, "Let's bring this meeting to order. We're here to review the academic performance of Midshipman Fourth Class York Ballin."

He looked to Laski. "Commander, as Mr. Ballin's academic adviser, would you care to begin?"

Laski stood. "Certainly, sir." He took a dramatic breath, then continued, "I feel sorry for Mr. Ballin. It's not his fault that the academic rigors of the academy are simply beyond his abilities. I think we should show leniency upon his expulsion, perhaps allow him to take a position in the lower ranks."

Abraxa said, "As his battalion officer, I am, of course, familiar with his performance, but perhaps you could summarize it for us all, Commander."

Laski gave Abraxa a smarmy smile. "Certainly, Your Lordship. I should say that Mr. Ballin has performed poorly from the beginning, always in the bottom ten percent of his class. He tries hard, but he struggles. I even asked Midshipman Lord Simma if he could help Mr. Ballin by tutoring him, and he was kind enough to do so. But unfortunately, this young man is just not up to academy standards. As I say, it's not really his fault; his kind is just not up to the task."

With those words, Storch and Prescott both frowned.

Abraxa said, "Yes, that's clear to us all."

Prescott's frown deepened.

Laski continued. "Part of the problem is that Mr. Ballin does not understand or accept his own limitations. He thinks he is as capable as any of the rest of us. In fact, if you were to ask him, I wouldn't be surprised if he believes that he did better on his exams than the scores indicate. He might even have some paranoid delusion that his scores have been changed after the fact, as if that were possible."

"Yes," Abraxa said. "It's always easier to credit some conspiracy with one's problems than to accept one's own failings."

Clearly, Abraxa and Laski must have feared that York might accuse them of tampering with his scores. But while he'd briefly considered doing so, they'd anticipated him and effectively countered any allegations he might make. He couldn't prove anything, and it would only make him sound like a petty whiner.

Abraxa and Laski went back and forth with what appeared to be a carefully rehearsed dialogue. They dissected York's personality, parentage, intelligence, and moral character, establishing that all were clearly not up to academy standards. And while they had tried desperately to help the poor, dumb fool, it saddened them that they had failed.

Laski finished with, "I almost feel it's my fault that Mr. Ballin has done so poorly."

"Not at all, Commander," Abraxa said. "Don't even consider the possibility."

York was never offered the opportunity to say anything in his own defense, and he dare not speak without permission. He could only stand there and seethe.

Abraxa finished by thanking Laski, who sat down. Abraxa then said, "It's sad, but it's clear we have no choice. I recommend we offer Mr. Ballin an opportunity to resign his commission." He looked at Captain Martinson. "Shall we vote on it now, sir?"

Martinson smiled. "Yes, in a moment, but first I have one question. As I recall, his first-semester scores were reasonably good"—he looked Laski's way—"and yet you say his performance has been terrible throughout the year."

Laski stood again. "Oh . . . sir . . . those earlier scores were incorrect. . . . A glitch in the computer. We found the error and corrected it."

Storch grimaced and Prescott looked incredulous.

Martinson said, "Why wasn't such an issue reported to me? It could have affected everyone at the academy."

Abraxa said, "Sir, once we corrected the problem, we felt it wasn't necessary to bother you with it."

York wasn't sure what to think as Martinson nodded slowly and said, "Well, that was kind of you. It is time to vote on Mr. Ballin's continued tenure here at the academy. But given his father's sacrifice in defense of the empire, I recommend we give the young man one more year to see if he can improve."

Laski stepped forward. "B-but he's a liar and a cheat."

Prescott spoke for the first time. "Really? Now that is alarming. How did he cheat?"

"I don't know," Laski said. "But I know he did. That's the only way his kind could have done well."

Storch looked like he'd just tasted something quite foul. "I agree with Captain Martinson. Let's give the young man another year."

Prescott said, "I'm good with that."

"I vote nay," Abraxa said.

Murtaugh looked back and forth between them, his eyes wide. "I . . . ah." Abraxa gave him a furious look. "I . . . ah . . . vote nay."

"Then it's done," Martinson said. "By three to two." He looked at York. "Mr. Ballin, you get another year, but see to it you take advantage of our generosity and show us some improvement. You're dismissed."

York saluted, turned and walked to the door, his legs feeling a little weak. Out in the hall, he tried to recall everything he'd just seen and heard, and was quite certain he didn't understand any of it.

After finals that year, they were all granted a twenty-day leave. The plebes who had made it through the year all celebrated with a couple of loud and boisterous off-campus parties, then they went their separate ways, most to visit family. Karin and York spent a couple of days together, then she went back to her father's estate.

Alone, York did some sightseeing. He took a guided tour of some of the ruins of the civilization that had long ago occupied Terr, but all the major cities were still too hot to enter without shielded radiation suits. And the sites they could visit were so old there wasn't much to see. He grew bored and was quite pleased when his leave ended.

He then spent four tendays on his third-class cruise, supposedly his first time in uniform on a real naval vessel and part of a real naval crew. He and a couple of dozen other plebes were assigned to a patrol ship that made the rounds of the Lunan System, where they were exposed to the day-to-day life aboard ship. Some of York's classmates were quite excited by it all, but for York, most of it was not new. He did enjoy the chance to actually stand on the bridge of a ship and put navigation and ship-handling skills to use; until then, it had all been purely academic.

Following the cruise, the plebes were shuffled into different platoons. They spent one tenday on the surface of Terr running through a series of physically demanding ground-combat exercises. Almost everyone suffered an injury or two, some quite serious, but only a few fatal.

When York returned to Luna, he had another twenty-day leave before it would be time to report for his second year at the academy. He wasn't looking forward to the time off because he knew he'd be wretchedly lonely. He took a shuttle up to Luna Prime and went to one of the bars near the docks. As he had suspected, while they didn't openly advertise it, there were plenty of prostitutes available for the asking, and for the right price. He struck up a conversation with a pretty young girl in a bar, but his heart wasn't in it, so he bought her a drink, had a couple himself, then left and took the next shuttle back down to the surface.

He did get one pleasant surprise: Karin showed up several days early, and they renewed their friendship most vigorously. They weren't in love, and they both knew they couldn't allow it to go that far, but there was something about sex with Karin that meant far more than just the simple physical act. And he also had a thoroughly good time with her when not under the sheets.

CHAPTER 21: JUST FRIENDS

When York checked in for his second year, he was assigned to a room that he would share with three other second-year midshipmen. It had a private fresher, with a shower and toilet facilities, and closets—not lockers—for their uniforms. York had never had a closet before, or a room for that matter. As a child, he'd slept on a cot in the corner of the main room of Maja and Toll's government subsidized housing. As a spacer, he'd slept in his coffin or in a large bunk room not unlike that in Plebe Hall.

"I'm assigned to the same room," Karin said. "How'd that happen?"

York looked around the room. "I don't know, but we're going to have to be very careful."

"Oh," she said. "That's right—roommates, strictly off-limits." She gave him a conspiratorial look. "If we're going to share a room, we may have trouble confining our extracurricular activities to off-campus venues."

Muldoon showed up, and to their surprise, he, too, had been assigned to their room, which they all agreed could not be coincidence. When Tony arrived, also assigned to the room, they got their answer. "I pulled some strings," he said. Only Tony could get away with that.

"Ballin."

At the sound of Abraxa's shout, they all cringed.

Abraxa conducted a white-glove, black-sock inspection of York's bunk and study space. Since they hadn't begun to move in yet, and the room had been unoccupied for some months, he uncovered enough dirt to start York's year off with a healthy dose of demerits. The four of them stood at attention for ten minutes while Abraxa shouted in York's face, and it was then that York realized that, for all intents and purposes, his plebe year would never end.

"Sorry, York," Tony said. "Wish there was something I could do."

Now that they were upperclassmen, they were free to harass the incoming plebes, but York's memories of his own plebe year were a little too fresh for him to do so with any enthusiasm. He recalled how some upperclassmen overdid it a bit and resolved not to do so himself. Tony, Karin, and Muldoon took their cues from York, and like him, they moderated their participation in the education of plebes.

Lying in bed beside Karin in a hotel in town on one of the few lazy afternoons they could steal, York traced a finger along the curve of her bare hip, and recalled doing the same with Sissy in his coffin what seemed an eternity ago.

Karin said, "You look sad. What's wrong?"

"Oh," York said. "I was just thinking of my first love."

"Ballin, you're not supposed to think of her when you're with me." She sat up, not a hint of modesty about her nakedness. "Not that we're going to fall in love or anything. But it bruises my ego if you can think about her when I'm sitting here like this." She held her hands out to either side to better display her attractions.

"Don't worry," he said. "She's dead."

"That's even worse. You can think of a dead woman when I'm here, naked, available, and drop-dead gorgeous."

He said, "You reminded me of her, though she was really very different from you."

"How did she die?"

"I wasn't there, got a letter from one of the marines in her platoon telling me she was gone."

She swung her legs out of bed, stood, crossed the room, and threw on a robe, then sat down on the bed beside him. "You promised me you'd tell me about yourself before graduation. I learned a little when I saw all the chest candy you'd earned, but I don't want to wait two more years to hear who the real York Ballin is."

He could trust her not to spread his secrets, but he wondered how she'd feel when she knew the truth. He decided to just hit her over the head with the worst. "Shortly before my twelfth birthday, I was convicted of felony murder and sentenced to life on a prison mining asteroid."

Her jaw dropped and her mouth opened into a wide, incredulous *O*. He got a little satisfaction from seeing the always unflappable Karinina Toletskva struck so completely speechless.

"They really didn't give me a choice when they pressed me into the navy, told me they'd fake my signature if I didn't willingly sign the enlistment papers."

He told her about his first months aboard *Dauntless*, and the mistakes he'd made. When he told her of the lash, she reached out and touched the scars on his shoulder, and he saw a tear in her eye. He told her about Sissy, the pain of their separation, the pain in his soul when he heard she'd been killed. He told her all of it.

"I'm the only survivor of the *Andor Vincent* who hasn't shown signs of mental instability. Apparently, they want to keep an eye on me, and the academy is a good place to keep me alive while they do so."

"Wow," she said. "You've already lived a whole fucking lifetime."

He leaned toward her, brushed his lips across her cheek, and said, "By the way, you were right about being drop-dead gorgeous."

"Well then, I guess you're forgiven for thinking about her. But don't do it again."

During the second year at the academy, they were required to take more advanced courses, so from an academic standpoint, it was even more demanding. And there was no slackening of the physical requirements, so sharing a lazy afternoon with Karin in a hotel in town proved to be a real rarity.

York thought he did rather well on his first-semester finals, though it came as no surprise when the results were reported that he was again near the bottom of his class. Tony noticed the discrepancy and mentioned it. "You're tutoring me, and yet I'm at the top of the class and you're at the bottom."

York didn't have the heart to tell him the truth, so he said, "I guess it just sometimes works out that way."

Tony accepted that answer, but he frowned in thought, as if it had finally occurred to him that all was not as it seemed.

Even though York knew it would make no difference in the end, he continued to study and work hard. If nothing more, he stubbornly refused to give Laski and Abraxa the satisfaction of seeing him fail without their intervention. At year-end when the finals scores were released, there were no surprises. He dreaded the inevitable academic review board. At the last one, Martinson had given him another year on the condition that he show improvement, and now he had shown none, at least as far as his official scores were concerned.

At the appointed hour, he went to the same conference room in the Administration Building, knocked on the same door, and stood before the same table. As before, Laski sat in a chair to one side, and again, Martinson, Abraxa, and Murtaugh sat behind the table as members of the review board, though Storch and Prescott had been replaced with two officers named Charter and Minkowski.

Martinson opened by reading the minutes of the last review, which were a dry recitation of the facts. Laski grew visibly uncomfortable when, in a monotone, Martinson read, "Commander Laski then accused Mr. Ballin of being a liar and a cheat, and when asked how Mr. Ballin had cheated, he stated, 'I don't know. But I know he did. That's the only way his kind could have done well.' The board agreed that that was not sufficient evidence, so the accusations of lying and cheating were not acted upon. And by a vote of three to two, Mr. Ballin was given another year on the condition he show improvement."

"Well, there you have it," Abraxa said. "That's the key: He was supposed to show improvement and he hasn't, so this meeting should be rather short. I move we vote on expulsion."

Martinson said, "Excellent idea, Nathan. But first there's a discrepancy I'd like to clear up. You said Mr. Ballin has shown no improvement, but I believe he has."

Laski stood and said, "No, Captain Martinson, he hasn't. Mr. Ballin was in the bottom ten percent of his class last year, and he's in the bottom ten percent again this year."

Martinson hit a switch and a small screen appeared in the desk in front of him. He manipulated something on the screen, frowned, and said, "I don't know where you got your information, Commander, but while you're right that he was in the bottom ten percent last year, the records show that he finished in the bottom fifteen percent this year, a nice five percent improvement."

Abraxa frowned and leaned over to look at the screen in front of Martinson.

"That's not possible," Laski said. "I entered his scores myself."

Minkowski leaned forward and said, "Commander Laski, you're his academic adviser, but not one of his instructors. You're not supposed to be entering his scores into the system."

Laski's face turned red. "I . . . I misspoke. I meant that I *reviewed* his scores myself."

By that time, all five members of the board had each pulled up a screen and were apparently reviewing York's scores as entered in the system.

Charter said, "Well, Commander Laski, it appears you mis-read them. Captain Martinson is correct about Mr. Ballin's progress."

York wanted to laugh and cry and shout and scream all at once, because when he'd checked the night before, he'd been in the bottom 10 percent. Had Martinson somehow done that, or maybe the retired Chief Petty Officer Parker?

Abraxa tried to argue that 5 percent wasn't enough progress, so they should still expel York, but by a three-to-two vote of the board, York got one more year in the academy.

He, Karin, Tony, and Muldoon went out and celebrated rather noisily.

At the beginning of their third year, Karin returned wearing an engagement ring. That saddened York a little because he'd assumed they'd continue their relationship as long as they were both at the academy. They had a few days before classes began so York, Tony, and Muldoon took her out to dinner to celebrate. She was quite excited about it all.

In the middle of dinner, Muldoon asked her, "When's the big day?"

"Not until after graduation and my evaluation tour," she said. "I told my father I want to do this right, and as long as I don't get anywhere near the real action, he's okay with that."

Tony ordered some very nice wine, and York's eyes popped when he saw the price tag. They killed the bottle, ordered another, killed that, and ordered another. York figured he'd be in debt for the rest of his life before the night was over, but Tony picked up the tab.

Outside the restaurant, Karin told Tony and Muldoon, "You two go on without us. I want to talk to York."

York figured she wanted to explain her engagement, let him

down without hurting him, which wasn't necessary since they'd both been very careful to allow no emotional attachment between them. When they were alone, he said, "You don't have to explain. I understand."

She frowned and looked at him oddly. "What are you talking about? I've missed you."

She stepped in and wrapped her arms around him, kissed him hotly, pressed her body against his. He couldn't help but respond, and when their lips parted, she whispered, "Oh, I've needed that."

"But . . ." he said. "But . . . you're engaged. Isn't it over between us?"

She frowned again and looked quite perplexed. She cocked her head as if she needed to take a moment to process his words, then she threw her head back, and laughed. "I'm not going to see my fiancé for close to a year. Do you think I'm going to remain celibate that long?"

"I . . ." he said. "I guess . . . I figured . . ."

She held up her hand, displaying the ring, which looked like it probably cost more than York would make during his entire life. "This thing," she said. "This is a corporate merger. He and I are friends, even fond of each other, but we're not in love. The sex is okay, but you're better. We'll bear heirs for his family and mine, and our marriage will act kind of like a treaty between nations. His family's interests and mine will compete, but no nasty stuff, and we might even merge certain operations. He'll have his mistresses and I'll have my lovers. You see, I'm as constrained by my father's fortune as Tony is by his father's titles."

She kissed him again, almost defiantly. "I meant it when I said he's not as good as you, and I've built up a backlog of need. Let's get a room."

Karin was quite vigorous that night.

As a second-class midshipman, York took a greater role in the education of plebes. He'd come to realize that the sniping wasn't just hazing. If he excluded the occasional sadist, or those with a hidden agenda like Abraxa, the harassment and all the strange little customs had bonded York and the rest of his class as nothing else could. And as he gained more distance from his plebe year, he realized that the constant pressure had taught him to evaluate quickly and react instinctively, to think on his feet under the most stressful of circumstances. Still, he was careful not to overdo it when it was his turn to dish out the grief.

Abraxa kept the pressure on, sniping York like a plebe at every opportunity. Tony had previously expressed his concern over Abraxa's behavior with a quiet comment or two to York, but at the beginning of their third year, he grew more open about it. It came to a head in the middle of that year when Abraxa cornered York in front of their dormitory and upbraided him in front of a large crowd.

Tony stepped in and said, "See here, Abraxa. Your abuse of an upperclassman makes us all look bad."

In the middle of shouting in York's face, Abraxa froze and turned a cold look upon Tony. York thought Tony had been unwise to speak in the first place, would be wise now to shut up and leave it at that, but apparently Lord Anton Simma thought his titles and position would protect him, and he continued. "Your petty sniping demonstrates a level of intolerance I find exceedingly distasteful."

Abraxa was silent for a moment, then he exploded and turned his abuse on Tony. He heaped a wealth of demerits on both Tony and York, and hopefully Tony learned a valuable lesson that day.

Laski continued to ensure that York remained in the bottom 10 percent of the class, and at the end of the year, York faced another academic review board, same conference room, same table with Martinson, Abraxa, and Murtaugh serving on the board, Laski sitting to one side. Charter and Minkowski had been replaced by two officers named Sokolov and Kensington. Martinson read the minutes of the last two boards, and like their predecessors, something in them appeared to trouble the two men.

When Martinson finished, Abraxa said, "I believe there's no question this time that he's in the bottom ten percent of the class."

Martinson checked the screen in front of him and said, "That he is."

It appeared there'd be no magic pill to save York this time.

"Well, then," Abraxa said. "It's clear we need to expel him."

Kensington said, "But that would be most unusual. His class began with just over fifteen hundred cadets, and we've winnowed it down to less than a thousand."

Martinson said, "Excellent point. That means he's in the top sixty or seventy percent of the class in which he started. Someone has to graduate at the bottom of the class; I suppose it will be Mr. Ballin."

By a vote of three-to-two, York was allowed to start the coming year as a midshipman first class. It almost seemed as if Martinson and Kensington had orchestrated that, and York walked out of the meeting not sure what to think.

As firsties, Karin and York had more opportunity to spend time together, and Muldoon came out of his shell a bit more. Abraxa didn't let up on York, and Tony brooded on that. The four of them were studying together one day, and York had to carefully explain one of the navigational exercises to Tony, who turned thoughtful, leaned back in his chair, and said, "I'm going to graduate at the top of the class"—he looked pointedly at York—"and you're going to graduate somewhere near the bottom, but you know this stuff much better than me. It just doesn't add up."

"Oh, Tony," Muldoon said. "Now you're being naive. Haven't you noticed that the number-one student in every graduating class is always the most titled?"

That obviously bothered Tony quite a bit, but nothing was ever said about it again. After graduation, Tony, Karin, and Muldoon were assigned to evaluation tours on large ships in Home Fleet. York had requested a posting on a large cruiser, but graduating at the bottom of the class meant he had to take what he could get. He was assigned to *The Fourth Horseman*, a small hunter-killer under-going refitting on Muirendan and scheduled to ship out to the front in two months.

He had a few days before shipping out, so he and Karin spent the time together. They walked through the parks near Mare Crisia, did a few touristy things, and York realized that it didn't really matter what he did, as long as he did it with Karin. The day of his departure, they had breakfast at a small café in town, and only then did he realize how much he would miss her.

"The evaluation tour is half a year," she said. "Since we have to return here after that, let's meet up then." Her eyes glistened with tears, but she held them back.

They'd been very careful not to fall in love. They parted with a kiss.

CHAPTER 22:
BACK TO THE
LOWER DECKS

York rode deadhead on a military transport that couldn't do more than a thousand lights. It took almost forty-three days to get to Muirendan, and with no duties, he had nothing to do but think how much he missed Karin. He tried to read, to study, anything, but his thoughts always drifted back to her.

When the transport docked at Muirendan Prime, he packed up his gear. He now owned all the required uniforms of an officer of the Imperial Navy. If he could transport his twelve-year-old self forward in time, the young boy would be quite impressed.

When he logged in to shipnet to check the location of *The Fourth Horseman*, he noticed *Dauntless* was in port. In the typical fashion of *hurry up and get there so you can wait* naval orders, he had six days before he had to actually report for duty. He sent a message to *Dauntless*, learned that Cath was there and still alive. They agreed to meet at a small bar just off the docks.

York got there early and took a small table against one wall where they'd have a little privacy. To keep the waiters happy, he ordered a drink and nursed it while he waited for her. He knew he had changed considerably—after all, he'd been only fourteen years old when she'd last seen him. He wondered if she'd be different.

When she walked through the door, the first thing to draw his eye was that she'd let her blond hair grow to chin length. He stood, waved to her. She was slight of build and pretty, and she spotted him from across the room and walked his way. He'd always been attracted to her, but when he considered that now, he thought only of Karin.

She stopped a few paces from him, put her fists on her hips, and said, "Well look at you, kid, all grown up and practically an admiral. You know I ain't gonna salute you, or call you *sir.*"

He now towered over her, stood at least twenty centimeters taller. She looked up at him and said, "I will stop calling you *kid*, though."

When they sat down at the table, she said, "Sorry about Sissy."

He grimaced. "That's okay. That hurt scabbed over long ago."

He asked about Marko. "I didn't see Marko's name on the crew roster. He isn't . . ."

He feared what her answer might be, but she shook her head and said, "Nah. That old coot put in his forty years and retired. Married a young whore on Cathan, and with his pension, I hear they're real happy."

Zamekis had transferred to another ship, Durlling had finished her enlistment contract and left the navy behind; no one had heard from her. Tomlin hadn't learned anything from Sturpik's demise or the rather brutal training session the marines had given him. He continued to be a problem for everyone. Then, one night on fourth watch, he slipped while negotiating one of the steep ladders between decks and cracked his skull on a bulkhead. Their medical technology might have saved him, but it was late, and no one was around or aware of his accident until it was too late.

"What about Bristow?" York asked. "He wasn't on the roster."

Cath flinched and grimaced.

He asked, "What's wrong?"

A tear drizzled down her cheek and she wiped it away angrily. "Ah, I let that limp dick get in my pants, found out I liked him there, made a habit of it, and then that stupid fuck had to go get himself killed."

"I'm sorry, Cath."

They talked for a couple of hours and she got a little drunk. Then he walked her back to *Dauntless* and said good-bye.

York reported for duty five days early. *The Fourth Horseman* was a one-hundred-meter hunter-killer with a complement of sixty-four men and women. It was all power plant, drive, and transition torpedoes. It had a half dozen pods for defense, but its primary means of protecting itself was speed and stealth. If it had to depend on the pods for anything more than the occasional defensive shot, the ship was in serious trouble.

York stepped through *The Fourth Horseman*'s aft personnel hatch, his duffel over one shoulder, turned to the imperial ensign draped from a bulkhead, and saluted it. He turned to the officer of the deck, a gangly lieutenant junior grade with a name tag that read PAULSON. He saluted, saying, "Ensign York Ballin reporting for duty. Permission to come aboard, sir."

Paulson appeared to be York's age, maybe a year or two older. He hesitated before meeting York's eyes, then returned the salute. "At ease, Ensign Ballin. And welcome aboard."

He extended his hand and York shook it. Paulson spoke softly, almost shyly. "You're early."

"They probably didn't want me to miss the boat," York said. "And I had a long way to travel, sir."

"All the way from Luna, right?" Paulson seemed a little awestruck by that.

"Yes, sir."

York heard some noise outside the hatch, so he stepped aside. A master chief, medium height and slightly overweight, stepped through the hatch, followed by a man and a woman, both enlisted. The chief saluted the imperial ensign, then saluted Paulson. "I'm coming aboard, Lieutenant," he said.

York looked the chief over carefully. His uniform was clean, neat, and crisp. He had a black mustache and a dark shadow of a beard, but appeared to have shaved recently, and there was nothing about him that gave the impression of sloppiness. But regardless of his time in service, he should have followed the custom of formally identifying himself and asking permission to board the ship. York was careful to keep the look on his face neutral as the enlisted man and woman accompanying him both did it properly.

The chief hooked a thumb over his shoulder and said to Paulson, "There's a heavy crate of spare parts on the dock. Make sure they get loaded right away."

Paulson said, "Yes, s—" He'd almost said *sir*, but apparently caught himself and said, "Chief Vickers."

Vickers turned away from Paulson and spotted York. "And who are you?" he demanded.

The complete failure to follow military customs and etiquette surprised York. But he'd seen it a time or two before, a very senior NCO who had little patience for inexperienced junior officers.

York said, "I'm Ensign York Ballin, just reporting for duty, Master Chief."

"You are, are you?" he said. "Well we'll get along fine as long as you stay out of my way."

Vickers turned and marched away, followed by the two ratings.

Paulson watched him leave, then lowered his voice and said, "Do stay out of his way. He can be very difficult."

York said, "I'll take that advice to heart."

"You and I'll be sharing a stateroom," Paulson said. "We're short-staffed on officers, just the captain, XO, Lieutenant Kirkman, me, and you, so we're using senior NCOs as department heads where we have to."

A ship the size of *The Fourth Horseman* usually had a complement of seven to eight officers, so they were badly understaffed in the officer ranks. A posting on a hunter-killer was the least desirable service in the navy, and York had heard that officers with influence or connections found a way to be assigned to a larger ship.

York unpacked quickly in the stateroom he and Paulson were assigned, then found the master-at-arms, Senior Chief Carney, a middle-aged female with a bit of gray in her dark hair. The old-fashioned slug-thrower he'd purchased many years ago after leaving *Dauntless* was now part of the radioactive cloud of gas that had once been *Africa*. He'd purchased a new one after dropping Cath off, and he handed it to Carney now. "I need to register this," he said.

She looked the weapon over doubtfully. "Why carry this thing?"

He'd been through this before and had learned what to say to minimize questions. "I had a brief stint with the marines on a cruiser when I was twelve. They taught me it's a good backup sidearm."

She pointedly looked at his rank. "Twelve? Didn't you just come from the academy?"

"Yes, Chief, I did."

She looked again at the sidearm, then again at him. She entered something into her shipnet terminal, handed the gun back to him, and said, "Very good, sir. It's registered."

York returned to his stateroom. He'd just finished stowing the gun when his implants informed him he was to report to the captain.

He stopped outside the captain's stateroom door, and announced through his implants. "Ensign Ballin reporting as ordered."

"Enter."

York stepped through the door. Seated opposite each other in the only two spaces at a small fold-down table were a man and a woman with mugs of caff in front of them. York had done his homework. Lieutenant Commander Hensen, the *Horseman*'s executive officer, had light brown hair and would have been handsome had his features not been so sharp and angular. The captain, Commander Hella Gunnerson, had bright blue eyes and prematurely gray-white hair. She was quite pretty.

York announced himself with the traditional formula and saluted. Gunnerson returned the salute casually. "At ease, Ensign Ballin."

York spread his feet and put his hands behind his back.

"We've been going over your record," she said. "Most unusual. A lower-deck pod gunner must have had a hellish time at the academy."

Apparently, Martinson had modified his record only in the academy's system. "It was difficult at times, ma'am, but I have some good memories, too." He thought of Karin, Tony, and Muldoon.

Henson said, "No doubt you requested something more interesting than a hunter-killer posting."

"Yes, sir, I did, though I knew from the beginning I wouldn't get it."

Gunnerson said, "Graduated at the bottom of your class. Are you going to be any good to us?"

York suspected he would face that question for the rest of his life. "I studied hard, ma'am, and learned everything I could."

"But still," she said, "bottom of your class."

York chose his words carefully. "The scoring system at the academy doesn't necessarily represent one's abilities."

Hensen laughed. "That was diplomatically put."

Gunnerson looked at him for a moment, then nodded. "Okay, Ensign. No one on this ship but Commander Hensen and I know your past. I'm sure it'll get out eventually, but you start here with a fresh slate. Make use of it."

She touched a switch on a small com plate. She could have vocalized into her implants, but York guessed she wanted him to hear her words. "Master Chief Vickers," she said, and York knew what was coming.

"Yes, ma'am," the speaker said.

"As you know, we have a brand-new ensign on board. He'll be reporting to you immediately. Please start him at the bottom."

It was customary to put new ensigns through a bit of friendly hazing, assign them to a lower-deck pod crew so they could see the ship from the bottom of the crew roster. But Gunnerson knew York's record and hadn't told Vickers about it. York wondered if she was setting him up for something.

"One more thing," she said. "Commandant Martinson sent me a message, said that any time we put into furthering your training would not be wasted. Make sure you live up to that statement."

"Aye, aye, ma'am."

She smiled and looked at Hensen. Without looking at York, she said, "Ensign Ballin, you're dismissed. Report immediately to Chief Vickers. And obey his orders as if they were coming directly from me."

Vickers was waiting for York on the gunner deck with an unpleasant grin on his face. "Stand at attention," he barked.

York stiffened and threw his shoulders back.

Several enlisted men and women gathered as Vickers walked slowly around York. It was not uncommon that new ensigns fresh out of the academy added non-regulation embellishments to their uniforms, like gold piping and decorative stitching. If Vickers found anything abnormal about York's, he would tell York he was out of uniform, make him strip down then and there, and York would have to finish the watch in his underwear, all part of a little fun. But as a gunner, York had seen the custom enacted a number of times, and had made sure his uniform could be used as a textbook example of naval propriety.

Vickers completed his inspection and stopped in front of York. "Hmmm," he said. It was also customary that if the newbie's uniform passed muster, there would be no special effort to trump up a reason for that little bit of humiliation.

"Well," Vickers said. "Let's see how well you do in a pod."

Behind Vickers, York saw one of the enlisted men cover his mouth and snicker. York knew what was coming.

Vickers showed him a pod hatch and introduced him to it much as Straight had done ten years ago. York didn't want to blind-side Vickers, thought he should say something about his experience. "I already—"

"Shut up," Vickers snapped, saying it in front of a group of ratings and NCOs. "You don't talk; you just listen."

York was careful to nod politely and listen. Vickers helped him get strapped into the pod, briefed him quickly on its controls, then said, "We're going to run through a simulation now, throw a lot of stuff at you. Don't worry if you don't do well."

When Vickers closed the pod hatch, York sealed it, ran the pod through its boot sequence, and brought it online. Then he quickly checked all the settings, found that most of his controls had the gain set to either maximum or zero. If he tried to target on anything, the pod would swing about wildly. He corrected the settings.

They started out by giving him two targets at once. He killed them both. They gave him four and he killed one and deflected the others. They gave him six. He killed two, deflected three, and one got through.

"Hold on there," Vickers voice said in his implants. "Ballin, get out here."

Vickers was waiting for York when he climbed out of the zero-G tube and out onto the pod deck. Vickers grabbed York's left arm and slid the short sleeve of his service khakis upward, exposing twelve gunner's chevrons there. One of the enlisted women said, "Shit, twelve of 'em."

York smiled at her and said, "The total is twenty-four and a half. It should be twenty-five and a half, but at Sirius Night Star they tanked me before I could attend my last gunner's blood."

He looked Vickers in the eyes. "I tried to tell you, Chief."

Vickers sneered. "No one came back from Sirius Night Star."

York recalled Nathan Abraxa saying almost exactly that at the reception when Martinson had exposed his past. "A few of us did."

Vickers said, "Get out of here and go back to the captain."

Gunnerson was on the bridge running the ship through static drive tests, but Hensen intercepted York in the corridor outside. York snapped a crisp salute. "Sir."

Hensen said, "What the hell did you say to Vickers to piss him off?"

"I don't think it was what I said, sir. Perhaps more what I did."

"Then what did you do?"

"I think he didn't like that I did well in the pod."

Hensen shook his head. "No, I don't think that's it. I know you're an ex-gunner, but . . ." One of Hensen's eyebrows shot up. "How many gunner's chevrons you got?"

"Twenty-four and a half, sir, but it should be—"

Hensen laughed and said, "Oh, that's rich. Vickers is no longer the most senior gunner on the *Horseman*."

It was then that York realized Gunnerson had not set him up for a fall, she'd set Vickers up, let him make himself look bad in front of his people. York wondered if he would be the one to pay the price for that.

CHAPTER 23: SPACE TRIALS

Gunnerson assigned York to assist Lieutenant Kirkman and Chief Soletski in engineering. When they first met, Kirkman asked York, "You come up through the ranks, huh?"

Apparently, word had spread. "Basically," York said. "Though it's a little more complicated than that, sir."

"That's pretty rare in this navy. But you started on the lower decks, right?"

York wondered if that would be a problem with Kirkman. "When I was twelve, sir."

"Then you've got what, ten years' seniority?"

York had never thought of it that way. Officially, even the two years in the *Vincent*'s tanks counted as hazardous duty. "Yes, I guess I do, sir."

Kirkman slapped him on the back and grinned. "That means you've got more seniority than I do."

It took another twenty days for the *Horseman*'s crew to finish the refitting, then run static tests while still in dock. York spent the time wrench in hand, frequently on his back beside Soletski beneath a piece of heavy equipment. The most important test came when they fired up the ship's systems and stopped drawing power from the station. The entire engineering crew watched nervously as Kirkman brought the power plant up to standby. Nothing went wrong, so they held it at standby for a few hours and ran more tests, then carefully brought it up to operational levels. They held it there for two days while they measured and checked everything possible.

"So far, so good," Soletski said. "Now let's see if she'll handle redline."

Since they weren't using the power they'd be generating, Kirkman contacted Muirendan Prime's engineering department and warned them the *Horseman* would be feeding power to the station for a couple of hours instead of taking from it, then Gunnerson put the ship on Watch Condition Yellow.

Kirkman brought the power up in small increments. At each elevated level, he paused, York and the rest of the engineering crew ran a series of tests, then Kirkman went to the next level. At 70 percent of maximum, the sound coming from the core changed from a low, bass hum to an irritating whine. Soletski had warned York that using his implants to dampen his audio response would not be sufficient, so like everyone else, he wore ear protection and communicated exclusively through his implants. He now understood why implants were required to work in the engine room. When they brought the power back down to standby, everyone breathed a sigh of relief.

The day before they were scheduled to depart, Gunnerson called York up to the bridge. "You're going to work with me now, Mr. Ballin. You're going to learn how to drive this boat."

She pointed to the captain's console and said, "Take a seat, Mr. Ballin."

York's stomach knotted with butterflies as he sat down on the most sacred acceleration couch on the ship. He strapped in and sat there waiting for Gunnerson to tell him what to do.

She said, "We always wear headsets, York. They're a good backup to your implants, and they filter out excess noise that your implants can't scrub."

York pulled on a headset and adjusted the wire-thin pickup in front of his mouth. Again, he waited for Gunnerson.

"Tomorrow," she said, "when we depart, if you show me now that you learned anything at the academy, you're going to be sitting in that couch in command of this ship when we go live. So show me now that you can take this ship through a full departure sequence. You're now in command, so command."

York froze for a moment. He'd done this in bits and pieces, in simulations and on training cruises, and he realized he could do it now. He keyed his implants to allship. *All hands, stand by to cast off.*

Gunnerson had set up the entire bridge as a large simulation, with the bridge crew supporting him in what amounted to a training exercise. The hours of practice and study kicked in, and York settled into a comfortable rhythm of issuing orders, though he was constantly in fear of doing something wrong, so the butterflies didn't go away. It all went nicely until he backed the ship away from its mooring. In the simulation, the bow clipped the edge of the dock, causing considerable damage to both.

York buried his face in his hands.

"Not bad," Gunnerson said. "I don't like losing a couple of meters off the bow, but not bad for a first try. I like the way you asked for, and took, the advice of your crew. But don't forget that you have to make the final decision and bear the responsibility for it."

York was surprised to learn that he hadn't failed miserably. The next day, he again sat at the captain's console, and took the ship through a real departure sequence. Gunnerson and Hensen were both there to correct or countermand any faulty order he gave, and the *Horseman* departed Muirendan Prime without incident.

Gunnerson and Hensen didn't stand a standard watch rotation, and since they took York's training quite seriously, neither did he. On that first drive out-system from Muirendan, he spent every waking moment on the bridge or down in engineering. The captain or the executive officer would ask York what command he would give next. If he guessed right, they would give the command, then have York explain why he'd chosen that particular order. If he guessed wrong, they'd give the proper order, then explain to him why his choice had been incorrect, and the horrendous consequences that would have resulted. He guessed right most of the time, and it occurred to him that maybe he wasn't really guessing.

Before they stressed any of the ship's systems, they had to put it through space trials. They drove out-system for several hours on sublight drive at one G, a bare crawl for a ship capable of twenty thousand G's. But while they'd stressed the ship's power plant, they hadn't yet tested its drive. After a little more than three hours, they'd put a million kilometers between them and the space station. York had spent a good portion of that time down in engineering helping Kirkman run tests. Satisfied that they weren't going to turn into an enormous fireball, Kirkman gave the all-clear to Gunnerson.

She ordered the sublight drive up to ten G's. Kirkman ran tests for a half hour, then Gunnerson upped it to a hundred and they ran more tests. In that way, they cautiously pushed the sublight drive to its maximum rated acceleration, and by that time they were close to heliopause with a relativistic dilation factor well over two.

They cautiously tested the transition drive in the same way, by up- and down-transiting several times and slowly pushing it to the limit. They ran crash-drive and crash-stop tests in which they started from a dead stop, accelerated at max drive in sublight until they could up-transit, then accelerated in transition as fast as they could up to three thousand lights. They coasted at that speed to run further tests, then reversed the process to get to down-transition in the shortest possible time. After they'd done that a few times and were confident the main ship's systems were operating reliably, they settled a few light-years out from Muirendan. There they test-fired all the pods and the transition launchers, tested every system on the ship, ran through simulated

damage-control exercises and every possible emergency Gunnerson and Hensen could come up with.

York had previously qualified on the helm, but now he had
to do so again while they practiced what they called a "*hunter-
killer approach*," an exercise in which they slowly decreased their
transition velocity as far as possible while approaching a solar
system. The combination of low transition velocity, and the
nearby presence of a large gravitational mass, produced instabilities in the transition drive, and at a certain point the ship
would spontaneously down-transit. York did rather well, held
them in transition all the way down to ten lights, though young
Petty Officer First Class McHenry held the record at close to
nine.

A tenday after departing Muirendan, Gunnerson declared the
ship and crew ready for duty as an imperial ship-of-the-line, and
they set course for Cathan, an intermediate stop on the way to the
front lines.

It took more than a month to get to Cathan, and during that
time, Gunnerson drilled the crew relentlessly. She told York,
"After more than a year on liberty, your crew loses its edge. And
we've got new members to integrate and rookies to train."

During that month, York served in just about every function
on ship, the notable exception being pod gunner since he already
had plenty of experience there. He enjoyed the new experience of
training with one of the transition launcher crews, regretted that
he wouldn't get the chance to train in a main transition battery
since hunter-killers didn't have any. He even worked with Lieutenant Paulson in supply and provisioning.

One day, the two of them sat down in the wardroom for a mug
of caff during a short break. "I envy you," Paulson said.

"Me?" York said. "Why me?"

He seemed a little sad. "The captain and XO gave up trying to
push me as hard as they're pushing you long ago. I'm really not
cut out for command, and I think they realized it before I did."

York had noticed that Paulson was rather timid, especially in the way he let Vickers push him around.

"I might get promoted to full lieutenant on this tour, but I think the captain's going to classify me as unfit to command. That means I'll never go beyond that."

York asked him, "What will you do?"

Paulson shrugged. "My enlistment contract is up in two years. I guess I'll look for something else."

Vickers walked in at that moment, hooked a thumb over his shoulder, and said, "Paulson, I need you down in supply."

Kirkman walked in an instant behind Vickers and frowned, his brow furrowing and his eyes narrowing with anger. "Chief Vickers," he said sharply. The NCO turned, clearly surprised Kirkman was there. "What did I just hear?" Kirkman demanded.

Vickers said, "I just asked the lieutenant—"

"No, you didn't," Kirkman said. He stepped forward and stood over Vickers. Kirkman and York were of similar height, which gave them several centimeters over the chief and allowed the engineer to tower over the man. "Stand at attention when I'm addressing you."

Vickers's eyes turned to hard, cold slits. He slowly threw his shoulders back and said, "Sir."

"You issued an order to a superior officer," Kirkman said. "And you did not address him properly. I believe you and Commander Hensen have talked about this before, so I'm putting you on report."

Kirkman spun about and marched out of the room. Vickers relaxed, then turned and looked down at Paulson and York. The look he gave them told York that he would pay for seeing the master chief upbraided by an officer.

They took on supplies at Cathan and, along with three other hunter-killers, two destroyers, and a medium cruiser, were assigned to escort a large convoy to Dumark. Hensen had the bridge watch when they started out. He told York, "It would be pretty unusual for an enemy hunter-killer to sneak this far behind the front lines, but not unheard of, so we play it cautious."

The larger military ships stayed with the slower convoy while the hunter-killers shot ahead. The four of them down-transited a quarter light-year apart in a line along the convoy's course, which stretched them out over one light-year. With their drones out, they scanned that space carefully, and when the convoy caught up with them, the hunter-killer in the rear pulled its drones in and up-transited. Using its faster drive to stay ahead of the convoy, it leapfrogged past the other hunter-killers and down-transited again. The process required each hunter-killer to up- and down-transit a little more than once a day, and York found it nerve-racking and exhausting.

Twenty days after departing Cathan, they put into Dumark without incident. Gunnerson set up a rotating skeleton crew and gave everyone else liberty. York didn't know what to do. He didn't want to go down to the surface, didn't really want to see Maja and Toll, didn't think they wanted to see him, and in any case, he'd been gone for more than ten years. He couldn't go to a bar with the enlisted men and women, and was still too junior to fraternize with the other officers. He considered going to a whorehouse, but that just didn't appeal to him, and he realized how much he was looking forward to seeing Karin at the end of their evaluation tours. York spent his liberty on ship studying, and five days later, they departed for deep-space patrol. Their destination was classified, which meant they were probably going behind enemy lines to disrupt shipping.

"It's a close approach shot," Hensen said.

York was sitting at Navigation with Hensen looking over his shoulder. They were coasting sublight and running silent two parsecs off the feddie system Stulfanos, a major transit point for supplies going to the front. At the *Horseman*'s maximum drive of three thousand lights it had taken six days to cross the fifty light-years from Dumark to the front. Once there, Gunnerson had grown cautious, dropped back to a thousand lights, and taken almost twenty days to get to their present position.

Hensen continued. "If we drive at two thousand lights, they can detect our transition wake while we're one to two parsecs out. Drive at half that, and their detection range is cut in half. So we start out fast and steadily decrease our transition velocity so we're always just outside their detection range."

York turned from the data on the navigation screens and looked over his shoulder at Hensen. "But that's an exponential decay curve, sir. We'll be steadily approaching zero velocity and we'll never get there."

"We don't need to get there," Hensen said. "We need to get close, maybe a light-month out. At that range, we can catch incoming ships just before they down-transit into the system, and outgoing ships just after up-transition out of it. If we do our job, we'll wreak absolute havoc with their supply lines."

"But that'll still take more than a month, sir."

"And it'll be the most boring month you've ever spent. Well . . . I take that back. You're not going to be bored, because we're going to work your ass off, but the rest of us'll be bored shitless."

CHAPTER 24:
A LONG WAIT

"Sixty lights and closing, ranging at one-tenth light-year."

A gravity wave washed through the ship and York swallowed hard to keep his lunch down. He'd been warned not to eat a large meal, and he'd carefully obeyed, but the gravitational instabilities had become so intense and frequent that everyone suffered.

"Mr. Ballin, start dumping lights," Gunnerson said. "But remember, slow and steady wins this race. Dump too much too fast and we'll light up their screens like a holiday, make us a real easy target and ruin everybody's day."

York and McHenry were teamed at the helm. To everyone's delight, it turned out that the two of them complemented each other nicely. York was good at estimating how rapidly to dump lights, while McHenry excelled at keeping them in transition as they approached the sublight boundary. McHenry had a dark complexion and unruly, curly black hair. He was about York's age, but looked a lot younger, and York had to force himself not to think of him as *the kid*.

York checked his screens and announced, "Forty lights and holding."

Their transition wake was now weak enough that it could easily be mistaken for one of the many natural transition phenomena, like a burst of matter-antimatter annihilation events. But it was imperative they quickly get to down-transition because such natural events were transient in nature, and if they showed up as a weak event on someone's screens for too long, the enemy might grow suspicious.

York's eyes were locked to his screens as he read the information there out loud. "Twenty lights. How's she handling?" he asked McHenry.

He glanced at York and grinned. "Sweet and steady."

York now slowed down his deceleration curve, hoping to sneak up on ten lights. "Fifteen lights," he announced.

"Don't forget," Gunnerson said, "when she down-transits, hold on to all the sublight velocity you can, keep our transition flare to a minimum."

York gave them a countdown. "Thirteen lights . . . twelve . . . eleven . . ." He backed off on the deceleration curve even more as a cluster of gravity waves rolled through the ship, was surprised they weren't kicked into sublight. "Ten lights," he said. "Nine . . ."

He was about to say *eight*, but Hensen beat him to it. "Down-transition. Stand by all hands."

They all waited for the verdict, and York realized he was holding his breath. He forced himself to breathe as Hensen announced, "Clear to fifty thousand klicks. Drones out."

The hull thrummed with the launch of the combat drones.

Another breathless hush, and then Hensen said, "We're clear, no surprises."

Standing bridge watch alone on first watch and closely monitoring the scan console, York was technically in command of the ship, but he knew better than to fool himself with any such delusions. It was the first watch-rotation after down-transiting off Stulfanos. To minimize their transition signature and the possibility of detection, they were coasting toward the system at nine-tenths light, running silent with no gravity or drive, just the barest minimum drain on energy to maintain life support and all critical systems. They'd positioned their six combat drones in a static sphere about the ship at a distance of a hundred thousand klicks, and York's only responsibility was to monitor the scan data for incoming or outgoing ships. It was quiet, lonely, and boring, and drowsiness slowly crept up on him.

He unstrapped from the acceleration couch and floated upward. He moved carefully through the cramped confines of the *Horseman*'s bridge, using small handholds specifically intended for weightless maneuvering. To keep alert, he made the rounds of the bridge's command stations, had to duck and twist a bit to make sure he didn't bang his head on an overhanging instrument cluster. The power plant was on a standby trickle so they could bring it up in a heartbeat, which was always a gamble since it had a finite transition signature, but it was low enough that detection by the Federals was highly unlikely. Since they were coasting, the helm was dark and silent. He was about to check on environmental control when a faint, repetitive beep from the scan console drew his attention. He'd set an alarm to start at a comfortably low volume; if he didn't respond to it, the sound would increase slowly until quite loud, a little assurance against dozing off.

At the scan console, he killed the alarm then strapped into the couch. He looked at the summary on one of his screens, which indicated some sort of transition wake approaching from interstellar space. He brought up a detailed report on another screen, which showed a faint trace about four light-years out. It wasn't strong enough to get a sharp signature, so he couldn't tell if it was military or civilian, man-of-war or transport, but it was approaching at close to two thousand lights—probably military.

He keyed his implants. "Computer, priority message to Commander Hensen. Wake him if necessary. Message as follows: Incoming transition wake, driving at two thousand lights, about fourteen hours out. Nothing urgent. End message."

It took close to a minute for Hensen to respond. "I'll be up shortly, York."

York spent the time cleaning up the incoming signal and

trying to analyze it. Five minutes later, Hensen floated onto the bridge, strapped into the captain's console, and said, "Okay, let's see what you've got."

York sent a summary to the captain's console as he said, "At close to two thousand lights, it's probably military. In fact, I'm fairly certain it's a single ship, most likely a destroyer, but at this range I can't be certain."

Hensen leaned toward York, a smile on his face. "You don't have to whisper, Mr. Ballin. Trust me, the Federals can't hear you speak."

Only then did York realize what he had been doing, and he felt his face flush.

In ten minutes, Hensen confirmed York's analysis. "Good work, Mr. Ballin, but we're not going to do anything about a lone destroyer. We want supply ships, preferably a convoy."

Hensen stretched and yawned. "Why don't you take a break, go down to the wardroom, and get a mug of caff. I'll cover the bridge until you get back."

Hensen snapped a quick salute that, had he not been strapped in, would have sent him into a weightless spin. "I relieve you, Ensign Ballin."

York saluted back, "I stand relieved."

He unstrapped and made his way down to the wardroom. On a hunter-killer, the small complement of officers shared the wardroom with senior NCOs, but at that time of night, it was empty. York strapped into a seat, sucked on a mug of caff, and chewed on some sweetened, flavored protein cake. He was about ready to leave when Chief Vickers floated into the wardroom, looked surprised to see York there, and said, "What are you doing here? I thought you're on bridge watch."

York said, "Commander Hensen relieved me for a short break."

"You're good buddies, huh?"

York shook his head. "Commander Hensen is my superior officer."

"Ya, and you kiss his ass, don't you?"

York decided not to answer.

Vickers continued. "You listen to me, punk. You made me look bad, and I won't forget that."

York said, "If I made you look bad, it was not intentional."

Vickers sneered at him, twisted about, pushed off, and floated out of the wardroom. York finished his caff, tossed the rest of the protein cake in the recycler, and unstrapped. Out in the corridor, he ran into Chief Carney. Gripping a handhold, she said, "Good morning, sir."

When running weightless, no one saluted unless strapped down in a couch.

York smiled and said, "Good morning, Chief. I didn't know you were standing this watch."

"Couldn't sleep," she said. "So I thought I'd just check up on things."

It sounded almost as if she meant she was checking up on Vickers.

"Sir," she said tentatively, looking worried. "May I offer you a little . . . advice?"

That surprised York. "Certainly."

She grimaced as she said, "Be careful around Vickers. I think he's AI."

"Admiralty Intelligence?" York asked.

"Yes. They report directly to the Admiralty, not through the normal chain of command, kind of a law unto themselves. I can't prove it, but I have my suspicions. You would be wise to be careful what you say around him."

York nodded slowly. "Thank you, Chief. I will."

When York returned to the bridge, Hensen instructed him to watch the incoming destroyer closely and alert him if it defied all the gods of probability and looked like it might pass too close to the *Horseman*.

After he'd left, York thought back to Vickers and Carney. Two senior chief petty officers, both up and about on first watch when neither was on duty. Coincidence, or was Carney watching Vickers, keeping an eye on him?

"How many ships, Mr. Ballin?" Gunnerson asked.

Seated at Scan, York looked at his screens one more time. "I would guess about twenty, ma'am, ranging at one light-year and driving at nine hundred lights."

"And why are you guessing? I don't like guessing."

York tried to keep the tension out of his voice. "Many of the transition wakes overlap, and they're strung out, the leading wakes obscuring those following."

Hensen stopped behind York and looked over his shoulder at the scan data. "I couldn't have guessed any better, Hella." He turned away from York and looked at the captain. "I'm sure Mr. Ballin will have better data for us as they get closer."

"Ma'am," York said. "I think I've identified their military escort."

York had been glued to the scan console for the last day, watching the convoy approach. "There are three ships that can do better than the convoy's nine hundred lights. They're leapfrogging, up- and down-transiting, shooting ahead and falling behind, with always at least one in sublight. It looks like two are destroyer or cruiser class, and one hunter-killer."

Gunnerson asked Hensen, "Did you teach him that, Jack?"

"No," Hensen said, a smile forming on his face. "I think he figured that out on his own."

"Nice work, Mr. Ballin," she said. "How far is the escort ranging ahead of the convoy?"

"A light-year when we first spotted them yesterday, but they've pulled in a bit and are now leading them by only a tenth of that."

"They're getting cautious as they approach their destination. And what's their ETA?"

"A little over eight hours, ma'am."

"Then let's stand down."

York asked, "Permission to remain on the bridge, ma'am."

Both Hensen and Gunnerson grinned. Gunnerson shook her head. "No, Mr. Ballin. Go get something to eat, get some rest, and don't come back here for at least four hours. Mr. Paulson, you've got the bridge. Keep a close eye on the situation, and if anything changes, I want to know soonest. Mr. Ballin will relieve you when he returns. And then, Mr. Ballin, please be certain to sound Watch Condition Yellow two hours before they get here."

York ate a light lunch in the wardroom, then returned to the stateroom he shared with Paulson and tried to get some sleep. But he lay there staring at the deck overhead.

They'd been coasting off Stulfanos for eight days, had passed up several opportunities at single ships, waiting for just this kind of opportunity. York tried to think through how Gunnerson and Hensen would handle it. But with his lack of experience, all he could think to do was punch a lot of torpedoes into transition, then run like hell.

Somehow he did sleep, and his implants woke him at the appointed time. He choked down a mug of caff in the wardroom, then returned to the bridge and relieved Paulson.

When he sat down at Scan, nothing had really changed; the convoy was merely closer. But over the next two hours, as they approached and the resolution of his instruments improved, he eliminated most of the guesswork: twenty-two ships incoming, three of them warships, the rest probably cargo transports. It was possible, even likely, that at least one warship hadn't been up- and down-transiting with the rest of the escort, and might appear at this stage to be no more than a merchantman. They'd have to be careful about that.

As instructed, two hours before the targets converged on the *Horseman*'s position, York elevated the ship's watch condition to yellow. Gunnerson's stateroom was closest to the bridge, so she arrived first. Hensen followed a moment later and strapped in at Fire Control, then McHenry at Helm and Paulson at Navigation.

"Mr. Paulson," Gunnerson said. "Compute multiple escape scenarios, all driving at flank speed and up-transiting as soon as possible on a course perpendicular to our present track. Commander Hensen and I will review them with you shortly."

Gunnerson had to lean a little to one side and peer past an instrument cluster to see York. "Mr. Ballin, is your data any better at this point?"

"Yes, ma'am," York said. He sent a summary of his results to her and Hensen's consoles, then gave them a brief verbal summary. He mentioned his concern that there might be military vessels he hadn't identified because they hadn't done anything to stand out from the merchantmen.

She said, "That's a very good concern to have. As they get closer, Commander Hensen will show you how we might be able to identify them by their power-plant signature."

York and Hensen played with several targeting solutions while Gunnerson reviewed the escape scenarios Paulson had computed. It occurred to York they were just trying to keep their two most junior officers busy, keep their minds off what might really happen. But when one of the convoy's escorts down-transited one-tenth light-year out, they all paused for a moment and looked at their screens. Hensen glanced over at York. "The critical moment is going to be when the escort leapfrogs again, because the next one's going to be right on top of us. We've got about an hour."

Gunnerson brought the ship up to Watch Condition Red. The ship's systems operated much differently under the elevated status. "Commander Hensen," she said. "Arm and ready two ten-megatonne warheads, just in case we need them when that escort drops in on top of us."

At that point, it became a waiting game. The next jump by the escort would put one of them in the near vicinity of the *Horseman*, though *near* was a relative term. If the haphazard nature of war put the enemy warship within a few hundred million kilometers of their position, they might be detected and have to shoot and run.

There was something odd about the tension on the bridge, a level of fear York had never sensed before. He glanced around the confined space cluttered with instruments. Gunnerson appeared absolutely casual and unconcerned. Hensen's brow was furrowed in concentration, but not fear. It was when he looked at Paulson that he understood the stress that permeated the atmosphere of the bridge. The lieutenant trembled with obvious dread, his hands shaking, his eyes darting about worriedly. York glanced at McHenry and nodded toward Paulson. The young helmsman shrugged and rolled his eyes.

One transition wake broke out of the convoy and drove ahead of it at close to three thousand lights, definitely a hunter-killer much like the *Horseman*. It passed the leading escort, headed directly for the *Horseman*, and York felt a bead of sweat running down his spine. Paulson looked like he was about to break into tears.

York watched it approach on his screens, realized it would pass relatively close. Paulson sat at Navigation with his eyes closed, the muscles of his jaw visibly clenched. And even though they hid it well, Gunnerson and Hensen showed signs of strain in small ways, a nervous glance down at the screens, an unconscious tug on an earlobe.

When the escort passed over them, its transition wake sent a dozen gravity waves flooding in all directions through the ship. No one lost their lunch, but it was a near thing.

Hensen's eyes lit up and he counted, "One . . . two . . . three . . . four . . ."

The escort down-transited and Hensen said, "Hot damn!"

Gunnerson said, "You must be a lucky charm, Mr. Ballin." At the look on his face she added, "They overshot us by more than a billion klicks. They're not going to detect us, and we've got nothing between us and that convoy. That's incredible luck."

McHenry had a grin from ear to ear, and Paulson still looked sick.

"Okay, ladies," Gunnerson said. "We've got work to do."

The Fourth Horseman could spit torpedoes at a thousand lights and target accurately at distances up to twenty billion kilometers. But if they launched at extreme range, the approaching convoy would have eighty seconds to track the incoming torpedoes, time during which their military escort could target on the *Horseman*. Gunnerson wanted to cut it to under ten seconds.

"Mr. Hensen," she said. "Arm six ten-megatonne torpedoes for near-contact detonation. I'm sending targeting priorities to your console now."

"Aye, aye, ma'am."

"Also arm a one hundred megatonne torpedo to detonate immediately after launch at one million klicks off our bow, and another off our stern."

York frowned, wondering why she'd do that.

She must have seen the look on his face. "There'll be a lot of transition noise in that, Mr. Ballin, all nice and close to us, make it that much harder for them to get a targeting solution on us."

As York worked with Hensen to program the torpedoes for Gunnerson's targets, he glanced frequently at his screens, watching the enemy approach. The muscles in his shoulders tightened when they entered the limit of the *Horseman*'s targeting range, and he announced, "Ranging at twenty thousand megaklicks and closing. Just under two minutes out."

Gunnerson said, "Mr. Ballin, give us all a down-count on their approach at five-thousand megaklick intervals."

Paulson was almost dysfunctional at that point. York understood why Gunnerson had assigned him to Navigation. With their escape course precomputed, he wasn't needed once the action started, and if they had to make any last-minute changes, any one of them could handle it.

York looked at his screens again and announced, "Fifteen thousand megaklicks and closing."

They all had their implants tuned to a common command

circuit. Gunnerson said, "Engineering, stand by. I'll want launch power first."

The approaching convoy was now one minute out, but with the torpedo's transition velocity added to that of the oncoming enemy, their warheads would get to them in half that time.

York announced, "Ten thousand megaklicks and closing."

Gunnerson said, "Mr. Kirkman, when I give Mr. Hensen the order to fire, you know the drill: Power up, gravity up, and I want redline. And Mr. McHenry, you get us the fuck out of here."

McHenry said, "Aye, aye, ma'am."

York announced, "Five thousand megaklicks . . . four thousand . . . three—"

He didn't get to finish as Gunnerson shouted, "Fire."

The power plant went immediately to redline, then the hull echoed six times as the transition launchers threw warheads at the convoy. York felt the hum of the engines and McHenry firewalled the sublight drive. The transition launchers sounded two more times, and York's screens went blank as the two large warheads blew just off their bow and stern.

The power plant dropped out of redline, easily handling the demands of the sublight drive as they accelerated away at ten thousand G's, blind because of the transition noise their own torpedoes had generated. It was all up to McHenry now.

The hull of the *Horseman* groaned, and York actually felt a slight twitch in the internal gravity compensation. York's screens cleared as Hensen said, "That was a close one. That hunter-killer behind us must have got off a shot."

Once they could see through all the transition noise, it appeared they'd destroyed one cruiser class warship and three merchantmen, a rather successful shot. Now, they had to run like hell.

CHAPTER 25:
CHAIN OF COMMAND

Under the watchful eyes of Chief Petty Officer Harkness, and working with three other spacers, York sweated in the tight confines of the forward torpedo room. Orders had just come from the bridge to arm seven ten-megatonne and two one-hundred-megatonne warheads. The aft torpedo room would handle one of the larger warheads, while they were hustling to prep all eight transition launchers in the bow. Another close approach, another feddie system, this one named Joy of Dilosk; perhaps it had some meaning in some feddie dialect.

For this shot, Gunnerson had put Paulson in engineering, with York in the forward torpedo room. Gunnerson told him, "Before your evaluation tour is over, we're going to get you real live-fire experience in every critical station on this ship."

After Stulfanos, they'd set up another shot. York had gone through that one in engineering with Kirkman, and now, approaching the end of his evaluation tour, the Dilosk shot would be his last before returning to the academy and Karin. It would be the last time he'd see her, make love to her. After that, he'd probably be stationed on the front lines, while she'd get a cushy post near her father's estates. With light-years separating them, she'd get married, find other lovers, and they'd pretend their own relationship had never happened.

"Open the breech doors," Harkness ordered, yanking York back from his thoughts.

York had responsibility for tubes one and two, with Harkness looking over his shoulder to make sure he didn't screw up. He'd drilled on this routine for the last month, but under live-fire conditions, nerves could get the best of anyone.

York hit the locks on the two breech doors and popped them open.

"Load torpedoes," Harkness ordered.

York hit the switch above the first torpedo's trolley, and it slid smoothly into the launcher. He hesitated over the switch for number two. A telltale near the switch was still flashing red. Harkness frowned at his hesitation, glanced his way, saw the telltale, and nodded his approval. As long as it flashed red, the bridge was still downloading targeting information to the torpedo's onboard computer, and interlocks kept the trolley switch disabled.

It flashed from red to green, York hit the switch, and the torpedo slid into the launcher. They closed the breech doors, evacuated the launch tubes, and opened the muzzle doors. And now they waited.

Through York's implants Hensen's voice said, "Twenty thousand megaklicks and closing."

"Engineering," Gunnerson said, "you know the drill. On my order, power up, gravity up, and redline it so Mr. McHenry can get us out of here."

"Ten thousand megaklicks and closing."

In the torpedo room, no one spoke or moved, and York thought his heart might pound its way right out of his chest.

"Five thousand megaklicks . . . four . . ."

"Fire."

This close to the launchers, the thrum in the hull was deafening, and York was thankful for the headset covering his ears. The launchers rapidly spit out seven torpedoes, each accompanied by a wash of transition static and a gravity wave that turned York's stomach. The whine of the sublight drive kicked in, and an instant later the big torpedo meant to obscure their position with transition noise slammed out of the launcher.

As they closed the muzzle doors, they waited for any news from the bridge. But only a few seconds after the last launch, the hull screamed, the lights fluttered, and York's implants filled with damage control messages.

York looked at Harkness, knew he did a poor job of hiding the fear in his eyes. "We stay the course, Mr. Ballin," the chief said. "Wait for orders and be ready to comply."

York could tap into limited information on the situation through his implants, but Harkness had a full console, and updated them as he got information.

"Direct hit on the bridge, a transition shell, not a torpedo, or we'd be vapor. Bridge is under vacuum; Kirkman is in command operating from the auxiliary bridge in engineering. Power is good; drive is good. With the exception of the bridge, hull integrity is good, too. A rescue party is already on the bridge. So now we wait and see."

Gunnerson and two others were dead, with Hensen badly wounded. Word was, he might not make it. McHenry had lost a leg at mid-thigh, would wear a powered prosthetic until they got back to a naval facility and cloned him a new leg. On a hunter-killer, they didn't have a doctor, just a very highly trained medical corpsman, and the sick-bay facilities were nothing compared to that of a larger ship like a cruiser.

Kirkman called a meeting in the wardroom to include officers and senior NCOs. Beside Paulson and York, Vickers, Carney, Soletski, and Harkness attended, plus a chief petty officer York had met but not worked with: a woman named Garmin. The wardroom was a bit crowded, so York edged his way to the back of it.

Kirkman started the meeting by saying, "Looks like the Federals anticipated us, put on extra escorts, and a heavy cruiser managed to get in one shot with its transition batteries. After two close approaches and shots, we probably should have moved out of this quadrant before trying another."

Vickers said, "So Gunnerson fucked up, huh?"

Garmin nodded eagerly, agreeing with Vickers.

The look Kirkman gave Vickers did not bode well for the meeting. "First, Chief Vickers, *Captain* Gunnerson did not fuck up. Second, you'll keep a civil tongue in your head. And finally, you'll address me as *sir*."

The two men stared at each other for a long moment, until Kirkman said, "Well, Chief?"

Vickers looked like he was chewing nails. "Aye, aye . . . sir."

York noticed Garmin staring hatefully at Kirkman, apparently upset that Vickers had been upbraided.

Kirkman stared at Vickers until the chief lowered his eyes. Kirkman then continued, "To escape Dilosk, we had to drive deeper into enemy territory just when we needed to go back for supplies. We're now more than a hundred and fifty light-years behind the last known position of the front lines. We're heading back, but moving slowly so we don't broadcast too much of a transition wake, and we're zigzagging so we don't follow a predictable course. It could take us a couple of months to get there. The recyclers can provide all the water we need, so that's not an issue. But we're going to have to augment fresh food with synthesized protein cake out of the processors, so from here on, we ration fresh food. Everyone will receive the same ration regardless of rank."

Kirkman had each department head report on operational status. From what they said, the ship was in reasonably good shape. Even the bridge would soon be sealed up and operational again, requiring only a small amount of functional backup from the auxiliary bridge.

Kirkman had assigned York to the bridge crew, so when the meeting broke up he headed that way, but the medical corpsman stopped him in the corridor. "Ensign Ballin," he said, "a moment of your time."

York nodded, though he thought it telling that the man looked about carefully, almost fearfully, before speaking. He whispered, "Commander Hensen would like to speak with you."

"He's conscious?" York asked.

The corpsman said, "Not for long."

York followed the corpsman down two decks to sick bay. Hensen lay in an instrumented bed surrounded by a spaghetti of tubes and wires. His eyes were sunken, his cheeks hollow and pale, a greasy sheen of sweat covering his skin. From the shape of the sheets covering him, it appeared that the lower half of his body had been torn away.

"Commander," the corpsman whispered, "Ensign Ballin is here."

For the first time since York had entered the room, Hensen moved. He took a shallow breath, then another, as if building his strength for an effort, then he opened his eyes. He had trouble focusing them for a moment, then they settled on York.

"Ensign," he said, no hint of the strong, commanding voice York had come to admire.

"What is it?" York asked. "What can I do to help?"

Hensen said to the corpsman, "We'd like to . . . speak alone, please."

"Certainly, sir," the corpsman said. He walked past them deeper into sick bay.

Hensen reached out with his hand like a blind man. "Come close, York."

York leaned down so his ear was only centimeters from Hensen's lips. He felt the hot exhale of the commander's shallow breathing as he said, "Vickers . . . is AI. That's why we kept him . . . on the lower decks. Don't trust him."

York recalled how Garmin had supported Vickers's insubordination. He asked, "What about Garmin?"

Hensen shook his head, though it was an effort that cost him. "Not AI. . . . Probably wants to be. . . . Probably recruited by Vickers. Don't trust . . . her, either."

"Okay, sir," York said. "But why are you telling *me* this, and not Kirkman?"

"Last chance. They're gonna . . . tank me to keep me alive. And Kirkman already . . . knows. And Paulson doesn't count. Kirkman's gonna . . . need your help, gonna need you . . . to back him if Vickers tries anything. And Vickers . . . will try something."

Hensen's head sagged back against the pillow and he closed his eyes. His breathing grew shallow, so shallow that York wasn't sure he was breathing at all. York checked his pulse, was relieved to find he had one. He called the corpsman, then reported to duty on the bridge.

According to their orders of engagement, *The Fourth Horseman* had completed its mission. Even Dilosk had been a successful shot because they'd taken out a lot of feddie shipping, though it had cost them the lives of three crew, including their captain. They still had about twenty torpedoes left, but were running low on supplies, and with the chain of command badly impaired, it was time to get back to an imperial base. Kirkman planned to work their way slowly back to the front without engaging the enemy, then cross into friendly territory and let the Admiralty assign a new command structure to the ship. Unfortunately, he was forced to contend with Vickers at every turn.

The master chief was never again openly rude or impolite, was, in fact, textbook in the nuances of addressing a superior officer, even when it came to York. But the little slights were always there, a raised eyebrow subtly questioning any decision Kirkman made, an unvoiced smirk if their new captain showed even the slightest hesitation.

At first, morale plummeted into the toilet, yet as they cautiously made their way back toward the front lines, the bridge crew's confidence in Kirkman grew. And York saw firsthand how the engineering crew who'd worked under him trusted him, so parsec by parsec, day by day, spirits improved. But eighteen days later, a hundred light-years from the front lines, Kirkman slipped while navigating a ladder between decks and cracked his skull. It was in the middle of the night on first watch, with no one about to render assistance, and by the time they found him, he was dead. York thought it sounded a lot like the way Tomlin had died on *Dauntless*.

Kirkman's death made Paulson captain, and he immediately called a meeting of all officers and senior NCOs in the wardroom. York found it interesting that word of the meeting was spread by Vickers and Garmin, and that the two showed up at the meeting wearing sidearms.

"Captain Paulson," Vickers said before anyone else could speak, "we should drive straight for the front line and get back to friendly territory as soon as possible."

Soletski and Carney both looked warily at Paulson.

"Um," Paulson said, his eyes darting about the room. "But Captain Kirkman planned to approach it slowly, move cautiously. He—"

"He's dead," Vickers said. "And that's not the best way to handle this. We need to get back now."

Paulson nodded. "Okay. Whatever you say."

That was how the meeting went. Vickers ran it by issuing orders through Paulson.

As the meeting broke up, Paulson grabbed York's arm and held him back. When they were alone, he whispered, "Shit, shit, shit! I can't run this ship. Not with him running everything."

York said, "You have to. You're a line officer, and that makes you the CO of this ship."

Paulson looked like he was about to cry. "But I told you, Gunnerson was going to classify me unfit to command. You take command. I'll do whatever you say."

York shook his head. "It doesn't matter what Gunnerson was going to do, only what she did do. And since she didn't get around to classifying you as unfit, you're the captain of this ship. You have to take command back from Vickers, stop letting him walk all over you."

Paulson's voice trembled as he spoke. "I can't. I know I'm not fit for command. I can't."

York straightened and said, "Is there anything else, sir?"

"No," Paulson said, burying his face in his hands. "No, nothing."

Paulson refused to move into the captain's stateroom, but he did move Vickers into the executive officer's, and he assigned Vickers to bridge crew. Vickers did try to keep up the pretense that he wasn't giving the orders. He would say, "Captain, I recommend . . ." or "Captain, I would suggest that . . ." But occasionally, he slipped and threw out a direct order. The first time it happened to York, he was at the helm. They'd down-transited for a nav fix, and Vickers ordered, "Helm, maximum sublight drive. Get us into transition."

York didn't respond, but instead looked to Paulson, who was sitting at the captain's console and appeared preoccupied. York said, "Captain?"

Vickers's eyes flashed angrily. Paulson started, looked at Vickers, then at York. "Yes. Do what he said."

After that, York was taken off bridge watch and assigned to help Soletski in Engineering. The chief knew far more than York ever would about the ship's systems, so York kept his mouth shut and didn't try to run the department.

Driving hard at three thousand lights, the *Horseman* emitted a very large and visible transition wake, and that made many of them quite nervous. But there was nothing they could do about it. York did take the first off-duty opportunity to hunt down Chief Carney, the master-at-arms. He approached the subject carefully.

"Chief, I noticed you . . . issued sidearms to certain members of the crew."

Seated behind her small desk, she leaned back in her chair, steepled her fingers in front of her, looked at York, and smiled. "Captain Paulson came to me, accompanied by Chief Vickers and Chief Garmin. He ordered me to issue them sidearms."

The message she was trying to give York was that she had no choice. "Thank you," he said. "I was just wondering what the justification was for sidearms."

"The only justification needed: captain's orders."

York turned to leave, but as he did she said, "One more thing, Ensign."

He turned back to face her.

"Vickers also wanted a list of any non-issue weapons registered with this office, and since the captain ordered me to comply, I gave it to him."

York's gut tightened at the thought that Vickers knew of the old-fashioned slug thrower he had squirreled away in his stateroom.

Carney said, "The list is rather short, though. Just a competition piece I have, and a rather valuable antique of Commander Hensen's."

At the look on York's face, her smile broadened. York thanked her and left.

The next morning, York got up early and went down to sick bay, where the corpsman bunked. He kept thinking of the way Cath had described Tomlin's death on *Dauntless*, and he wanted to speak with the corpsman alone and unobserved. "I'd like to ask about Lieutenant Kirkman," York said.

The corpsman gave him a wary look. "What do you want to know?"

"How bad was the skull fracture?"

The look of wariness turned to open distrust. "Why do you want to know that?"

York shrugged. "Just curious."

"It was a skull fracture," the corpsman said. "You don't actually fracture a skull without some serious impact."

"How bad?" York asked.

The corpsman looked around the room fearfully. In many ways, his nervousness was all the answer York needed, but he wanted to hear it. He pressed on, "What kind of wound, how deep, and how bad a fracture?"

The corpsman leaned forward and hissed, "The back of his fucking skull was caved in, fucking brains all over the place. And that's all I'm saying."

He turned his back on York and walked away.

CHAPTER 26:
A SIMPLE SOLUTION

The situation deteriorated rapidly. Paulson hid in the stateroom he shared with York as much as possible, and every time York ran into him there, he was forced to listen to the fellow's litany of self-loathing. "I know you think I should stand up to Vickers, and I should, but I can't. He's probably better at running the ship anyway. Certainly better than I am." It got so bad York hoped Paulson would relent and move into the captain's stateroom so he didn't have to listen to him anymore.

Vickers stopped even pretending to consult Paulson, and gave orders on the pretense that he was relaying them from the captain. York was more tuned in to the ship's rumor mill than most officers, probably because he wore gunner's chevrons and many of the enlisted personnel were a little more comfortable speaking to him. Confined now to Engineering, he heard from one petty officer serving on the bridge crew that Paulson always sat silently at the captain's console with a morose look on his face. Vickers gave them orders by saying, "The captain wants you to . . ." or "The captain ordered me to tell you . . ."

The petty officer speaking to York said, "And Paulson didn't say a fucking word during the whole watch."

The fresh food didn't go as far as anticipated, even with rationing, and they had to eat more and more protein cake. At least it was textured and flavored—anyone who'd served a stretch in the brig knew how hard it was to choke down unflavored cake. One evening, York said to Paulson, "I'll sure be glad when we can get some real food again."

Paulson looked down at the deck and wouldn't meet his eyes.

With his suspicions aroused, York asked, "We are running out of real food, aren't we?"

Paulson shrugged, looked exceedingly guilty, and said, "I have to get to the bridge."

York stepped in his way, and in the narrow stateroom he completely blocked Paulson's exit. "Answer my question," he said.

Paulson straightened and stuck his chest out. "I'm the captain. I don't have to answer questions from an ensign."

York stepped forward and towered over Paulson, forcing him to take a step back. "Answer my fucking question, goddamn it."

Paulson lowered his eyes and looked at the deck. "Chief Vickers feels . . . it's more appropriate to . . . distribute the fresh food to those who have more demanding watch assignments."

"You idiot," York said. "If the crew hears this, you're going to have a lot of pissed-off spacers on your hands."

"You won't tell them, will you?" Paulson pleaded.

"No, of course I won't. But word will leak out somehow. It always does. And then you're going to have a real shitstorm to deal with."

The next day, York was working in Engineering, and he overheard the enlisted personnel grumbling about the food. He listened carefully, but didn't hear any accusations of unfair rationing, just general discontent with *the crap they're feeding us*. Soletski overheard it as well.

The hull shrieked, pulling York out of his dreams. The *Horseman* down-transited as emergency lighting kicked in and he floated up out of his grav bunk. "*Warhead off the port bow*," his implants said.

Paulson was on watch, so York was alone in their stateroom. In zero-G, he scrambled into coveralls, an exercise he'd practiced a hundred times in training. As he pulled his way down to Engineering from handhold to handhold, he listened to the developing situation.

"Must have stumbled across a picket."

"Big warhead, forced us into down-transition."

"Coasting at more than nine-tenths light."

When he got to Engineering, Chief Soletski said, "We've got this under control, sir, but we're getting nothing from the bridge. See what information you can get us."

York logged into a console, pulled up a scan report, and dug through the data. A feddie hunter-killer had spotted their transition wake, not hard to do with them screaming by at three thousand lights. The Directorate ship had taken a long shot and scored a near miss.

York briefed Soletski and the Engineering crew, then asked, "How much damage?"

"Not too bad," the chief said. "We'll have it fixed in three or four hours. What about that feddie?"

York looked at the scan report and shook his head. "We're going in opposite directions. It'll take him a day or two to kill his velocity, turn around, and head this way. I'll be surprised if he tries to come after us."

York met Soletski's eyes. "But he knows we're here. If they've got any transition relays in the area, he could spread the word quickly."

Soletski nodded and said, "And Vickers is too fucking stupid to take evasive action."

York grabbed a wrench to help the Engineering crew. Soletski had been optimistic. It took more than six hours to restore power, then get gravity, drive, and environmental control working again. Once they up-transited, everyone breathed a sigh of relief, though the ever-cautious Soletski wanted to monitor the power plant carefully for several hours, so York and the Engineering crew continued to stand watch until he was satisfied. Fourteen hours after they'd narrowly escaped the feddie warhead, York staggered up to his stateroom. He found Paulson dead.

York had his suspicions about Kirkman's death, but there was no question of any foul play with Paulson. Vickers would have been York's prime suspect, but Paulson had been giving him exactly what he wanted, letting him run the ship, so he had no motive. The cause of death was obvious. Paulson had tied a piece of plast cord around his neck, tied the other end to an overhead light fixture, then slumped down and quietly hanged himself. Just to be sure, York checked for a pulse and found none. In doing so, he also learned that rigor mortis had set in. He decided not to touch the body beyond that.

York called the corpsman down in sick bay to come up and dispose of the body. Then he called Carney and Soletski, the two senior chiefs who'd seemed tolerant and somewhat sympathetic. They agreed to come up right away.

The corpsman must have called Vickers, because the master chief arrived first. Standing out in the corridor, he demanded, "What the hell is going on here?"

York nodded toward Paulson's body, still hanging by the plast cord. "See for yourself."

The corpsman, Soletski, and Carney arrived at that moment. The small stateroom York shared with Paulson was much too small to contain them all, so they gathered just outside the door.

The corpsman edged past them into the room. "Looks like he killed himself," he said, examining the body.

Vickers shook his head angrily. "I don't believe it."

Carney shrugged and said, "I do. The longer he was in command, the more he fell apart."

Vickers pointed at York. "I think he did it."

"What do you mean?" Soletski asked, frowning.

"It's obvious. He wanted command of this ship, and the only thing standing between him and the captaincy was Paulson."

Vickers drew his sidearm and pointed it at York. "I'm placing you under arrest for the murder of Captain Paulson. You're a fucking traitor, and you're going to pay for it."

Convenient, York thought. With Paulson dead and him in the brig charged with treason, Vickers would be in command.

"Wait a minute," Carney said.

"Yes," Soletski said. He asked the corpsman, "How long's he been dead?"

The corpsman grimaced and shrugged. "I don't have the forensic capability to determine the exact time of death. But rigor mortis has set in, so at least two hours, maybe more."

"There you have it," Soletski said. "Mr. Ballin was with us down in Engineering for the last fourteen hours, left us only a few minutes ago."

"Bullshit. Somehow he did it and I'm arresting him."

In a flat, hard voice, Carney said, "No."

Soletski added. "I and the entire Engineering crew will testify that he couldn't have killed Paulson."

"Don't defy me," Vickers said. "I'm in command of this ship."

"No, you're not," Carney said. She pointed at York. "Now he is."

From the look on her face, York thought Carney was none too pleased that their new commanding officer was an ensign straight out of the academy. He suspected she'd acknowledged him only to thwart Vickers's grab for power.

By that time, a large crowd had formed in the corridor, spacers of every rank looking on. Vickers looked around, and York guessed he didn't like the idea of having so many witnesses. He holstered his sidearm and said to York, "Nothing's changed."

He spun about, catching a young, female petty officer by surprise. She was in his way in the middle of the corridor and didn't have time to move before he shoved her aside, knocking her against the bulkhead. Everyone else stepped aside and got out of his way as he marched down the corridor. Chief Garmin followed on his heels.

*   *   *

After the corpsman took Paulson's body away on a grav stretcher, the crowd in the corridor broke up. York asked Carney and Soletski to stay. "I didn't ask for this," he said. "But I'm not going to abdicate my responsibility. What's your opinion on Lieutenant Kirkman's earlier strategy of keeping our transition velocity below a thousand lights?"

Soletski said, "We'll have less of a transition wake and be that much harder to spot."

Carney said, "It'll take longer to get home, and we'll be eating more protein cake. But better that than eating a warhead."

There was a specific protocol for transfer of command under such unusual circumstances. Once the corpsman certified Paulson's death, and with signed affidavits by two senior NCOs, Carney and Soletski, the ship's computer gave York primary command access. He went up to the bridge and found Vickers seated at the captain's console. York could almost taste the tension there as everyone but Vickers and Garmin locked their eyes on the screens in front of them and refused to look his way.

"Chief Vickers," York said. If this was going to be a confrontation, it should be done in private. "If you don't mind, I'd like to have a private word with you."

Vickers didn't take his eyes off his own screens. "I mind."

"Then I'm making it an order."

Vickers looked York's way and rested his hand on the butt of his sidearm. In the corner of his eye, York saw Garmin doing the same. Vickers said, "You don't give me orders."

"Are you refusing a direct order from the commanding officer of this ship?"

"You're never going to be the CO of this ship."

"Don't speak in the future tense, Chief," York said. He had to get the man off the bridge, and had to do it without violence, so he offered him some bait. "Speak in the present tense, because I am now in command of this ship, and will be holding a meeting of the senior staff shortly. I'll let you know where and when."

York didn't wait for a response, but turned and walked off the bridge.

He went down to see Carney. "Can you come up with three NCOs who you trust to obey proper orders?"

She grimaced. "It didn't go well with Vickers, eh, sir?"

"I don't think any of us thought it would."

"As to your question," she said, "I can come up with quite a few more than three if needed."

York shook his head. "Three should be sufficient. And can you arm the four of you with concealable weapons, something you can hide in coveralls?"

Her eyes narrowed, and he wondered if the possibility of violence had shifted her loyalties. "I can do that, sir."

"Then please do so. I'll be calling a meeting of the senior staff shortly. Please come armed as we've discussed, and bring your three colleagues with you when you attend. If all goes well, the weapons will be an unnecessary precaution."

"Aye, aye, sir."

York went up to his stateroom and closed the door. From his locker, he retrieved the old-style chemically powered slug thrower and a box of bullets. He checked the revolving cylinder to make sure it was empty, dry-fired it a few times to remind himself of the feel, put five rounds into the cylinder, then carefully decocked the hammer and engaged the safety. It was small enough to conceal in the thigh pocket of his coveralls, though it would be obvious to anyone who saw him walking down a corridor that he'd placed something heavy in there. For that reason, he had to be in place before anyone else showed up.

On his way down to the officers' wardroom, he encountered a few spacers walking the other way. In the tight confines of the ship's corridors, it was necessary to turn slightly sideways for two to pass each other. York was always careful to turn his right side away from anyone he met. He noticed that none of them treated him like the commanding officer of the ship. That would soon change, or he'd be dead.

In the wardroom, he poured a cup of caff, then sat down on a long bench seat at one of the plast tables. He took care to sit at the far end with a bulkhead on his right, the door to his left on the other side of the room. He made sure his right thigh pocket was open and the gun easily accessible.

"Computer," he said into his implants.

"Acknowledged," the computer said.

"Please inform all senior NCOs that the captain is calling a meeting of the senior staff in the wardroom in ten minutes. Attendance is mandatory."

York knew Vickers could not resist such bait. If he didn't come himself, York might somehow turn the rest of the senior staff against him.

York waited with his elbow on the table, his left hand gripping his cup of caff, his right resting on his thigh below the table. Soletski was the first to arrive. He saluted York, grabbed a cup of caff, and sat down opposite him. Harkness followed, but didn't get any caff, and sat down next to York on his left. Carney came next, alone. York wondered if he'd misunderstood her loyalties. She didn't sit down, but leaned against the bulkhead next to the door.

Vickers and Garmin showed up together. Garmin sat down on the other side of the table next to Soletski, while Vickers stood at the end of the table and loomed over them. Garmin did not pretend to hide her actions as she lifted a small scanner and aimed it at York. She smiled, clearly satisfied that he was carrying no energy weapons like the grav gun at her side.

Vickers rested his hand on his sidearm and said, "So what's this about?"

When Vickers had wanted to arrest York, he'd backed down

in front of the others. York hoped that with them present, he'd do so now and they could resolve this with nothing more than a bit of tension.

York said, "I have to decide what our course of action is going to be, and I'd like the advice of my senior NCOs to do so."

"As we discussed earlier, I'm in favor of slowing down so we reduce our transition wake," said Soletski.

Carney nodded. "We'll be a lot less of a target that way."

Behind Vickers, a petty officer first class stepped quietly into the room and leaned against the bulkhead near Carney.

Garmin said, "We need to get back as soon as possible. I vote no." She grinned at York.

York said, "Chief Garmin, this is a naval vessel. We don't vote."

Her grin disappeared, and the tension in the room ratcheted up a notch.

Vickers leaned forward and put his hands flat on the table. "You want advice, I'll give you advice. You don't decide shit."

York raised the cup of caff to his mouth and took a sip, at the same time sliding his right hand into his thigh pocket and wrapping his fingers around the handle of the gun. He swallowed, leaned forward, and looked at the caff in his cup. "According to naval regulations and the laws of the empire, I do decide."

Because he was leaning forward, his right hand was hidden by his torso. He casually pulled the gun out of his thigh pocket and kept it beneath the table between his thigh and the bulkhead, then leaned back, lowered the cup back to the table, and rested his left elbow there. While he did that, another petty officer slipped quietly into the room and leaned against the bulkhead at the back of the meeting.

Vickers looked at each of the NCOs seated at the table. "Are we going to put up with this shit? A fucking ensign, straight out of the academy."

A hard, angry look settled on Harkness's face. "An ensign who has the right to wear more campaign ribbons than most of the crew on this ship."

Still leaning on the table, Vickers said, "I don't care how many ribbons he can wear. He has no right to command this ship."

Harkness said, "I don't know what you think—"

As another petty officer stepped into the room and quietly stood near the back of the meeting, York raised his voice. "Ladies and gentlemen, please." He took advantage of the momentary silence. "We have a number of issues to settle here, one of which is the unnecessary wearing of arms. Chiefs Garmin and Vickers . . ." He looked at each of them. "Our previous CO may have authorized you to carry arms, but I'm withdrawing that authorization now. When this meeting is done, you're ordered to return your sidearms to Chief Carney for return to the arms locker."

Vickers's eyes widened and he slammed a fist down on the table. "I'll do no such thing."

That was it; he'd just refused a direct order. York had to get him to back down, or to escalate it so far there'd be no questioning York's actions.

"Are you refusing a direct order from your captain?" York asked.

Carney and the three petty officers tensed.

Vickers shouted, "You are not now, nor will you ever be, my captain."

"But that's the issue before us," York said. "I am your captain, whether you like it or not. And there's nothing in *The Naval Code of Regulations* that gives you the authority to change that."

Vickers's lips turned upward in a sneer disguised as a smile. "Normal chain of command. If you're not physically able to perform your duties, then I'm in command."

At that point, York could think of no way to retrieve the situation. "I think what you're saying is that I could have an accident . . . like Lieutenant Kirkman had an accident."

Garmin grinned like a fool, while the others grimaced at having the truth of Kirkman's murder stated openly. Vickers's smile broadened further. "Accidents do happen," he said.

"Is that a threat?" York said, and while he spoke he cocked the hammer on the gun.

Spittle flew from Vickers's mouth as he said, "You take it to be whatever you want it to be."

Vickers had taken them down a path that was now irrevocable, so York needed to take him all the way. "I, your commanding officer, am giving you a direct order, and you're refusing it?"

"I'm not taking any orders from you. And you can take that space-lawyer bullshit and shove it up your ass."

"And you're threatening me?"

Vickers lifted his right hand off the table and rested it on the butt of his sidearm. "What are you going to do about it?"

York let the silence draw out as if he were trapped and had no recourse to counter the man. Garmin and Vickers believed he was helpless, and that moment of apparent indecision proved to them that they were right. Garmin visibly relaxed, and York's moment had come.

Answering Vickers's question, he said, "This." Then, without making any sudden, sharp movements that might elicit a reaction, he calmly raised the gun, aimed it between Vickers's eyes, and pulled the trigger.

In the small room, the explosion that came from the barrel was deafening. A small, round dot appeared in the middle of Vickers's forehead and behind him blood, brains, and bone splattered Carney and her three petty officers.

The impact rocked Vickers back and he straightened, his eyes wide, his lips forming a round *O*. His mouth opened and partially closed, opened and closed, like a fish York had once seen in a public aquarium. Then he toppled forward and his face smacked into the table with an unpleasant crack, nothing left of the back of his head but a steaming crater.

In the silence that ensued, York looked at Garmin. She sat

stiffly with her eyes wide, staring at the gun in his hand. Then she lifted her gaze and met his eyes. She must have seen something there, for she paled visibly, then slowly placed her hands palm down on the table in front of her and averted her eyes.

York cocked the hammer on the gun then laid it down on the table next to his cup of caff, careful to position it so the barrel pointed directly at her. He fought to keep the tremble out of his voice as he said, "We still have a meeting to conduct. I take it we're all in agreement we'll slow down and reduce our transition wake?"

They all nodded silently, even Garmin, though her eyes remained wide, round circles of fear and she appeared unable to look away from the steaming ruin of the back of Vickers's head. York considered killing her, too; he'd murdered an AI agent, and when they court-martialed him for treason, she'd surely be the first to testify. But he couldn't find it in himself.

He almost got up to leave, but then realized the best thing he could do was finish the meeting. He forced them all to stay, and he made up agenda items on the fly just to draw it out, the crater in the back of Vickers's head a centerpiece for their discussions.

It seemed like an eternity, but it was over in twenty minutes. York reached out, picked up his gun, and stood. Those seated jumped to their feet and they all stood at rigid attention. Carney quietly moved to a position behind Garmin, her hand hidden in a pocket of her coveralls. York looked at her. "Chief, please make sure all issue weapons are returned to the weapons locker."

"Aye, aye, sir."

He was rather proud that he'd managed to sound very like a captain, without the slightest bit of tremor in his voice. He looked at the gun in his hand and decocked the hammer, then engaged the safety. "And please confiscate all non-issue weapons. You can start with this."

He tossed the gun onto the table with a casual flick of his

wrist. They all jumped at the loud crack it made when it hit the plast and bounced a couple of times.

He stepped back from the table and something occurred to him. "Does Vickers have a family?" he asked, not aiming the question at anyone in particular.

Soletski said, "Um . . . I believe he does, sir."

"Then let the record show that Chief Vickers died honorably in defense of the empire. We'll let them draw his pension."

York edged past Harkness and walked to the door, trying to keep the tremble out of his knees and wondering if he'd make it out of the room alive.

CHAPTER 27:
READY TO COMMAND

Three days after York killed Vickers, they down-transited for a nav fix and spotted a transition wake coming their way, driving hard. After reviewing all the data they could gather, they decided it was most likely the feddie hunter-killer that had blown them out of transition shortly before Paulson hanged himself. At the time, they'd been going in opposite directions, and York thought it unlikely her captain would be stubborn enough to go to the trouble of killing his velocity and turning around to chase them. But now they were in sublight, running silent, with good telemetry and scan data, and the feddie captain must have assumed they were driving hard, because he came right at them in transition. They put a big torpedo into his bow and he went out with all hands.

It took them two months to work their way back to the front lines, moving slowly and cautiously. By that time, they were living almost exclusively on protein cake, though they had found a small cache of fresh food in Vickers's quarters, and some in Garmin's as well. But they'd used that up quickly by distributing it evenly among the crew. York could still remember choking down the unflavored, untextured cakes for a month in the brig on *Dauntless*. He considered the flavored stuff they were eating now a luxury, and had little sympathy for the grousing of his crew.

Once they crossed into friendly territory, they upped their

speed to maximum and made good time to Dumark, and then on to Cathan, where York was relieved of his command. They transferred Commander Hensen out of the tanks into a hospital ward on Cathan Prime, and York received orders to return to the academy for his final evaluation. He got a ride on a fast destroyer to Muirendan, then took another passenger liner to Luna.

York felt a certain sense of déjà vu as he waited in the shuttle lounge on Luna Prime, looking at the large observation screen that showed the same image of Terr he'd looked at five years ago. The feeling continued as he rode the shuttle down to the surface, hopped the subsurface transport to Mare Crisia station, then walked to the academy. And just like the first time he'd come through the main gate, a bored MP told him he was *to report to the commandant immediately upon arrival*. They didn't have to give him directions this time.

Since his evaluation tour had inadvertently been extended to more than a year, he'd missed Karin when she'd returned after the standard half year, and he knew he'd never see her again. She did send him a note:

> York:
>   Glad to hear the rumors of your death were greatly exaggerated. I'll always remember you.
>
> Karin

Martinson had a different secretary now, but like the first, she asked him to take a seat and wait—though unlike that first time, he didn't have to wait long. Martinson looked the same, seated behind his desk more rigidly than any cadet standing at attention. He returned York's salute and said, "At ease, Ensign. Pull up a chair and relax."

There were two simple chairs to either side of the desk. York grabbed one and sat down in front of Martinson.

The commandant said, "You know, we thought you were dead, thought *The Fourth Horseman* went out with all hands."

York shrugged. "We got lucky, sir."

Martinson shook his head. "From what I've heard, luck had very little to do with it."

Again York shrugged. "We took some damage, lost some crew, but we still had a functioning ship, even if a bit damaged. And we had a functioning crew. That was luck."

"By the way," Martinson said, "Commander Hensen is recovering nicely, though his injuries were so extreme it'll be a few months before he can return to active duty."

"I'm glad to hear that, sir."

"So you lost Gunnerson and Hensen, and Lieutenant Kirkman took command, but he was killed in a freak accident. Lieutenant Paulson took command after that, he was killed in a separate incident, and you finally took command. Chief Parker has spoken with the NCOs who were under your command. We know Kirkman was most likely murdered. We also know Paulson committed suicide. Why did you list him as killed in action?"

York wanted to shrug a third time, but he didn't. "He had a family, and I thought it would be nice to let them draw his pension."

"Are the rumors about you true, Mr. Ballin?" Martinson asked, changing the subject without warning.

"I haven't heard the rumors about me, sir."

"None of the NCOs under your command said anything directly to Parker—they're all rather loyal to you at this point— but he heard a few things in a roundabout sort of way. The most persistent rumor is that you crushed a mutiny by personally, and rather cold-bloodedly, executing its leader."

York wondered if they were now going to court-martial him. Garmin had probably reported everything to AI, and now they'd charge him with treason and be rid of him. "There might be a small element of truth to that rumor, sir."

"And yet there is no record of such a mutiny, Mr. Ballin, nor of any serious dissension among the officers and crew of *The Fourth Horseman*."

York had to assume Soletski, Harkness, and Carney had forced Garmin to keep her mouth shut. He tried to keep the surprise he felt from showing on his face as he said, "Once the instigator of the mutiny was . . . no longer an issue, and it was over, there was no need to tarnish the reputations of those involved."

"Let their families draw their pensions, eh?"

"Exactly, sir."

York wanted some answers to some old questions and knew he might be perceived as impertinent by asking them, but didn't really give a damn at that point. "May I ask a question, sir?"

Martinson smiled. "By all means, Mr. Ballin, but I think I already know what it is."

York wasn't going to play guessing games with Martinson. "Why did you expose me to Abraxa at that reception at the end of my first semester? You said it would be the hardest four years of my life. But you implied that if I worked hard, you wouldn't make it harder. I did work hard, and I did well up until then. You lied to me."

"I didn't lie to you," Martinson said. "This empire needs men and women who are capable of commanding people and ships under the worst of circumstances, and by that I mean when hampered by the incompetence of their own superiors. In every class, there are a few of you who have that potential. And for each one of you, I do something to make your life here hell, not just for your plebe year, but for your entire time here. As I said, we need you to be able to command independently under the worst of circumstances. And we need you to understand what fools you'll frequently be reporting to."

He leaned back in his chair, steepled his fingers, and regarded York with a faint smile on his lips. "It turns out my record is quite good; I'm rarely wrong about one of you. You, Mr. Ballin, are ready to command as only a very few of your classmates are."

"May I be blunt, sir?"

"Please."

"I would rather have had just the regular, ordinary, hellish time of it."

Martinson threw his head back and roared with laughter, which was incredibly unlike him. After he calmed down, he wiped tears from his eyes and said, "Thank you for that, Mr. Ballin. Have you never wondered why you didn't flunk out when your grades were so poor, why I didn't make your life even worse when you failed to perform?"

"I did wonder about that, sir."

"Up until that little reception, you were performing nicely. Then I exposed you, Abraxa and Laski put their heads together, and suddenly your test scores plummeted." He held up his hands and looked upward as if acknowledging divine intervention. Then he looked at York and said, "Do you think I'm a fool, Mr. Ballin?"

York opened his mouth to say something politic, but Martinson held out his hand. "Rhetorical question, Mr. Ballin. I knew what Laski was doing, and I kept track of your real scores, which continued to be in the top thirty percent. It was not a coincidence that every time you faced an academic review, there were officers on the panel who are just as disgusted as I am by the privilege and corruption in our system. And consider this: Had Laski and others like him not inflated the scores of people like Tony Simma, you would likely have made the top ten or fifteen percent."

Martinson hesitated for a moment and grinned at some thought. "By the way, Mr. Simma told his father that he didn't think he was properly ready to command, that he really hadn't applied himself as well as he could have, and he asked to return to repeat his final year. He then sent me a private message that he wanted me to ensure that he received no favoritism. He mentioned you, said you had quite an impact on him."

York couldn't help but smile, recalling that Tony had never been as full of himself as some of the others.

Martinson continued. "Many of your graduating class will eventually make good officers, and because of you, Mr. Simma might be among them. But you're ready to command now in a way that very few of them are, so go out there and command, Mr. Ballin."

He stood and extended his hand. Surprised, York stood and shook it.

Martinson released his hand and straightened. "That's all. You're dismissed."

York saluted, turned with parade-ground precision, and marched the short distance to the door. He opened it, but before he stepped through, Martinson said, "Oh, one more thing, Mr. Ballin."

York paused and turned to face him. "Commander Hensen has recovered sufficiently to write you a nice review. And since there were no superior officers left conscious and alive on *The Fourth Horseman* to provide an assessment of your performance during your final months of the tour, I'm adding to it myself. It will be quite glowing, though probably not enough to make up for the fact that you graduated at the bottom of your class. We'll give you a medal or something to compensate."

York didn't say what he wanted to say. He simply said, "Thank you, sir," and closed the door softly.

APPENDIX:
SOME NOTES ON TIME, GRAVITY, AND THE IMPERIAL NAVAL ACADEMY

The Lunan Empire and the Republic of Syndon operate on decimal (Base 10) not duodecimal (Base 12) time. The standard Lunan day, which is derived from our Terran day, is divided up into twenty hours, not twenty-four. Each hour is divided up into one hundred minutes, and each minute into one hundred seconds. Hence, in our present-day duodecimal time, the day is divided up into 24 x 60 x 60 seconds—we'll call them Terran seconds—whereas in York's time and place that same day is divided up into 20 x 100 x 100 seconds—for clarity we'll call them Lunan seconds. So 86,400 (24 x 60 x 60) Terran seconds is equal to 200,000 (20 x 100 x 100) Lunan seconds, which means:

1 Lunan second = 0.4320 Terran second.

Or, one Lunan second is a little less than half a Terran second. The table below compares hours, minutes, and seconds for the two timing systems.

Measure	Terran	Lunan
hour	1	0.83
minute	1	1.38
second	1	2.31

This is why the math may not appear to add up. During York's pod training, when Straight poses the question of:

- Enemy warship at 100,000,000 kilometers,
- Spitting transition shells at 100 lights,

doing the math in our Terran system of units, and given that light travels at 299,792.458 kilometers per second in a vacuum, yields a result of 3.34 Terran seconds, which is 7.72 Lunan seconds.

That's why York's answer is, "A little under eight seconds," not, "A little over three seconds."

In 1861 and 1862, James Clerk Maxwell published an early form of a set of partial differential equations that became the foundation for electromagnetic field theory, which details the interaction between electric and magnetic fields. To this day, Maxwell's equations, as they came to be known, are still the most elegant solution to an understanding of light and radio waves. But they cover only the interaction between electric and magnetic fields, with no consideration given to gravitational fields, though there is a wealth of experimental data that proves all three do interact. Albert Einstein spent the last thirty years of his life in a failed attempt to do the same for all three, which is referred to as the unified field theory.

In this story of the far distant future, scientists have long ago solved the problem of classical unified field theory. This so enhanced their understanding of the interaction of electric, magnetic, and gravitational fields that they gained extensive control of gravity, and quickly developed the means of artificially generating thousands of G's of acceleration. But the human body cannot withstand such forces for even a tiny fraction of a second, and even a large steel beam would fail dramatically, so all systems must be compensated internally.

It has been demonstrated that the human body can withstand accelerations of close to one hundred G's for a fraction of a second, if strapped into an acceleration seat and carefully protected. When one takes an elevator in York's time, it rockets upward at a hundred G's, taking its occupants up many floors in the blink of an eye. But if they are to survive the journey without broken bones and other ill effects, there must be an internal, opposing acceleration so they feel the force of only one G. And inside a ship or pod or turret, strapping in to an acceleration seat is simply a precaution against weightless maneuvering. At a thousand G's or more, without internal compensation there wouldn't be anything left of the seat's occupant but bug-squish.

The Imperial Naval Academy of York's time is *very loosely* based on the U.S. Naval Academy. The author freely selected certain aspects of the culture and traditions of the USNA and ignored others. The Imperial Naval Academy is corrupt, rife with privilege, and hampered by a class system that stifles equality and opportunity, while the USNA is a storied institution that strives to teach young men and women the highest qualities of leadership and honor. There have been mistakes and scandals at the USNA, for no institution of that size can be perfect. In fact, it should be noted that all branches of the military, as well as most civilian institutions, are still struggling with important issues like sexual equality and equal pay. But the U.S. Naval Academy's few missteps should not be compared to the widespread culture of corruption at the Imperial Naval Academy.

ABOUT THE AUTHOR

J. L. Doty is the author of eight science fiction and fantasy novels. A scientist with a PhD in electrical engineering, he became a self-publishing success and was able to quit his day job as a lackey for the bourgeois capitalist establishment to work as a full-time writer. Doty writes epic fantasy, hard science fiction, and contemporary urban fantasy, frequently with strong young-adult themes. His novels include *Child of the Sword*, *A Choice of Treasons*, and *When Dead Ain't Dead Enough*. Born in Seattle, Doty lived most of his life in California but now resides in Arizona with his wife Karen and their three cats.

THE TREASONS CYCLE

FROM OPEN ROAD MEDIA

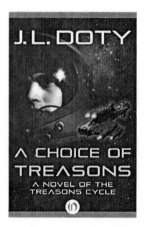
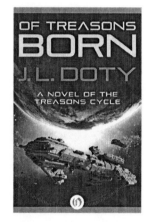

Available wherever ebooks are sold

OPEN ROAD
INTEGRATED MEDIA

Open Road Integrated Media is a digital publisher and multimedia content company. Open Road creates connections between authors and their audiences by marketing its ebooks through a new proprietary online platform, which uses premium video content and social media.

Videos, Archival Documents, and New Releases

Sign up for the Open Road Media newsletter and get news delivered straight to your inbox.

Sign up now at
www.openroadmedia.com/newsletters

CPSIA information can be obtained at www.ICGtesting.com
Printed in the USA
BVOW05s0229260316

441844BV00002B/2/P